> "We got a special treat tonight. All the way from San Francisco, with the voice of an angel, is Belle California."

There was a smattering of curious applause. Gabe found himself looking around for the glamorous entertainer. Just then Slade lifted a female in his arms and seated her on the piano. When she looked up, Gabe nearly swallowed his cigar.

Belle California was the girl he'd met that afternoon. Billie Calley. But this woman bore little resemblance to her.

The crimson satin gown fitted her like a second skin. Her freckled face had been transformed with makeup. Her lips were a dramatic red and her wide expressive eyes were outlined with black smudges.

Gabe couldn't take his gaze off her. She was absolutely mesmerizing. She appeared exotic, aloof and absolutely untouchable.

His eyes narrowed as he looked around and realized that innocent, shy little Billie Calley, in the guise of Belle California, had suddenly become the fantasy of every man in the room.

Ar

**Acclaim for *USA TODAY* bestselling author
RUTH LANGAN**

"Ruth Langan is a true master at involving
your emotions, be they laughter or tears."
—*Romantic Times*

"…another tautly written, fast-paced and
sensual romance. A fine example of why this author
is such a successful romance writer."
—Romance Reviews Today on **The Sea Sprite**

"Ruth Langan makes us believe
in the beauty of true love."
—*Romantic Times*

BADLANDS LAW
RUTH LANGAN

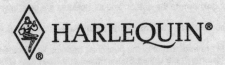

HARLEQUIN®

TORONTO • NEW YORK • LONDON
AMSTERDAM • PARIS • SYDNEY • HAMBURG
STOCKHOLM • ATHENS • TOKYO • MILAN • MADRID
PRAGUE • WARSAW • BUDAPEST • AUCKLAND

ISBN 0-373-29220-1

BADLANDS LAW

Copyright © 2002 by Ruth Ryan Langan

For Pat and Ed, Marg and Terry
Family and best friends.

And of course, for Tom
My very best friend.

Prologue

South Dakota, 1867

The little party of mourners stood on a sun-baked hill, sweltering under a relentless haze of heat that rivaled the fires of hell. There had been no rain for weeks, and the scorched earth had begun to split and crack. The silence was broken by the distant rumble of thunder, but the ranchers of South Dakota had given up looking to the heavens. Instead, they felt the ground under their feet shudder, and knew it was a herd of buffalo, thundering across the plains in search of precious prairie grass.

Gabriel Conover stood next to his mother at the gravesite of his grandfather, watching as the half-dozen neighbors took turns tossing a handful of dirt on the wooden box. In all of his ten years, this was the first time young Gabriel had ever worn a suit. His ma had been up all night sewing for him and his nine-year-old brother, Yale, and five-year-old Kitty.

Dorry Conover said she did it out of respect for his grandpa. After all, Deacon Conover, his father's father, a stern bear of a man, had taken them in when they'd had nowhere else to go.

Whenever her children asked about their father, Dorry told them proudly that after he'd finished soldiering in the Great War, Clay Conover had been sent on a secret assignment that had been authorized by President Lincoln himself before his untimely assassination.

Though he yearned for Clay's return, Gabriel found the loneliness tolerable, knowing his pa was a hero. One day, he figured, his pa would come riding up to the ranch, bearing a cask of gold from a grateful nation, and the Conovers would get back to the business of being a family again. Until then, as the eldest, Gabriel was his pa's right hand, and he took his job seriously.

Beside Gabriel, his brother Yale, always the troublemaker, was poking an elbow into Kitty's arm, and whispering that he was going to toss her into the grave with their grandpa. Seeing his Uncle Junior's withering look, Gabriel picked up the little girl and, ignoring the sweat running in rivers down his back, held her in his arms until the gaping hole was filled.

As the neighboring ranchers returned to their wagons, Dorry called out, "You're all welcome to come back to our place for supper. I killed a couple of chickens. They're simmering in a pot right now."

Several of them paused until, seeing the scowl on

her brother-in-law's face, they offered their apologies and hastened back to their own ranches.

As Dorry was climbing into her wagon Junior caught her roughly by the arm, stopping her in mid-step. "What right have you got inviting them back to eat my food?"

She seemed genuinely surprised by his outburst. "Junior, these are your neighbors. They came all this way just to pay their last respects to your father. Some of them will be on the trail for hours before they get home. It's only right that we offer them our hospitality."

"Oh, you'd be good at that, wouldn't you? You know all about accepting hospitality."

At his uncle's outburst, Gabriel, helping his little sister into the back of the wagon, turned around in surprise.

Dorry's voice took on that quiet, respectful tone she'd learned to use around her husband's older brother whenever he was on one of his tirades. "What are you talking about, Junior?"

"I'm not Junior anymore." His voice seemed as hot as the sun. As hard as the baked earth. "I've always hated that name. With the old man gone, I'm Deacon now. Deacon Conover. And don't you forget it."

Dorry nodded. "Whatever you say."

"That's right." He glanced at the mound of dirt, then back at her. "It's whatever I say now. Not the old man. I told him he was a fool to take on four more mouths. But you fed him that lie about Clay, and he swallowed it whole.''

"Lie? What are you...?'' She glanced toward the back of the wagon and could see her three children watching and listening in horrified fascination.

"That pretty little sugarcoated story about Clay carrying on some secret mission for the President. You and the old man both knew it was a lie. Clay's never coming back for you.'' His voice lifted to a whine. "You could have had yourself a solid, dependable husband, Dorry. You knew I wanted you. When we were kids, you were just about the prettiest girl around. With all that yellow hair and those big blue eyes.''

Junior's tone hardened. "But you just had to go and give your heart to my reckless little brother. And look what it got you. Three brats, and a husband who left you to run off with the most dangerous gang of outlaws in the land.''

From the back of the wagon came a cry, and Gabriel drew his little sister into his arms, pressing his hands over her ears, even though he knew it was too late. She'd heard. They'd all heard those cruel, cutting words. Words that had struck with all the force of a blow to the heart. A blow that flattened young Gabriel, causing pain beyond belief as it swirled around and around in his young mind, echoing and reechoing those hateful words.

An outlaw? His pa, an outlaw? It wasn't possible.

Still, now that the seed of doubt had been sowed, he couldn't completely deny it, either. His father was little more than a stranger to him. A man in a sol-dier's uniform who rode off to fight, and except for brief periods, was rarely seen again. Was that why Pa had left them? Had he given in to the lure of easy money?

For the space of several moments Dorry seemed frozen to the spot, unable to speak. Unable to move. Finally she drew in a long breath. "You'll be bur-dened with us no longer. We'll stay only long enough to fetch our things. Then we'll be through accepting your hospitality."

She climbed up to the wagon and flicked the reins. As they started across the hills, nobody spoke. Not the woman, the children, nor the man who rode his horse in stone-faced silence alongside them.

At the ranch Dorry moved from room to room, bundling up their meager belongings, supervising as Gabriel and Yale secured them in the back of the wagon. She walked the garden, taking care to pick only half the rain-starved crop, leaving the other half for her brother-in-law. She did the same with the chickens, tossing half a dozen in a pen, along with a rooster. She tied a young cow behind the wagon, then ordered her children to climb aboard.

Junior stood in the doorway, grinning foolishly. "You want me to beg, don't you, Dorry? That's what this is about, isn't it?"

She said nothing as she picked up the reins.

His smile faded as he ran down the steps and started racing alongside. "All right. I'm sorry for what I said back there, Dorry. But the brats had to hear it some time. Besides, you know you can't really leave. Where will you go?''

She reined in the horse long enough to say, "I'm heading for the Badlands. That's where Clay said he'd be. As for you, I never want to see you again, Junior." And then, because she'd been pushed to the limit, she added, "You'll never be Deacon Conover to me, Junior. You're not half the man your father was. Or your brother, Clay."

She urged the horse into a trot, leaving her brother-in-law standing in the dust, staring after her.

Gabriel Conover watched his mother's lips tremble, even as she held her head high.

And though his own heart was shattered beyond repair, he'd never been more proud of her than he was in that moment.

The euphoria of freedom lasted a few days. After that, their little odyssey became a test of endurance. To spare their horse, the family walked as much as possible until, drained by heat and exhaustion, they would make camp during the hottest part of the day and begin walking again after sundown. While Kitty slept in the back of the wagon, Gabriel and Yale would take turns leading the horse, with their mother walking beside them, telling them tales of her childhood in Missouri, or coaching them in spelling and sums.

"You owe it to me and your pa to make something of your lives, boys. You can't ever let life's trials beat you down."

"Yes'm." When Yale fell silent, Gabriel answered for both of them. He could see what this journey was doing to his mother. Every day, every mile, seemed to sap her energy, until, within weeks, she was going on pure will.

Their family witnessed a variety of bewildering extremes. There seemed to be limitless expanses of space, but almost no people. They traversed sweeping treeless plains and steep, forested mountains, but spent hours searching in vain for water.

To Gabriel, who saw himself as the man of the family, their odyssey had become a trial by fire. Each day seemed to bring new and greater challenges. But when Dorry Conover awoke one morning with a raging fever that gradually grew worse, he faced the greatest challenge of his young life.

"You ride in the wagon with Kitty, Ma." He helped her into the back and lay her down among the quilts, then took up the reins and began walking.

Yale, walking beside him, said softly, "What if Ma dies?"

Gabriel grabbed him by the throat, his eyes hot with fury. "She isn't going to die."

Yale shoved his hand away and lifted a fist, ready to stand and fight. "Who says? People die, Gabe. Gramps died, didn't he?"

"That was different. Gramps was old."

"Young people die, too. Remember Pa's friends who died in the war?"

"That was war. This is…" He shook his head,

struggling to find a word to describe the hell they were in.

"This is a different kind of war, Gabe." Because he was scared, Yale lowered his voice. "It's just us against the Badlands. But it's war all the same."

The two brothers fell silent, each lost in their own terrible thoughts.

By the time they stopped for the night Dorry was too weak to sit up. She clutched their hands and struggled to make herself understood.

"Your pa's a good man. An honorable man. Don't believe what your uncle said about him."

Gabriel spoke for all of them. "We know, Ma. You just rest and get your strength back."

She shook her head. "I'm not going to be with you. I can feel my strength ebbing. But I want you to know that my spirit will always be with you. Don't be afraid. You have your father's blood flowing through you. That Conover blood will make you strong enough to prevail over anything." She squeezed Gabriel's hand, and turned to look at her middle child, Yale, and then her baby, Kitty, as though memorizing their faces. "You take care of each other, you hear me?"

"Yes'm." Gabriel nudged his brother and sister, and the two answered in kind.

Even as they were speaking, Gabriel felt his mother's hand slip from his. Saw the way her eyes went sightless. And knew, in that one terrible moment, that she was gone.

* * *

They left the crude grave with its simple stone marker at first light and started out. Gabriel led the horse and turned for one last glimpse of his mother's resting place. Then, at the sound of laughter, he turned to see Yale carrying his little sister on his back and making her giggle as he trotted up a hill.

Gabe's heart was heavier than a boulder as he pondered how they could possibly survive alone. What if their uncle had been right, and their father was part of a gang of outlaws? What would happen to them, and especially to Kitty, if they wandered this wilderness forever?

They made camp that night by a mud hole that had once been a stream. Still, though the water tasted foul, Gabe boiled it over the fire and when it had cooled, passed it around.

In the morning when he awoke, he found Yale striding toward them, his face wreathed in smiles.

"Where've you been?" Gabe's features were tight with anger. Beneath the anger lay a deep well of fear, though he refused to admit it.

"Getting us some supplies." Yale held up a jug and uncorked it, filling a tin cup with milk. He passed it to Kitty and watched as she drank it down in long gulps.

Gabe knew his jaw had dropped. "Where'd you find milk out here?"

Yale grinned. "There's a ranch about a mile from here."

"And the rancher gave you milk and supplies?"

"In a way." Yale's grin widened. "'Course, he

doesn't know it yet. And I'd advise us to be long gone before he finds his prize calf slaughtered." He tossed a hunk of raw meat, as much as he'd been able to carry, in the back of the wagon and covered it with a blanket to hide the evidence.

"You stole his milk and butchered his calf?" Gabe looked horrified.

"That's right." Yale pushed him aside and lifted Kitty into the back of the wagon. "Now let's get. It'll be light soon."

They managed to cross a muddy creek and pass through a forest before making camp. But that night, for the first time in weeks, they went to bed with their stomachs full.

All through the night Gabe brooded about his younger brother's skill as a thief. Did he come by it naturally, through the blood of his father? He pushed aside that thought and focused on the perils that lay ahead. Would there ever be an end to their misery?

The answer came sooner than he'd expected.

Two weeks later, when they'd gone through the last of their meat, they came up over a rise and saw a small encampment of wagons and shacks. As they drew near they saw an old man tending a herd of cows. He looked up as their little party approached.

"'Afternoon, boys. Welcome to Misery."

The two brothers looked at each other.

It was Gabe who said, "Misery?"

Seeing their surprise the old man laughed, showing a gaping hole where his teeth had once been. "That's the name of our little place. We figure we're all sharing in it together. My name's Aaron Smiler.''

Gabe offered a handshake. "I'm Gabriel Conover. This is my brother Yale." He pointed to the back of the wagon. "And that's our little sister, Kitty."

At the sight of the little girl the old man touched a gnarled hand to his wide-brimmed hat in a courtly gesture. Then he turned back to Gabe, sensing that he was the spokesman for the family. "Where's your folks, son?"

"Our ma's buried along the trail. We're heading for the Badlands to join up with our pa." He looked at the old man hopefully. "You wouldn't happen to know him, would you? Clay Conover."

The old man shook his head. "Sorry, son. Never heard of him." He glanced at the weary little party before pointing toward a wood shack in the distance. "That's my place. Why don't you stop awhile and I'll make you some vittles."

At that the two younger ones perked up considerably.

Gabe held back. "We can't pay you, Mr. Smiler."

Aaron Smiler saw the range of emotions in these three. He could read disappointment in the little girl's eyes, and a simmering annoyance in the eyes of the middle brother. But it was this oldest that held his attention. There was such simple honesty here. Though he was little more than a boy, this one had the heart of a grown man. A man of integrity.

To appease his sense of honor, the old man said simply, "Well, now. Maybe you could lend a hand with some of the chores around here. I'm getting on in years, and I can't do all the things I used to."

"Yes, sir." Gabriel nudged his brother and Yale nodded his agreement.

"All right then." The old man led the way. "Maybe, if you decide you like it here, you'll make Misery your home for awhile. Just until you're ready to resume your search for your pa, that is."

"Thank you, Mr. Smiler." Gabe felt a trembling in his legs, and didn't know if it was weariness or relief. But this much he knew. For now, for as long as the old man would have them, they'd found a place to settle. To stay together.

He'd given his ma his word that their little family would stay together. He intended to keep his promise. Or die trying.

Chapter One

Misery, South Dakota, 1885

"Sheriff Conover."

"Yeah." Gabe looked up from his desk to see Roscoe Timmons, the bartender from the Red Dog Saloon bent almost double in the doorway, wheezing out a breath after racing through town. "What's the trouble?"

"You better get over to the Red Dog right away." Roscoe waited just long enough for Gabe to snatch up his rifle and wide-brimmed hat before falling into step beside him.

Whenever there was trouble in Misery, Sheriff Gabe Conover was the man everybody wanted standing beside them. It wasn't just his skill with a gun that had earned him a reputation as the toughest lawman in the territory. Though slow to anger, and famous for taking his time to think through every situation before acting, he was a straight shooter who never veered from his path as an honest, dedicated man of the law. He'd delivered more outlaws to the courts than any other sheriff in the Dakota Territory. Not an easy job, since the gold rush of seventy-four had swelled the number of people flocking into the region.

"Somebody drunk and causing trouble?"

"Yeah." The bartender cast him a sideways glance. "Buck Reedy."

Gabe gave a sigh of resignation and touched a hand to the gun belt at his hip. "Who'd he lose his money to this time?"

"Some cowboy from Montana who won six hands in a row, and then started bragging. You know Reedy's temper."

Everyone in the town of Misery knew Buck Reedy's temper. They'd seen the signs of it often enough on his shy, long-suffering wife, and on his timid son. A hundred different bruises, and a hundred different explanations for each of them.

As Gabe put a hand on the saloon door he said, "Try to keep everyone out of the line of fire, you hear?"

Roscoe, who had come to the territory young and eager for adventure, and had stayed on as bartender and sometimes piano player at the Red Dog, nodded and hung back as the sheriff strode through the doorway.

Inside, though it was still midafternoon, there was the usual smattering of cowboys scattered around the room, along with a couple of girls in scanty clothes.

All were staring at the big, rawboned rancher holding a pistol in his right hand, his left arm wrapped tightly around the throat of a girl who bore signs of having been pistol-whipped. Blood oozed from a cut over her temple. Her eyes were glazed with fear and pain.

Gabe aimed his rifle at the man and called, "All right now, Buck. Let go of the woman."

"So you can shoot me?" The rancher's tone was filled with scorn. "I'll let go of her when this cowboy gives me back my money."

"We're not going to talk about the money until you release the woman."

"This isn't your fight, Sheriff. Back off. All I want's my money."

Gabe cocked the rifle, letting the sound sink into the man's consciousness. "Any time there's a fight in this town, it becomes mine, Buck. Now let her go or I'll shoot you where you stand. Is your life worth hers?"

Gabe was aware that a crowd was beginning to gather in the doorway and mill about behind him. Word traveled fast in a town this small. And people were always eager for a little excitement. He knew it only made things more complicated. Buck Reedy, ever the bully, wouldn't want to show any sign of weakness in front of witnesses.

Still, it was important for the sheriff to forget the crowd and focus on Buck and the woman, hoping for any distraction that might give him the chance to wrestle her free.

"That cowboy cost me three hundred dollars.

That's all the money I saved for grain." Buck Reedy's hand was shaking with a temper that was quickly slipping out of control. His face was red and streaked with sweat.

"What's that got to do with the woman?" Gabe couldn't see much more than her eyes, wide with terror, and a few strands of red hair. Or was that blood? He couldn't be certain. But this much he knew. He'd never seen this female before. After eighteen years in Misery, he knew everyone in the entire town.

"It's got nothing to do with her." Buck was shouting now, slipping closer and closer to losing his last thread of sense. "But either I get my money back, or I kill her. And it'll be his fault. So you tell him to lay my money on the table right now or she's dead."

Gabe's voice was deadly soft. "Cowboy, do as he says. Set the money down."

The cowboy shook his head. "I won it fair and square. I won't give it back."

Gabe turned his rifle on the cowboy. "The folks in this town will tell you I never give an order twice. Now are you going to do what I say, or do you want to see your woman die over money?" His voice, though calm, seemed to reverberate in the silence of the saloon.

The cowboy swallowed, then reached into his pocket and set the bills on the table. His voice shook. "There, Sheriff. Satisfied? But you're wrong about one thing. She's not my woman."

"I don't care whose woman she is." Gabe faced Buck Reedy. "Turn her loose."

"After I've got my money. I don't trust that little skunk. He probably kept half in his other pocket." Reedy inched closer to the table, keeping the pistol at the woman's head.

In the blink of an eye things happened so quickly, nobody had time to sort them out. The cowboy swore and pulled a pistol from his boot, while at the same instant making a grab for the money. In his agitation Buck Reedy's finger tightened on the trigger of his gun. Sheriff Gabe Conover knew he had only a second or two to save the woman's life. With his left hand he caught her by the arm and yanked her free while at the same moment firing his rifle. Then, to shield her from harm, he flung her behind him, putting himself between her and the cowboy as he fired again.

The first bullet ripped through Reedy's shoulder, knocking him back against the wall. His pistol dropped to the floor.

The second bullet sliced a strip of skin off the cowboy's fingers as it tore the gun from his hand.

Before Reedy could reach for his weapon, Gabe kicked it aside, then scooped up the cowboy's gun, tucking it into his waist before pressing his rifle to Reedy's chest.

Gabe's voice was pure ice. "You move a muscle, Buck, you know what'll happen. This isn't a good day to die."

The crowd held its breath, knowing the burly

rancher loved nothing more than a good brawl. If his opponent were anyone else, a bullet to the shoulder wouldn't stop him. But even Buck Reedy's famous temper was no match for Sheriff Gabe Conover when his temper was up.

Buck was breathing heavily and studying the lawman through narrow, slitted eyes, as though weighing his chances. Finally he closed his eyes and lifted his hands in a signal of surrender.

Everyone who'd been watching heaved a sigh of relief.

Gabe turned to the saloon owner, Jack Slade, who'd watched the entire scene unfold without leaving his place at the poker table. "Did the cowboy win Buck's money fair?"

Slade nodded.

Gabe motioned with his rifle to the cowboy. "Pick up your money and get out of town."

The cowboy's eyes were hard and sullen. "What about my gun?"

"It's mine now. You use it on a man of the law, you lose the right to ever use it on another man."

With a string of oaths the cowboy scooped up the bills.

"And if you're smart," Gabe added softly, "you'll pick a town other than Misery next time you're in the mood to gamble."

The furious cowboy left without a backward glance.

Gabe turned and saw the girl still sitting numbly on the floor, holding a hand to her head.

He walked closer and bent down. "What's your name?"

"Billie. Billie Calley." Her voice was little more than a breathy whisper, and he could see that all the color had drained from her face.

"Where's your home, Billie?"

She looked away. "I don't have one."

"All right. Where are you from?"

She stared at a spot on the floor.

Gabe knelt in front of her, forcing her to look at him. "What are you doing here?"

"I..." Her lips were trembling and she looked like she might pass out any second. "I work here."

Gabe flicked a glance at Jack Slade, who shrugged. "She just hired on today."

"Are you crazy, Slade? She's no more than a kid."

The saloon owner stood, shoving back his chair. "She said she's eighteen. You calling her a liar?"

Gabe got to his feet and tossed a key to the bartender. "Take Buck over to the jail and lock him up. I'll send the doc over to see him after he's tended to Billie here."

"I'm the one with the gunshot," Buck said hotly. "All she's got is a measly little cut."

Gabe rounded on him, his eyes as hard as flint. "You're lucky I didn't kill you, Reedy. While you're lying in your cell, you think about that. You think about why you've been given another day to live."

In one smooth motion Gabe lifted the girl in his

arms and was shocked to realize she weighed less than a sack of grain.

He turned to Slade. "Show me to her room. And send somebody to fetch Doc Honeywell."

The saloon owner led the way up the stairs.

There were a dozen small rooms on the second floor, which could be rented by the hour or by the night. Since there was no boardinghouse in the town of Misery, this was the only place a stranger could sleep. It guaranteed Jack Slade a thriving business.

This was also where Gabe Conover slept most nights, since room and board were included in his pay.

They climbed to the third floor, which was off-limits to anyone but the girls employed at the Red Dog. If Slade found one of the girls with a man on this floor, he docked her a day's pay. That way, he made certain he collected the room fee, and was also able to keep track of how much his girls were earning, so that he could take his cut.

Gabe strode down the hall until Slade paused and pushed open the door to a small, cramped room. Gabe brushed past him and lay Billie on the bed.

"If you don't mind, Sheriff, I'd like to get back downstairs." Slade barely glanced at the girl before walking away. "I have a business to run."

When they were alone Gabe poured water into a basin. Wringing out a cloth he sat on the edge of the bed and began washing the blood from her forehead.

"Your ma know you're here, Billie?" He deliberately kept his tone soft.

She shrank from his touch and looked like she'd rather jump out the window than tolerate having him this close. "I got no ma."

Gabe paused, then forced himself to proceed even more slowly. It was obvious this female didn't like being touched by a man. "How about your pa?"

She darted a look at him, then away.

He decided to try again. "Got any brothers or sisters?"

She shook her head.

He caught sight of the ugly bruises on the top of her arm and wondered if there were more on other parts of her body. "Your pa do this, Billie?"

She clamped her mouth shut.

He sighed. He'd seen so many of them. Girls running from the isolation of ranch life, or wives hiding from husbands who beat them. Women old before their time, thinking they'd find something better in one of the rough towns that had sprung up all over the landscape. But the only work they ever found was in places like this, where, a few months from now, their old lives would seem like heaven compared to what they'd taken on.

"You know what Slade expects you to do here?"

She shook her head. "I didn't ask. I don't care. He promised me a place to sleep, and enough food to stay alive."

He glanced at the way the faded old gown hung on her. From the looks of her she'd never had a decent meal in her life. "In return, you'll have to flirt with the cowboys who come in here.'' He studied her closely. ''And…other things.''

He could tell, by the way her expression never changed, that she had no idea what he was talking about.

Just then a heavyset man waddled into the room, breathing heavily from his climb.

''Hey, Doc.''

''Gabe.'' The doctor set down his black bag and looked at the girl on the bed. ''This our patient?''

''That's right.'' Gabe stood up to make room for the doctor. ''Her name's Billie. Billie, this is Doc Honeywell.''

''Billie.'' The doctor sat on the edge of the bed and examined the wound to her temple, which still oozed blood. ''How'd this happen?''

When she remained silent Gabe said, ''Buck Reedy went on another rampage. Said he'd kill her if some cowboy didn't give back the money he'd lost to him.''

''Why the girl?'' Doc asked as he opened his medical bag.

''I guess 'cause she was handy.''

''What were you doing in the saloon, Billie?'' Doc began applying disinfectant.

When she didn't answer Gabe watched her face. Though the ointment the doc was putting on her must have burned like the fire of hell, she made not a sound. The only indication she gave of any discomfort was the way her hands clutched at the blanket beneath her.

Gabe answered for her. "She says she's going to work here."

Doc Honeywell paused to look into her eyes. "You got any idea what you're getting yourself into here, Billie?"

She shrugged. "The sheriff says I'll have to flirt with the cowboys. And other things."

The old man took his time closing the ointment and returning it to his medical bag. "It's the other things I'm worried about, Billie." He glanced up at the sheriff. "If you don't mind, Gabe, I think Billie and I will have a little talk before I head on over to the jail to tend to Buck."

Gabe looked greatly relieved. "Thanks, Doc. You might want to look at those bruises. They're not as fresh as the cut. Could be more of them under her clothes." He nodded toward Billie, then let himself out.

He was halfway down the stairs before he heard a little cry, and realized that Doc Honeywell had, in his own brusque manner, apprised Billie Calley of the duties of a saloon girl.

He hoped he never saw her in Misery again.

"Sorry, Sheriff." Lars Swenson came hurrying into the jailhouse. "I didn't mean to be so late. But my father said that as long as I was riding out to the Reedy ranch, I may as well deliver a wagon load of supplies to the Sutter place."

The Swenson family owned the dry goods store in Misery. Lars, just turned twenty, was the big, strap-

ping son of Olaf and Inga, and worked the family
business. In addition Lars stayed nights at the jail
whenever there was a prisoner, giving Gabe a chance
to get some dinner and some sleep.

Despite his size, Lars was a gentle man who would
be useless in a fight. But he had a quick mind and
was completely honest. Those two traits were enough
for Gabe Conover, who was grateful for his assis-
tance.

"That's all right, Lars. I had a lot of paperwork
to see to." Gabe shoved the latest wanted posters in
a drawer and strapped on his gun belt. "How did
Mrs. Reedy take the news that her husband was
spending the night in jail?"

"She seemed fine with it."

The boy blushed, and Gabe could only imagine
the relief of Reedy's wife and son. They probably
wished he could always cool off in jail before taking
that temper home to them.

"Well, maybe I'll hold him another day or two,
so the doc can take a look at his bullet wound. And
give her and the boy some breathing room." He
picked up his hat and walked to the door. "See you
in the morning."

"Yes, sir." Lars picked up a broom and began to
sweep as the sheriff made his way along the dirt path
that served as the main street of Misery.

The notes of a tinny piano could be heard long
before Gabe paused outside the doors of the Red
Dog. He'd hoped to ride out to the Smiler ranch for
supper, and maybe spend the night with his sister and

old Aaron, but it hadn't worked out. He figured in a day or two, if things remained quiet, he'd do just that.

He missed Kitty. He smiled, just thinking about how she'd grown. His smile faded at the thought of his brother Yale. No one had heard from him in months. Not since he'd taken up with that band of outlaws.

Without warning the weariness and guilt crept into his soul. What did he do wrong? How could Yale have been tempted by such a life? Hadn't he seen the pain their father's choices had caused all of them? It was, Gabe knew, the reason he was a man of the law. He needed somehow to atone for the sins of his father. His jaw tightened. But he'd be damned if he'd pay for the sins of his brother, too. It was Yale's life. Yale's choice.

He shoved open the doors of the saloon and stepped inside, pausing as he always did to assess the room full of people. He was assaulted by the music from the piano, and the voices raised in raucous laughter from one corner, where a rancher was relating a funny story. A gambler at a nearby table cursed loudly and several others moaned as one of the men gathered up a pile of chips. A peddler sat alone, devouring a bowl of stew. The steam wafted up, reminding Gabe that he hadn't eaten since early that morning.

As he took a seat in a corner of the room one of the saloon girls hurried over and he inhaled the cloying fragrance of cheap perfume she always wore.

"Hey, Sheriff." Dyed yellow hair had been knotted on top of her head with a ribbon in which she'd tucked a gaudy purple feather. Her purple gown was cut low enough to display her ample bosom. She called herself Cheri, insisting that it be pronounced Sheree, because she thought it sounded exotic. She bragged that she'd been working in saloons since she was ten, and knew more about men than they knew about themselves. She'd taught herself to walk with one hand on her hip, so that she could lift her skirts and give the customers a view of shapely thigh. "Something to drink tonight?"

"No, thanks, Cheri. Just supper."

"It's stew."

He knew by the face she was making that she'd had some complaints from the customers. Red Dog's cook, named Grunt, was capable of making only two things. Burned steak or stew. Nobody ever asked what went into the stew pot. But the regulars always hoped for steak, no matter how badly it was burned.

Gabe sighed, too hungry to care. "Make it a big bowl."

She hurried away and returned minutes later with his meal, which he attacked. A short time later he sat back, feeling almost human again. Tipping back his chair he removed a cigar from his pocket and held a match to the end.

Despite the stew, life didn't get much better than this, he thought as he gave a satisfied glance around.

Just then Jack Slade walked to the bar and clapped his hands for attention.

When the crowd fell silent he called, "We got a special treat tonight. All the way from San Francisco, with the voice of an angel, is Belle California. Let's hear it for the beautiful Belle."

There was a smattering of curious applause. Gabe found himself looking around for the glamorous entertainer. Just then Slade lifted a female in his arms and seated her on the piano. She tipped down her head and the wide gauzy brim hid her face while she adjusted the yards of lacy petticoats until they'd modestly covered her exposed ankles. That brought a roar of protest from the cowboys seated nearby. When she looked up, Gabe nearly swallowed his cigar.

Belle California was the girl he'd met that afternoon. Billie Calley. But this woman bore no resemblance to her.

The crimson satin gown fitted her like a second skin, hugging small, firm breasts, and an even tinier waist, before spilling down into row after row of flounces, and ending with layers of flirty white lace petticoats. Her red hair was hidden beneath a black wig. Over that, the hat was red satin with black plumes that dipped over one side of her face, hiding the marks of the pistol-whipping she'd taken earlier. Her freckled face had been transformed with makeup. Dramatic red lips. Wide, expressive eyes outlined with black smudges. Gabe suspected that the twin spots of color on her cheeks were natural. Though she lifted her head, she avoided looking at the cowboys directly in front of her, who were now hooting and hollering, and urging her to show some leg.

Roscoe Timmons at the piano tickled the keys, then glanced up expectantly. But though she opened her mouth, nothing came out.

Nerves, Gabe thought with a trace of pity. From where he was sitting he could see that the poor thing was scared out of her wits.

Roscoe went through another riff, and this time held the note until she took a deep breath and began to sing. At first it was impossible to hear her over the calls of the cowboys. But as she continued singing, they gradually fell silent.

She wasn't singing; she was speaking the words. All in that soft, breathy voice he'd heard earlier. This wasn't one of the bawdy saloon songs they were all familiar with. It was a tender ballad a wife might sing to her cowboy husband before he left on a cattle drive.

Gabe couldn't take his eyes off her. She was, he thought, absolutely mesmerizing. Though she was far too thin, and her eyes looked too big for her face, there was just something about her that tugged at him. Little wisps of red hair peeked out from beneath the outrageous wig, giving her a waiflike appearance. She refused to strike a suggestive pose, choosing instead to hold herself rigid while she stared at a spot on the far wall. It was, he realized, amazingly effective. She appeared exotic, aloof and absolutely untouchable.

By the time the song was finished, the cowboys

were on their feet, tossing money at her, shouting for more.

She was so surprised, she didn't seem able to move. Then, as the money floated around her on the piano, she gathered it into her hands, unsure what to do with it.

When Jack Slade lifted her down and announced smugly that Belle California would give another performance in one hour, the saloon roared with protests. But not a single patron walked out, which left Slade beaming his approval. For the next hour the cowboys would spend their money on drink and cards, biding their time until they could get another glimpse of the glamorous Belle.

Slade dropped an arm around her waist, hauling her roughly through the crowd toward the stairs.

As they passed Gabe's table, Billie caught sight of him. For a moment she hesitated, her eyes going wider than ever. Then Slade muttered an oath and dragged her out of the reach of an overzealous cowboy who made a grab for her.

Gabe saw the way she shrank from the contact with the drunk before allowing herself to be escorted from the room.

His eyes narrowed as he looked around and realized that innocent, shy, little Billie Calley, in the guise of Belle California, had suddenly become the fantasy of every man in this room.

And though it shamed him to admit it, he was no exception.

Chapter Two

Billie was shaking so hard she could feel her knees knocking under the voluminous petticoats. But she allowed herself to be hauled through the crowd of drunks until she was safely up the stairs and in her own room.

Jack Slade closed the door and leaned against it, watching as she sank down on the edge of her bed. "That was good. I didn't know if you'd get through it, kid. But you did just fine."

"Thanks."

He was studying her with new respect. "I wasn't sure just what I was going to do with you, but I thought I recognized something. And I was right. You're different."

He folded his arms over his chest, his mind working overtime. He'd originally intended to introduce her with that little song, and then throw her to the wolves. But as soon as he'd seen the reaction of those drunks downstairs, he'd come up with a better idea. It had come to him in a flash of brilliance.

This girl had something special that appealed to men. Not beauty or a great body, though in the right clothes she proved to have both. But she had something even more precious. Innocence. Even the fact that she'd been too nervous to sing had helped that image. The image of a wounded bird that made every man in that room want to help her fly. So Slade had decided to play on that. He'd keep her untouchable for as long as possible, so the cowboys and ranchers would keep coming back for more.

Eventually he'd have to turn her loose with the other girls, to earn her keep. After all, he wasn't running a charity here. He wasn't about to give her free room and board, not to mention glamorous clothes, without getting something in return. So when the interest dimmed, she'd survive the way the other women did. In the meantime, as long as she kept his saloon filled at night, and the men drinking while they waited around for more, she could hold on to her precious innocence. It was, he knew, something that couldn't be faked. Once lost, she'd never be quite as appealing again. And since she didn't appear to have any other talent, he'd have to play this up for all it was worth.

"You've got an hour to rest up and make yourself glamorous again. See that you keep that bruise covered. It would spoil the image."

She nodded. "All right." She held up the fistful of money. "What about this?"

"That belongs to the house. I'll give you your share when I pay you." He stuffed the money into his pocket before opening the door and letting himself out.

Billie carefully removed the hat pins and set the plumed hat on a night table, and the wig beside it. Then she slipped her feet out of the soft kid slippers, before sinking back against the pillow and closing her eyes until the trembling eased up.

She'd done it. She'd actually gotten through the song, though the truth was, she couldn't recall a single word of it now. In fact, that entire display downstairs was a blur to her. A blur of men's faces and voices. The sounds of their hands clapping and their feet stomping the wooden floor. Coarse words muttered as she'd passed them. The smell of sweat and horses and whiskey and leather. All a blur.

Except for one thing. The sheriff.

She'd thought earlier today, when that rancher held his gun to her head, that she wouldn't live to see another sunrise. She'd actually resigned herself to dying. And then Sheriff Gabe Conover had walked in and everything had changed.

She'd never seen a man so brave, so sure of himself. He'd looked like something out of a dream, dressed all in black, except for that shiny star pinned to his collar. She could still see the way he'd looked, so tall and muscled, with that strong, jutting jaw and those ice-gray eyes, striding across the room right into the face of danger.

Grown men had been cowed by his power.

It wasn't just the power of his gun. She'd seen

men with guns before. Had seen how much destruction they could cause.

Nor was it the power of his badge. She was well aware that there were corrupt men who wore the badge of the law. Some of them were worse than the men they considered outside the law.

No. It wasn't the gun or the badge. It was the man. The way he walked through a crowd, tall and proud, expecting them to part for him. The way he looked down the barrel of a man's gun without flinching. The way he stared a man in the eye when he gave an order.

She had the feeling that whatever Sheriff Conover set out to do, he'd see it through, no matter what the odds against him. When he'd yanked her out of that drunk's arms and put himself between her and danger, she had just about fainted from the sheer courage of the man. Like everyone else in that saloon she'd watched with a sort of horrified fascination as he'd calmly taken charge of two men who, by all rights, should now be dead.

And when he'd lifted her in his arms and carried her up the stairs to this bed, she'd felt as if she could just wrap her arms around his neck and hold on forever. It was the strangest sensation. For the first time in her life she'd felt safe. Protected.

She thought about the way he'd tried to talk to her about her job at the Red Dog. She hadn't understood. And when the doctor had explained her duties, she'd been not only horrified, but humiliated, to think that any man could expect such behavior from her.

And now the sheriff thought she was that kind of woman.

But what could she do? She'd run as far as she could. There was nowhere left to go. She was desperate.

Besides, Mr. Slade had assured her that her only duty consisted of wearing these clothes and speaking the words of the only songs she knew. One was a song her pa used to sing. The other was a lullaby she could vaguely recall hearing her grandmother sing when she was a little girl.

She shivered, wondering what would happen when the cowboys downstairs grew tired of her songs.

She pressed a hand to her eyes and tried to rest. She wouldn't worry about that right now. For now, for this night, she was safe and warm.

She'd come so far. Had been through so much. Tomorrow was soon enough to deal with whatever was to come.

When a knock sounded on her door, Billie awoke with a start, then raced to the chipped mirror to paint her lips the way Cheri had taught her, before securing her wig and hat and slipping her feet into the fancy kid boots.

As she followed Slade down the stairs he shouted gruff orders and she obeyed, fluffing up her skirts and petticoats. By the time they reached the bottom step the roar from the crowd was almost deafening.

Billie felt Slade's arm around her waist as he hustled her through the maze of hot, sweaty bodies. She was aware of faces slipping in and out of her line of vision. Men shouting, cheering. One held up a fistful of money and muttered something that had her face flaming. But Slade had a firm grasp on her as he kept moving resolutely toward the piano, never pausing long enough to allow the cowboys to come between them.

When they had maneuvered their way across the room Slade lifted her to her perch and the crowd fell strangely silent.

After Slade's announcement, Roscoe went through his usual introductory notes on the piano and gave her a signal to begin.

As she modestly adjusted her skirts Billie could almost feel the men in the room breathing. Could sense the eager, expectant hush as she opened her mouth and began to speak the words of her childhood lullaby.

At first she avoided looking at their faces, choosing instead to stare at a spot over their heads. But her gaze was drawn to a wiry old man in the back of the room who was mopping at his eyes with a filthy rag.

It took her a moment to understand the implications. Was he crying? Because of her song? Stunned, she allowed herself to look at the faces of these men. To really see them. Several of them were openly weeping. Others were staring at her with looks that ranged from mild interest to pure lust.

She was not only startled but also repulsed to realize she was the object of such attention.

And then one face caught her eye, and she found she couldn't look away.

Sheriff Gabe Conover was still seated at the same table where he'd been earlier. He was watching her with an intensity that caused her heart to take a sudden hard bounce. Was that anger in those icy eyes? Not that she could blame him. He'd tried to warn her about the perils of working here, and she'd chosen to disregard his advice. To a man of the law that was probably the worst possible insult.

She felt a wave of sadness. There was no way to explain her dilemma. What would he know about feeling powerless? Desperate. Without even a shred of hope left. A man like Sheriff Conover, who had the respect of an entire town, couldn't possibly fathom what she was feeling.

Seeing the way he was looking at her had her forgetting the words. She was forced to start over. Nobody except the piano player seemed to notice the mistake, and he recovered at once. Gamely she plowed ahead, reminding herself that if she could pull this off, she could take refuge in her room. There would be no one there watching her. No one expecting her to display herself for the enjoyment of some drunken cowboys.

But as she mouthed the words she began to think about how she'd felt as a little girl, safe and secure on her grandmother's lap, while that quavering voice lulled her to sleep. Without realizing it a dreamy smile played on her lips and her voice took on a faraway look.

When she spoke the last words, and the final notes of the piano faded, she was surprised at the sound of men shouting and stomping their feet, demanding more. She realized that she'd managed to get through yet another trial through sheer force of will.

Again the men tossed money at her and she gathered it up as quickly as possible.

As Slade reached for her a shrill, feminine voice lifted above the din.

"Women of the Red Dog Saloon. Come with me and leave this den of iniquity behind."

Billie looked over to see a young woman standing in the doorway. Despite the warmth of the night she wore a dark cape over her long dark dress. Her hair had been pulled back in a severe knot, and covered by a hat. Her eyes glittered with indignation behind round spectacles.

"Do not let Jack Slade use you in this manner. If he had his way, all women would become his harlots. He is an evil man, and this is the devil's own house."

Slade let out a hiss of breath and said tiredly, "Come on, Belle. Let's get out of here before we have to hear the same tired lecture."

As he lifted her down from the piano, Billie caught sight of Sheriff Conover still watching her in that quiet, intense way.

She felt shivers along her spine as she was hauled roughly through the crowd, while the drunken cowboys reached out to touch her hair, her face, her skirts as she passed by. She held herself stiffly, unable to relax her guard until she was safely out of their reach and up the stairs.

Once in her room Slade closed the door and looked at Billie standing uncertainly beside her bed.

"Who was that woman in the doorway?"

"Emma Hardwick. Fancies herself a missionary, and sees me as the devil incarnate. Don't pay her any attention." He wiped away his frown. "You did real good, kid. That's all for tonight."

"That's...all?"

"Yeah. I'll take that money now."

As she handed it over Slade said, "Maybe tomorrow night you'll do three shows, depending on the size of the crowd." He studied her a moment before asking, "You know how to cook?"

"Cook?" She couldn't seem to grasp this abrupt change of direction. But she was so delighted to know that the nightly entertainment was over, she merely nodded her head.

"Good. I'll expect you downstairs early in the morning. You can help old Grunt in the kitchen."

"Grunt? Is that a man or a woman?"

"Grunt's a man."

She hesitated. "That's his name?"

Slade grinned. "If he has any other, I've never heard it. We call him Grunt because that's how he talks. Mostly he just grunts. See that you're down there early. We'll have a lot of hungry cowboys to feed after the whiskey they managed to drink tonight."

As he turned away Billie glanced down at her gown. "Should I wear this in the morning?"

"No." Slade opened the door and said over his shoulder, "That's special. It's just for evenings. You'll have to make do with what you own." He realized she hadn't yet caught on to what had happened downstairs. "During the day you're just Billie Calley, who slings stew at the Red Dog. None of the cowboys who see you will realize you have any connection to the exotic Belle California who entertains at night."

"They won't?"

He shook his head. "Trust me. Your secret's safe."

When he left her, Billie did as before, unpinning the hat and wig and setting them aside so they wouldn't get damaged. But this time she didn't lie down. Instead she undressed and carefully hung the gown. Then, dressed in nothing but a flimsy chemise, she filled a basin with water and began to scrub her only dress until all the dust of the trail and the blood caused by Buck Reedy's outburst had been washed away. After that she removed her chemise and washed it as well, hanging both on pegs to dry.

She glanced at the bed and knew that she ought to get as much rest as possible for the day ahead. But she found herself pacing the length of the tiny room, too agitated to sleep.

What had she gotten herself into here? How long would Jack Slade allow her to help the cook and speak her little songs, before he ordered her to do more? She crossed her arms over her chest, tapping a finger against her elbow as she worried and thought about Emma Hardwick's warning. Was Jack Slade a tool of the devil? He'd admitted to her that he wasn't a patient man. And that he didn't run a charity for wayward orphans.

Still, her luck had held tonight. And she was reluctant to think beyond the here and now.

She paused at the window and stared up at the night sky before closing her eyes. In an instant everything was wiped from her mind except the way the sheriff looked downstairs as he'd watched her. That handsome, rugged face perfectly composed. Those big competent hands folded together on the table. Those fierce eyes narrowed with concentration.

He'd been the only man in the saloon who had remained both silent and watchful, while the men around him had behaved like a pack of coyotes, wailing at the top of their lungs. If he'd felt anything at all, it wasn't apparent.

She had the sense that he was a man who gave away nothing of his feelings. But then, she thought with a shiver, maybe it was because he had none. Especially for her. She was, after all, a saloon girl now. What man of the law could ever feel anything but contempt for her kind?

Gabe pushed away from the table and headed toward the stairs. Before he'd taken two steps he felt a light touch on his back and a low, feminine purr.

"Want some company tonight, sheriff?"

He didn't even bother to turn. "No thanks, Cheri."

"Just thought I'd ask."

"Sure. I appreciate it." He climbed the stairs and stepped into his room.

Instead of lighting the lantern on his night table as he usually did, he undressed in the dark, with just the light from the full moon streaming through the dirty window. He carefully placed his pistol under his pillow and his rifle beside him on the bed before climbing naked under the covers.

He folded his hands under his head and closed his eyes, seeing again the way Billie had looked in that fancy gown. She was such a contradiction. Part child, part woman. An innocent and a temptress. A lost soul who, with a few spoken words, was able to control an entire room full of hardened men. Some of them had actually cried while she spoke the words of that lullaby.

Probably remembering their childhoods, he thought with a flash of pain. For most of them it was no doubt a place they'd like to revisit. A time when they'd been carefree and happy. As for himself, he had no desire to return to those boyhood memories. They gave him no pleasure. When a fleeting scene did manage to intrude on his sleep, all he seemed able to recall was the incident at his grandfather's grave. That had been the moment when all his innocent illusions had been shattered, and he'd learned the truth about his father.

He turned on his side, determined to shut out the

sound of his uncle's voice and the pain in his mother's eyes.

Her heart had been broken. But no more than his. In that one moment all their lives had been altered forever.

He had long ago decided that there had been no life before Misery, and no family before Aaron Smiler, who had opened his heart and his home to three lost children.

Gabe clenched his jaw. He'd made a good life for himself here. It had been a long, hard climb, but he'd earned the respect of the people of Misery.

He had no intention of getting sidetracked by one skinny female who didn't have a lick of sense. What Billie Calley did with her life was her business.

As long as she didn't break any laws, he had no intention of meddling in her affairs. And when Jack Slade was through with her, as he surely would be when she lost her appeal, she'd just have to find someone else to pick up the pieces of her shattered life and broken dreams.

Chapter Three

Morning light was just inching over the horizon when Billie slipped out of bed and hurriedly dressed in her chemise and shabby calico dress. The neckline drooped over one shoulder and she had to keep pulling it up. The waist fell somewhere around her hips. The skirt was so long the hem dragged on the ground.

For a moment she stared hungrily at the soft kid slippers she'd worn the previous night. She'd never before worn anything brand-new, and she'd felt so elegant walking in them. But they belonged to Belle California. Billie Calley had no right to wear them. With a sigh she stuffed her feet into the scuffed hand-me-downs she'd been wearing for the better part of a few hundred miles. They were big enough to fit a man twice her size, and smeared with mud and dung. But they served their purpose. And they'd carried her over some very unforgiving land in the past few weeks.

For lack of a comb she ran her fingers through the

tangles of her hair. Minutes later it was falling over one eye. With a sigh of resignation she shoved it aside, tucking it behind her ear.

She carefully made up her bed, smoothing the blanket and plumping the pillow. It gave her a sense of pride to know that it was her bed. Her room. For as long as she worked here it was all hers, and she intended to see that it was kept clean. She gave a glance around, and seeing that everything was tidy, let herself out the door and tiptoed past the other rooms on her way to the stairs.

She'd heard the girls coming up to their rooms at various times during the night, after they'd finished whatever they'd had to do. Billie wondered what time they would get up. Not that it mattered. She figured, with all the distasteful work they did for Jack Slade, they deserved to sleep as long as they wanted. As for her, she was delighted to be up early and facing another day.

Another day.

She paused. Thanks to the quick thinking of Sheriff Conover, she'd been given another day.

As she walked through the deserted saloon she could hear sounds coming from the kitchen, signaling that the cook was already up and about. She pushed open the door and was assaulted by heat from the cookstove, and the smell of stale grease sizzling in a huge iron skillet.

The cook had his back to her, stirring something in a kettle. She was startled by his size. He stood head and shoulders over any man Billie had ever seen. And what shoulders. They were wider than two axe handles, and bigger than most men's thighs. His hair was snow-white and flowing nearly to his shoulders.

"Mr. Grunt?"

She saw his head whip around, blackbird eyes wide with surprise. Seeing her, they narrowed suspiciously.

She gave him a timid smile, thinking he looked like some sort of prophet from ancient times with that flowing mane and stern, unforgiving eyes. "My name's Billie. Mr. Slade said I was to help you."

"Huh. I ask for help and Slade sends me helpless." He looked her up and down, then pointed to a blob of dough on a scarred wooden table. "Know how to make biscuits?"

"Yes, sir."

"Then make 'em." He cocked his head toward a smoking oven. "If you burn 'em I'll make you eat every last one of 'em."

She felt a trickle of sweat down her back. "Yes, sir."

He pinned her with a look. "There's no sirs here. Just me."

"Yes, si—" She felt foolish saying his name, but she had no choice. "Yes, Grunt."

He made a sound and turned away, busying himself at the kettle.

They worked in absolute silence, except for the sounds Grunt made as he sawed off chunks of beef with a rusty saw. It soon became apparent to Billie that he'd been aptly named. He sawed and grunted. Slapped meat in a skillet and grunted. Mopped sweat from his face with the end of his filthy apron and grunted.

After the first batch of perfectly browned biscuits had been removed from the oven and dumped into a bowl, Billie cleared her throat.

"How do you know how much food to make?" When he merely looked at her she felt a need to explain. "The saloon was empty when I walked through a little while ago. What if nobody eats all this food?"

"Huh. You going to talk or work, girl?"

"Work."

"Then get to it." He pointed to a bushel of sandy potatoes.

While Billie began peeling, she kept glancing over, wondering if he ever spoke.

Grunt slapped another steak on the griddle, sending grease and flames leaping everywhere. Finally, sensing her impatience for answers he said, "You see that crowd of drunken cowboys last night?"

She nodded.

"Slade told me most of 'em stayed the night, filling up his rooms."

"Why didn't they ride back to their ranches?"

He shrugged. "Too drunk, I guess. Slade says they kept hoping for a glimpse of some fancy woman he had here."

Her face flaming, Billie turned away, pretending to check the progress of her next batch of biscuits.

"Anyway—" Grunt lifted a steak from the fire and tossed it onto a platter "—when the whiskey wears off, they'll want food, and plenty of it. And what's left will go for supper tonight. Nothin' goes to waste in my kitchen, you hear me, girl?"

"Yes, si— Grunt." She kept her back to him, still too embarrassed to meet his eye. "When did you talk to Mr. Slade?"

"Just before he took himself off to bed this morning."

"He stays up all night?"

She glanced over her shoulder and could see that Grunt was getting tired of her questions.

He stirred the kettle, mopped sweat. "Slade always counts the profits before he turns in. That's just about the time I'm starting, so he gives me a tally of rooms being used."

"But how do you know that everyone who sleeps here will eat here?"

He growled, grunted. "Where else would they eat?"

She shrugged. "But why do you start cooking so early?"

Grunt frowned. "You ever see a nest of hornets when they're all riled up?"

Billie nodded.

"Well, that's nothin' compared to a cowboy just comin' off drink if his food isn't ready the minute he sits down to eat. Now, when you finish that batch of biscuits, you can take this tray over to the jail."

"The...jail?" She was so startled she burned her hand and gave a yelp.

"Bet you'll be more careful next time. Put some of this on it." Grunt nodded toward a can of congealed grease.

Billie reached in and slathered grease on the angry red welt that was beginning to form.

Grunt indicated a huge tray covered with a none-too-clean square of linen. "That's for the sheriff and his assistant and his prisoner." He watched as she struggled to lift it. "Think you can manage?"

"I've lifted heavier." Billie struggled under the weight, balanced it, then staggered toward the back door. "Where's the jail?"

"End of town." Grunt stood mopping his sweaty face and watching in silence as she squared her shoulders and stepped outside.

Cool morning air slapped her face and she drank it in. After the heat of the kitchen, this was a refreshing change. She made her way along the dusty path between crude wooden buildings bearing the names of Swensen's Dry Goods, Doc Honeywell's Surgical Clinic, Jesse Cutler's Barbershop and Bath, and Eli Moffat's Stable.

There was also a tidy little cabin, no bigger than a chicken coop, with crisp white curtains billowing at the open window, and a broom standing alongside a freshly swept stoop. A hand-lettered sign on the door read, Rescue Mission.

Billie found herself wondering just who was rescued, and from what.

At last she came to the end of the town, and paused outside the door of the jailhouse. Just as she was pondering how to juggle the heavy tray and knock on the door, it was thrown open by a young giant with pale yellow hair and sunny blue eyes.

The minute he saw her he whipped his hat from his head. "'Morning, miss."

"Good morning." She was out of breath, and nearly tripped over the hem of her dress as she stepped through the open doorway.

Gabe Conover looked up just as the young man grabbed the tray with one hand and caught her arm to keep her from stumbling. For a moment Gabe was too startled to move. Then he hastily cleared his desk and said gruffly, "You can set that here, Lars."

"Yes, sir." The young man set it down, then turned to Billie. "You all right, miss?"

"Yes. Thanks to you." She gave him a big smile. "I'm Billie Calley."

"Pleased to meet you, Billie. I'm Lars Swensen." For a moment he was so blinded by her smile he nearly forgot his manners. Color crept up his neck and blossomed on his cheeks. Then, remembering his manners, he added, "And this is Sheriff Gabe Conover."

Gabe was frowning at the two of them. "I've already met Miss Calley."

She felt suddenly awkward in the sheriff's presence. Her cheeks turned nearly as red as her hair. "Good morning, Sheriff. Mr....that is, Grunt sent over your breakfast."

"So I see." He didn't move. Couldn't. His gaze was fixed on the way the neckline of her dress had slipped off one shoulder, revealing a good deal of milk-white flesh dotted with freckles.

When he glanced over at Lars, he could see the youth staring, as well. And why not? It wasn't often they were treated to the sight of a female in a gown several sizes too big, wearing men's muddy boots on her feet, her red hair tumbling in her eyes. Eyes which, up close, looked as green as prairie grass.

Last night, in that skintight gown and flirty hat, she'd looked like some exotic creature straight out of every man's fantasy. This morning she looked to be an innocent who belonged back on a farm.

He frowned. "I didn't know you were working days at the Red Dog, too."

She swallowed. "Mr. Slade said I had to earn my keep somehow. And I don't mind. I'd rather this than—" She saw his frown deepen and realized she'd said the wrong thing. Now she had him thinking about last night.

"Well." She could feel herself growing hotter under the sheriff's stern gaze. Obviously he wasn't about to forget what he'd seen in the saloon. "Grunt didn't say if I was supposed to wait and bring back the tray."

"I'll see that you get it back later."

She nodded. "Okay. Well, then…" She started to back away and bumped into a chair, knocking it over with a clatter.

That had the prisoner, Buck Reedy, leaping off his bunk in the cell and cursing loudly.

Billie's face flamed.

Gabe was grateful for an excuse to release the temper that flared the minute he'd seen this female and realized he was attracted to her—a saloon girl. He was across the room in quick strides and reaching through the bars, dragging the prisoner by the front of his shirt until his face was pressed against the cold metal. "Shut your mouth, Reedy. Or I'll add another two days to your time."

Cowed, the man held up his hands in a sign of surrender.

Gabe released him and turned to Billie. She was backing toward the door, looking like a rabbit about to bolt. Just then he caught sight of the angry welt on her hand.

"What's this?" He walked over to lift it to the light of the open door for a closer inspection.

The moment he took her hand in his, he realized his mistake. A jolt of energy shot through him with all the force of a lightning bolt. He stared down into her eyes and saw them widen with sudden fear.

His own narrowed, to hide whatever feelings might be obvious. "How'd this happen?"

"The oven. I...got careless. It'll be all right. I put some grease on it." She pulled her hand away as though his very touch repulsed her. "I've...got to get back."

He curled his hand into a fist at his side. "Thank

you for the meal.'' He spit the words between clenched teeth.

She nodded, sensing that what he'd really like to do was yell at her the way he'd just yelled at his prisoner. Confused and more than a little afraid, she whirled and fled.

As Lars uncovered the tray he said, ''She's new to Misery, sheriff. Where'd she come from?''

''I don't know.''

''How'd you meet her?''

''She was the one Reedy pistol-whipped yesterday.''

''Her? Why, she's no bigger than Cutler's cat.'' Lars picked up a biscuit and popped it in his mouth. ''I wonder why a sweet little thing like that would work at the Red Dog?''

''I guess you'll have to ask her.'' Gabe unlocked the cell door and stood aside as Lars carried Buck Reedy's meal inside.

After the cell was locked, he and Lars uncovered their own plates.

''She's got a sweet smile,'' Lars remarked as he dug into his food. ''If it weren't for those clothes, she'd probably be a pretty little thing. Don't you agree, sheriff?''

Gabe suddenly pushed aside his tray and got to his feet.

Lars looked up. ''What's wrong?''

''Nothing. Guess I'm just not hungry this morning.'' Gabe picked up his hat. ''I'm going to take a turn around the town. When you and Reedy are through, you can leave the tray on my desk. I'll be going to the Red Dog later anyway, so I'll return it to the kitchen.''

Lars shrugged. In all the time he'd been helping out, he'd never before known the sheriff to volunteer to return the breakfast tray. But maybe he had business to discuss with Jack Slade. ''Whatever you say, Sheriff.''

Gabe stepped outside and could just see the hem of a calico gown swirling inside the doorway of the saloon. He decided to take his time walking. Maybe it would help cool the temper that was simmering.

A temper that had risen several notches as soon as Reedy had opened his mouth. Of course that was the reason. It certainly wasn't because of that jolt when he'd touched Billie. Or because of the fact that he'd caught sight of Lars Swensen staring at her with big puppy-dog eyes. What that fool did was none of his concern.

As for Billie, she was an even bigger fool. She had to know she was playing with fire every day she stayed at the Red Dog. And sooner or later she was bound to get burned.

''About time you got back here, girl.'' Grunt was ladling leftover stew into several bowls. ''Now get that skinny hide out to the other room and see if we got any business.''

Billie hurried away and returned minutes later to say, ''There are half a dozen cowboys already sitting out there, waiting to eat.''

While Grunt loaded up a platter with blackened steaks, he pointed to a stack of tin plates and another wooden tray. When the tray was filled to capacity with food, coffee and utensils, Grunt stood back, considering. "You think you can lift that?"

"I managed the other one, didn't I?"

She staggered under the load, and once in the saloon, was helpless to do more than watch in dismay as the cowboys seated around the tables grabbed steaks off the tray, as well as bowls of stew and biscuits before she even had time to set it down in the middle of the table.

At first, as she circled the room, filling tin cups with coffee, she fretted that one of them might recognize her as Belle California. But she soon realized that she'd become invisible to these cowboys. The girl in the tattered dress and muddy boots, her hair hanging in strings from the heat of the kitchen, was just hired help. Instead of looking at her, they seemed to look right through her. She was just there to satisfy their hunger.

And Belle California, she realized, satisfied a very different sort of hunger.

For the next two hours she wore a path between the saloon and the kitchen, carrying enough food to calm the queasy stomachs of a dozen cowboys and peddlers, as well as several of the men in town who, with no women to cook for them, made it a habit to start their day at the Red Dog.

When they'd eaten their fill, she poured coffee as

thick as mud, and watched as the bartender, Roscoe Timmons, offered whiskey to make it more palatable.

By the time the last straggler had left, she loaded the tray with dirty tin plates and cups and utensils and carried them to the kitchen, where buckets of water were heating over the fire.

Grunt was already busy carving chunks of meat for fresh stew and simmering it in a huge blackened kettle. He paused to mop his forehead. "Washing up is your job."

If he expected any complaint, he was pleasantly surprised when Billie merely nodded and poured hot water into a basin. Through sheer force of will she ignored the pain each time she immersed her burned hand in hot water. By the time she'd washed a mountain of dishes, her face was slick with sheen, and her gown was plastered against her like a second skin.

She was startled by a woman's voice from the doorway. "Turn away from this place. It's the house of the devil."

Billie looked up to see the same woman she'd seen the night before. She was wearing a long navy skirt and a crisp white shirtwaist. Her hair was pulled back in a severe bun, and she looked like an owl in those round spectacles. But in the light of day it was obvious that she was young. Not much older than Billie.

"Go on," Grunt shouted. "Take your preachin' elsewhere. Nobody here's interested."

The young woman fixed Billie with a piercing look. "Let this lamb speak for herself."

"L…lamb?" Billie swallowed. She pulled her hands from the dishwater and it ran in little rivers down her arms to the floor.

"Like a lamb to the slaughter. Do you have any idea what becomes of women in this place?"

"Go on," Grunt shouted. "I told you to git. Now git."

The young woman turned. But not before she sent Billie a long, knowing look. "If you ever need help to escape this prison, come to me at the rescue mission."

When she was gone Billie turned to Grunt. "Mr. Slade told me her name is Emma Hardwick. Why does she come here and say those things?"

"Some say her pa was a gambler, who left her and her ma destitute. I say she's just a crazy female who's out to take all the pleasure out of a man's life."

Billie and Grunt both looked up when Gabe Conover stepped through the open doorway. In his hand was the wooden tray.

Grunt looked surprised to see him. "Lars Swensen sick, sheriff?"

"No." Gabe felt suddenly foolish for being here and was quick to cover himself. "Lars had work to see to. So I told him not to worry, I'd bring back the tray."

He offered it to Grunt, who shook his head. "Got to see to the stew. You can give it to the girl to wash."

Gabe walked closer and handed it to Billie without a word.

She began scrubbing it, aware that he was still standing beside her. How she wished he'd say something. But all he did was stare at her in that way that made her so uncomfortable. Did he think, like Emma Hardwick, that she was evil for working here?

Grunt looked over. "Is there something else, Sheriff?"

Gabe was startled. "No. Nothing else. Thanks. That was a fine breakfast." He felt the need to add, "And the biscuits were better than ever."

"The girl made 'em," Grunt covered the kettle and turned away to add more wood to the cookstove.

"You did?" Gabe looked at her with interest. "You can cook?"

"Yeah. Well, some." She smiled. Blushed. Lowered her voice. "I had to be really careful with those biscuits."

"Why was that?"

"Grunt said I'd have to eat all of them if I burned them."

He nearly smiled before he caught himself. Everybody in Misery knew of Grunt's famous temper. In the years he'd spent in this town the old man had made few if any friends. He was more apt to hit a man than shake his hand.

"Well, they were good biscuits." Gabe took a step back. "You working again tonight?"

"You mean as...?" She couldn't say the name. She was too mortified.

She saw the way his look hardened and busied herself drying the tray. Around and around the rim with the dirty towel, to avoid looking at him. She knew if she met his eyes, her face would turn every possible shade of red.

She lifted her chin, determined not to let him intimidate her. "Yes. I'll be working tonight." She spoke in a whisper, so that Grunt wouldn't overhear.

"Well, then." Gabe coughed. Cleared his throat. His gaze was drawn to the burn on her hand, but this time he was smart enough to keep from touching her. "Take care of that."

"I will."

"I guess I'll be seeing you." He turned and sauntered out. As an afterthought he called, "See you, Grunt."

"Yeah." The old man shot a puzzled glance as the lawman started up the dusty street. He turned to Billie. "You in some kind of trouble, girl?"

"Of course not. Why do you ask?"

He shrugged. "Just wonderin'. Never saw the sheriff in my kitchen before."

So. She'd been right. The sheriff was of the same mind as Emma Hardwick.

She took out her temper on the blackened skillet, rubbing until her knuckles bled. "You probably won't see him in here again, either."

At least not if she could help it. If Sheriff Gabe Conover thought he could shame her out of his town, he had another thought coming.

He could stare at her in that cold way, and she'd

just stare back. And if he tried to push, she'd dig in her heels. She had the right to do whatever work was offered, as long as it kept her from starvation.

She wasn't going to let him run her off.

She'd already been to hell and back. After a journey like that, she didn't scare easily.

Chapter Four

Billie pressed a hand to her stomach, churning with nerves. She'd hoped it would be easier tonight, now that she knew what to expect. But seeing the sheriff at his usual table, staring at her with such stark intensity, had ice skittering along her spine.

She looked away and tried to put Gabe Conover out of her mind, concentrating instead on the words of the song. But tonight it made her sad to think about a young wife saying goodbye to a husband leaving on a cattle drive. She could see, as she glanced at the faces of the cowboys gathered around her, that it made them sad, too. Some of them had gone so still and quiet, they looked like statues. A few had dropped an arm around the shoulders of one of the saloon girls and dragged her close as they listened to Belle California speak the words to the tinny sounds of the piano.

It occurred to Billie that her simple songs helped ease the loneliness of some of these men. Wasn't that a good thing? Why, then, did Sheriff Conover look so angry whenever she glanced at him?

Maybe it was just his nature, she thought. Maybe a tough lawman like him couldn't help but expect the worst of people, and especially strangers to his town who refused to heed his advice.

She'd had to endure the arrival of Emma Hardwick as well. Just as her song had begun, the young woman had stood in the doorway, offering her warning to the crowd, before being drowned out by a chorus of shouts from the angry cowboys. Emma had left as silently as she had arrived. And though the others had laughed, Billie had felt a rush of sympathy laced with admiration for the young woman's courage.

As her song ended the crowd erupted into thunderous applause. For a moment Billie seemed startled. She'd forgotten, just for an instant, that she was the object of everyone's attention. She gave a hesitant smile and began gathering up the money that had been tossed at her. Just then a young, lanky cowboy, unable to contain himself any longer, dashed toward the piano and hauled her into his arms, swinging her around and around as he let out a joyous hoot of enthusiasm.

She was caught completely by surprise. And though she struggled against him and tried to break free, she was no match for his strength.

The rest of the men seemed electrified by his boldness, and began laughing and shouting their approval.

"You git her, Jase. Go ahead. Kiss her good. And when ye'r done with her, let me have her."

"I want some of that, too, Jase. Don't hog her all to yourself."

"I'm next." A big burly cowboy shoved his way through the crowd and lifted his arms above his head in victory. "The rest of you will have to get in line behind me."

Jack Slade had been pushed aside by the frenzied crowd and was now fighting to break through the logjam of bodies blocking his way. But it was impossible. Even when he clapped his hands and shouted for silence, he couldn't make himself heard above the din that was growing more thunderous by the minute.

Billie resorted to kicking and biting as the cowboy pinned her in his arms and brought his face close for a kiss.

He let out a yelp when her dainty little slipper connected with his groin. Suddenly his laughter faded and his eyes were no longer smiling as he lowered his mouth to hers. "When I'm through with you, Belle California, you'll know you've been kissed by a real man."

She pushed against his chest with all her might and turned her face aside, so that his mouth merely brushed her cheek. But it was enough to have her breathing in the strong smell of whiskey on his breath, and the stench of horses and leather. Her gown was already growing damp from his sweaty body.

The crowd of men around them were encouraging him, shouting crude suggestions and surging forward, eager to join in the fun.

Just then there was a gunshot and the men fell back in absolute silence, stepping quickly away as one man strode through their midst.

One minute Billie was being held in a viselike grip. The next she saw the cowboy's eyes widen with surprise before he released his hold on her and dropped to the floor like a stone.

She gave a smile of relief when she saw the sheriff step over the cowboy's limp body. But her smile turned into a gasp of humiliation when, in that same instant, she caught sight of the look of fury on Gabe's face as he picked her up and carelessly tossed her over his shoulder like a sack of grain. His dark eyes dared any man in the room to defy him as he took aim with his pistol.

"Step away now. All of you." The words, though spoken softly, had a thread of steel that commanded respect.

Every man in the room took a step back, as the sheriff strode toward the stairs, still carrying his burden over his shoulder.

When he reached Slade he nodded with his head. "By the time I get downstairs, I expect Jason Blodgett to be on his way back to his ranch. If he isn't, he'll spend the night in jail. Is that understood?"

Jack Slade nodded. "Thanks, Sheriff. I'm afraid they caught me unprepared."

"I don't know why." Gabe's tone deepened.

"You should have seen this coming. You hold food just out of reach of starving dogs long enough, you've got to expect them to finally decide to just rush in and take what they want."

He brushed past Slade and stormed up the stairs. This time he didn't have to ask where Billie's room was. When he reached her door he thrust it open and strode inside before setting her unceremoniously on her feet.

"You didn't have to carry me." She took a deep breath and pushed the black plumes out of her eye before running her hands down the ruffled skirts in an attempt to calm her nerves. She wasn't sure whether to thank him for saving her, or curse him for embarrassing her. "I was perfectly capable of walking."

"I wasn't taking any chances. I wanted you out of sight as fast as possible, so none of the other cowboys would be tempted to try what young Blodgett just tried." He gave her a long, slow look from her head to her toes. A look that had the blood rushing to her cheeks. "I figured you just might be thinking about sticking around to see how many more men you could get to make fools of themselves over you."

Her eyes went wide. "You..." She struggled for breath, "You think I enjoyed that scene downstairs?"

He shrugged. "I'm thinking a woman could start liking that kind of power. One song and you have an entire saloon full of cowboys fighting over the priv-

ilege of being the first to kiss you. That must be some
kind of feeling for a girl like you.''

"A girl like me?" Whatever gratitude she'd experienced briefly was now gone. In its place was a
slowly simmering fury. "You think I not only enjoyed that, but encouraged it?"

"Didn't you?"

She brought her hands to her hips and faced him.
"This is a job, Sheriff. Just like yours. Can't you
understand that? As long as I do what Jack Slade
tells me, I get a bed to sleep in and all the food I
want."

"And what'll you do when sitting on that piano
and speaking the words of some songs isn't enough
to satisfy Slade?"

He saw the heat that came to her cheeks and knew
he'd struck a nerve.

"I...haven't figured that out yet. I guess I'll just
cross that desert when I come to it."

He couldn't seem to help himself. He had to just
keep pushing her until her back was to the wall. His
voice was a deep, angry growl. "Then be warned,
Billie. There've been plenty of people who started
across a desert, only to find themselves without
enough food and water to survive. This saloon, like
the desert, has a way of eating people alive."

"Don't you worry about me surviving, sheriff. I'm
stronger than I look. Now if you'll excuse me..."
She sent him a withering look, expecting him to step
out of her room.

He fully intended to. But there was just something

about the way she looked, her hands on her hips, her chin jutting like a prizefighter, and wearing that sexy gown and silly, flirty hat.

Maybe it was all the long lonely hours he'd spent watching her with the rest of the men, while that smooth velvet voice washed over him, touching something buried deep in his soul. Maybe it was the way she'd crept into his dreams last night, robbing him of sleep. Maybe it was simply a moment of weakness. Whatever the reason, he surprised even himself when, instead of turning away, he stepped closer, his eyes narrowed in concentration.

"Now what?" she demanded. "Is there some other point you were hoping to make?"

"Just this." He hauled her roughly into his arms, staring down at her mouth with a hunger that had her heart leaping to her throat.

Before she could react he covered her mouth with his in a kiss that had her gasping for breath.

He couldn't for the life of him figure out how it had happened. One minute he was preparing to leave. The next he was kissing her. A kiss that seemed to go on and on, heating his blood, clouding his mind, until all he could taste was her. All he could feel was the way those soft, delicate curves fitted themselves to his body.

He ran his hands across her shoulders, down her back, pressing her firmly to the length of him.

She was so tiny. So small and thin, she more resembled a child than a woman. But now that he was holding her, kissing her, he was achingly aware that she was all woman. And like Slade's whiskey, she was going straight to his head.

He knew he had to stop. Now. This instant. Before he did something he'd regret. But all the blood seemed to have left his brain and rushed to his loins, creating a heat, a need, that had him actually trembling.

No woman had ever had this effect on him before. Stripping him bare. Stealing his sense. Making him ache with need.

And all in the space of a single kiss.

She tasted surprisingly sweet. Like a cool spring rain sweeping down from the Black Hills on a hot summer day.

He fisted his hands in her hair and drew her head back, drinking her in. As he took the kiss deeper he imagined himself sinking into her, filling her, and filling himself with her sweetness. The taste of her, the feel of her hair against his hands, had him wanting her with a desperation that left him gasping.

He jerked back, shocked at the intensity of his feelings. Feelings that were completely alien to him. He'd never before wanted anyone the way he wanted her.

What in hell had just happened here? How had she robbed him of his common sense?

He certainly didn't need this woman in his life. But there it was. Right now, right this minute, he wanted her. Despite whatever complication that might involve.

To cover his embarrassment he shoved her aside

and turned toward the door, hoping she wouldn't notice the evidence of his arousal.

His voice was rough with impatience. "Remember this, Billie. I'm getting tired of coming to your rescue. One of these nights I won't be around to save your hide. Then what'll you do?"

Billie stared at the rigid line of his back, and felt the sting of rejection. She wasn't about to let him see just how affected she'd been by that kiss. Especially since it seemed to mean nothing at all to him. "Don't waste your time worrying about me, Sheriff. I don't want to be a burden to you. If I get myself into trouble, I won't expect you to get me out."

"You remember that." He yanked open the door and stepped into the hallway without looking back. "If you're smart you'll…"

"I know. Take your advice and get out of town. But it looks like I'm not very smart, because I have no intention of leaving Misery. Not for you. Not for anybody."

He slammed the door and strode toward the stairs. But instead of descending them he leaned a hip against the railing and stared at the closed door of her room.

What in hell had come over him? He'd behaved worse than young Blodgett. After all, as a man of the law he'd always held himself to a higher standard. He'd never before taken advantage of a helpless woman. In fact, he'd always prided himself on his respect for the gentle sex. But there was just something about Billie that seemed to bring out the worst in him.

He knew, by the way she'd kissed, that she'd had little experience at such things. That made it even more imperative that he keep his distance. If he was a betting man, he'd lay money that her innocence wasn't merely an act.

He took in a long, slow breath and realized that he could still taste her on his lips. Could still feel the imprint of her lithe young body on his.

As he started to walk he was still vibrating with need. A need he hadn't even known was there until he'd touched her. How had she managed to stir up so many feelings in him, and all in the space of a single heartbeat?

By the time he returned to the saloon he found himself looking toward the poker tables, hoping a fight would break out. It would give him an excuse to work off this edgy restlessness that had taken hold of him. There was nothing like a good knock-down-drag-out fistfight to clear a man's head and cool his blood.

It occurred to Sheriff Gabe Conover that he would no doubt be spending a long, sleepless night. And all because of one skinny, ornery female who had him tied up in knots.

In the predawn light Billie paced the length of her room. She'd put in a night of sheer misery. And all because of Gabe Conover's unexpected kiss.

She'd replayed it over and over in her mind. The

way she'd felt when he'd hauled her against his muscled chest. The way his arms had felt, holding her
close. The way those powerful thighs felt pressed to
hers. She'd never felt such amazing strength in a
man.

Then there was his mouth. She touched a finger to
her lips and closed her eyes. She'd never been kissed
like that. Oh, there had been a cowboy or two, on
some of the ranches where she'd worked. But they'd
been mere boys, doing what boys always did when
they were feeling frisky. Gabe Conover was all man.
And he'd kissed her the way a man kissed a woman.

Her reaction to it had left her absolutely devas-
tated. She should have been repulsed by his rough
behavior, the way she'd been repulsed by that cowboy who'd grabbed her. Instead, she'd been excited
by it.

She'd spent hours trying to figure out why this
man's kiss should have such a compelling effect on
her. He didn't like her. He'd made that quite clear
from the moment they'd met. He disapproved of
what she was doing here in Misery. And if he should
learn of her past, he'd like her even less.

So why then was she letting herself get all worked
up over a single kiss? Maybe it was because of the
control she'd sensed in him. As though a part of him
had wanted to do much more than kiss her, while
another part of him was shocked by such a human
weakness. She had the idea that Gabe Conover was
a man of strong principles. Any weakness, real or

imagined, wouldn't sit well with him. That thought intrigued her.

What would it be like to see him lose all that cool control?

She sank down on the edge of her bed, trying to imagine the dour, angry sheriff being anything except strong and fearless and reasonable. It was impossible to contemplate anything less. And it was that strength, that absolute fearlessness that she found most appealing.

Even his abrupt rejection couldn't dampen the fire that seemed to flow through her veins when she thought about him.

Was he right about her? Were these feelings proof that she was some kind of wicked woman, bent on self-destruction?

She pressed a hand to her stomach and gave a little moan of disgust. Of all the men in the Dakota Territory, why did it have to be the sheriff who had unlocked such feelings?

If he ever found out the truth about her, he would destroy her. And if she didn't keep her distance, she might be the one to unwittingly give him the key to unlocking all her dark secrets.

She decided it was time for a tough decision. She would avoid the sheriff as much as possible. That wouldn't be easy in a town as small as Misery. But considering her job and his, it shouldn't be too difficult for them to maintain a polite distance. After all, he made no secret of his disapproval of the way she lived her life. And the last thing she needed was to get close to a lawman. Whenever she absolutely had to deal with him, she would do so with as little fuss as she could manage. And when she saw him in the Red Dog at night, she would look the other way.

No matter how good it might have felt to be held in his arms, she had to see that she gave him no opportunity to repeat that little scene. There was no telling what she might do if she allowed him to kiss her like that again. Just thinking about it caused her heart to give a funny little flip.

She closed her eyes a moment, then took a deep breath and got to her feet. She was wasting time. There was work to be done. She didn't have time to moon over a man who was nothing but trouble.

Chapter Five

Billie crawled out of bed, feeling like a slug, and struggled to face another morning. She'd been working days and nights at the Red Dog for over a week now, and the pace was beginning to catch up with her. Especially since Jack Slade had added several more hours to her evening routine. Instead of singing twice, she was now doing four shows. That meant that she had to stay awake until well past midnight. Still, there had been no cutting back on her kitchen duties that began each day at dawn.

She slipped into her tattered dress and boots and headed down the stairs. In the kitchen, the wood stove was fired and the stew was already simmering.

"'Morning, Grunt." She pulled out a bowl and started preparing the biscuit dough.

"Huh." It was his usual response to her cheery greeting.

She and the old man had begun dividing the chores. She made the biscuits and coffee, while he heated up whatever was left over from the previous

night's supper and sawed off fresh steaks from a hide
of beef provided by a nearby rancher. Because Grunt
seemed annoyed by her chatter, she'd learned to say
as little as necessary while they worked.

Billie glanced around. Every available space in the
steamy room seemed to be packed with dirty tin
plates and utensils. She sighed, and realized that the
girls responsible for cleaning up the kitchen the previous night had neglected their tasks. That meant that
she would have to see to it before she started serving
breakfast.

She heated water over the stove and began washing and drying, until the dishes were clean and
stacked neatly on a tray.

Wiping damp hair from her eyes she glanced at
the potatoes heaped on a sideboard. "Want me to
peel those?"

Grunt made a sound which she took for approval.
She began peeling the potatoes and tossing them into
a bucket of cold water.

A short time later he looked over and frowned.
"You peeled too many, girl. What am I supposed to
do with all those? In case you haven't noticed, this
isn't potato stew, it's beef stew."

She thought a minute, then brightened. "I could
fry some up in the skillet for breakfast."

He shook his head, sending white hair dancing on
his shoulders. "Just a waste of time. The cowboys'll
never eat 'em."

She shrugged. "It's worth a try."

She began cutting up chunks of potatoes, before

frying them in a little grease. A short time later, when the biscuits were baked and the steaks sizzling, she placed a clean linen square over a tray and started toward the jail.

She was grateful that there was only one plate on the tray today. With no prisoner spending the night there was no need for Lars Swensen to work. Even without the other plates, the tray felt heavier than usual, and Billie had to force herself to put one foot in front of the other and keep moving. By the time she reached the jail she could feel sweat trickling between her shoulder blades, despite the coolness of the morning air.

She braced herself for the stilted reception she anticipated from the sheriff. Ever since the night of their kiss, they had danced lightly around each other, avoiding all contact except for this morning routine which couldn't be avoided. Every night while she entertained he sat at his usual table and watched without expression. His presence had a calming effect on the cowboys who now flocked to the Red Dog in droves, as her reputation grew. But Gabe's presence had the opposite effect on Billie. Knowing he was there, watching and listening, simply added to the pressure, especially since she was trying so hard to ignore him. He had, after all, made it abundantly clear that he'd regretted kissing her. She wished she felt the same. But the truth was, there had been several times these past few nights that she'd fallen asleep with the thought of that kiss playing through her mind.

Balancing the tray against her hip she opened the door and stepped inside. Gabe looked up from his desk, wearing his perpetual frown.

"Good morning." She avoided his eyes as she crossed the room.

"'Morning." He stuffed papers in a drawer, making room on his desktop for the tray.

As she began to set it down she swayed slightly, sloshing coffee over the rim of the cup and down her skirt.

"Here." Gabe reached out to steady it, and set it on his desk before turning back to her.

She looked oddly flushed.

He hurried around the desk and caught her elbow. "You all right?"

"Yes. Fine." She felt the quick rush of heat at his touch, then blinked when his image became blurred.

Gabe was watching her closely and could see the color draining from her face until it was as pale as milk. "You're not fine. Something's wrong."

She felt the room begin to tilt at the same moment that she heard a strange buzzing in her ears. Her legs had turned to rubber, refusing to hold her. Just as she started to sink to the floor Gabe scooped her up and cradled her against his chest. Again he was startled by how little she weighed as he carried her across the room and gently set her on a bunk in the cell.

He sat on the edge of the mattress, rubbing her hands between his. Despite the heat of the day they were cold as ice.

She struggled to sit up. "I can't be wasting my time here. I have work to—"

"Not yet, Billie." He touched a hand to her shoulder, forcing her to lie back. He was watching her in that quiet way that always made her so uncomfortable. "Have you taken time to eat this morning?"

She avoided his eyes. "I'll eat later."

His tone grew stern. "You can't keep doing this to yourself."

"Doing what?"

"Working day and night, without ever taking time for yourself."

"I don't need time."

He caught her chin, forcing her to meet his look. "Everybody needs time to restore body and soul, Billie. Even you. And when you don't, this is what happens. You faint dead away."

She slapped his hand aside and scrambled to a sitting position. "I didn't faint. I'm not the kind of woman who faints."

"Maybe not. But I know what I saw."

"All right. Maybe I am feeling a little weak." She got to her feet and prayed she wouldn't lurch like a drunken cowboy. "I'll eat as soon as I get back to the saloon."

"You'll eat now." With a firm grasp on her arm he led the way to his desk and pressed her down onto his chair. While she perched on the edge of the seat he pulled a second chair beside her and removed the linen, revealing a blackened steak, a bowl of stew and several biscuits, as well as some fried potatoes.

He grinned. "Grunt always fixes more food than I could ever eat. We'll share."

Without giving her time to argue he broke a biscuit and handed her half, then began cutting the steak into bite sizes. He took his time eating and made certain that she did the same.

He was relieved when, after only a few minutes, he saw the color slowly return to her cheeks.

After chewing several bites of steak she glanced over and gave a tentative smile. "I must have been hungrier than I thought."

"Why do you say that?"

Her smile grew. "Because this has to be the worst food I've ever tasted. Is it always this bad?"

He seemed surprised. "You mean you've never tasted Grunt's cooking?"

She shrugged. "I've tasted some. Mostly I just eat whatever I've fixed. But this..." She shivered, causing Gabe to roar with laughter.

"Everybody in Misery knows Grunt is a terrible cook. But since he's the only one around, we have no choice but to eat whatever slop he fixes."

He took a bite of fried potatoes, and his laughter suddenly faded. With a look of concentration he took another bite, swallowed, then slowly shook his head. "I take that back. These are really good." He held out the fork. "Taste."

Billie tasted, then smiled. "They could use something." She thought a minute. "Onions. And maybe some seasonings. Other than that they're pretty good."

"Pretty good? They're the best I've ever tasted."

She turned to look at him. "Thank you."

"You mean you made them?" At her smile he shook his head. "I should have known. They're way beyond anything Grunt could have fixed."

"He won't be happy to hear that. He was really annoyed when he saw how many potatoes I'd peeled for his stew. I only fried them so they wouldn't go to waste."

"I'll bet when the cowboys at the saloon taste these, they'll want them every morning."

"The cowboys." She leapt out of the chair. "Grunt will be mad as a hornet if I don't get back to the Red Dog right away."

He stopped her with a hand to her arm. "You sure you're feeling up to it?"

She nodded, determined to ignore the quick sizzle of heat along her spine. "Really. I'm sure."

"Just see that you eat again later. You've got to keep up your strength."

She gave him a shy smile. "I will. Thanks, Sheriff."

As she started out the door he called, "I'll be by later with the tray."

She didn't bother to answer as she lifted the hem of her gown and began running along the street.

Gabe stood in the doorway and watched. His frown was back. What she needed, he decided, was a keeper. Someone to see that she not only ate enough to keep up her strength, but also to see that she got away from that rough saloon from time to time. Otherwise, she might forget that there was another world beyond the one she'd so eagerly embraced at the Red Dog.

Billie finished up the last of the dirty dishes and stacked them on the scarred wooden counter. Then she tackled the greasy stewpot and blackened kettle, scrubbing until she could see her reflection in them. Not a pretty sight, she thought as she pushed damp hair out of her eyes. Nobody seeing her would ever confuse her with Belle California, who had performed the night before to a packed house.

It had been, according to Jack Slade, the best Saturday night ever. Cowboys had come from as far away as Bison Fork, which was a good three-hour ride on horseback. They'd been more rowdy then most, but then, they'd come here hoping to spend their paycheck on whiskey and women, and they hadn't been disappointed. Best of all, they could go home boasting to their friends that they'd seen the famous beauty, Belle California.

Billie glanced down at her sagging dress and hitched up the neckline. A minute later it slipped back down, baring one shoulder. She was sick of washing it every night, but until Slade gave her some of her wages, she had no way of buying a second one. He'd promised to pay her at the end of the month, after figuring out how much she'd earned. But Cheri had warned her that Slade had all kinds of ways of withholding their money. He charged them for the food they ate, the bed they slept in, even the number of bed linens they soiled. But, since Billie scrupulously washed her own bed linens along with her dress and undergarments, and was careful to eat only what she absolutely needed, she figured Slade would have no way of deducting a thing.

Her own money. The thought had her smiling as she carried the bucket of wash water to the back door of the kitchen and tossed it on the tiny row of seeds she'd planted in the rear of the building.

"Is that a garden?"

At the sound of Gabe's voice she turned and felt herself blushing.

"Not a garden, exactly. Just a few things I wanted to grow. Onions. Chard. Turnips. Beets." She couldn't help staring. He was wearing a dark coat over a white shirt and dark pants. Even without his silver badge that caught and reflected the sunlight, it would be obvious that he was a man of authority. It was there in the guns worn low on his hips. In the way he stood, so tall and proud and unafraid. In the way his eyes narrowed in the bright sunshine as he looked at her.

"Did you want to see Mr. Slade?"

He shook his head. "I came to see if you'd like to go for a ride."

"A...ride?" Her smile faded. "Why? Is there something wrong?"

"Nothing's wrong, Billie." He frowned, wondering why he'd ever talked himself into this. Now that he was standing here he felt like a fool. "I'm driving out to visit my sister, and thought you'd like to get away from town for awhile."

"You have a sister?"

He nodded. "Kitty. She's about your age." He

glanced behind him. "I thought I'd take the buckboard. That is, if you'd like to go along."

She'd been caught completely by surprise. She stood, clinging tightly to the washbasin. "I suppose I could go. I don't have any more chores until tonight when I…" Seeing his frown deepen she let the words trail off. When would she learn not to mention her job in front of him?

"I guess so." She glanced around. "Should I tell somebody?"

"I don't see why. It's nobody's business what you do with your time, as long as your chores are done."

"All right. I'll just—" she looked down "—put this away." She stepped into the kitchen and set the basin on the table, then gave a last look around before stepping out into the sunlight.

When she reached the battered old wagon Gabe helped her up to the seat. She felt the press of his hand under her elbow and was forced to absorb the most amazing rush of heat.

She sat holding to the wooden seat as he settled himself beside her and picked up the reins. When they rolled along the dusty street she saw the people milling about Swensen's Dry Goods.

"What brought so many ranchers into town today?"

He glanced over at her. "It's Sunday. Emma Hardwick arranged for a traveling preacher to hold services in the back of Swensen's once a month. Afterward, most of the ranchers load up their wagons before heading back home. It gives their wives a chance to visit, and their children time to play together."

She understood now why he was dressed like that. "You were at the services?"

He nodded. "The preacher's pretty good. Not all fire and brimstone. And the songs bring back a few memories. I'll bet you recall a few hymns from your childhood."

She looked away, but not before he caught the flush on her cheeks.

"Well." He covered quickly, hoping to ease her embarrassment. "Growing up way out here, most folks don't get to see a preacher very often. The people of Misery are grateful for even one hour a month. Is your pa a rancher?"

"My pa's dead."

"I thought that was your ma."

She swallowed. "She's dead, too."

"You got any family, Billie?"

She shook her head and he could see that this was something else that embarrassed her.

He struggled to find something, anything that would put her at ease. He glanced up at the sky. "Fine day."

She nodded, but he could feel her withdrawing from him. He pulled the brim of his hat low against the sun. "I think you'll like Kitty."

"Does she look like you?"

He shook his head. "She resembles our ma. Yellow hair. Eyes the color of that sky."

"Does she live with your ma and pa?"

"They're both gone. She lives with Aaron Smiler, who's like a grandfather to us."

"She lives with a man who isn't kin?" Her eyes went wide and something flashed in them before she blinked it away. A fleeting memory that had her gripping the edge of the wooden seat.

"Not really. But he may as well be." Gabe slowed the horse as their rig crested a ridge. "There's his place."

Billie looked down on the barren land dotted with cattle, and then at the crude wooden shack in the distance. It looked no better or worse than most of the ranches in the area.

Cattle looked up from their grazing as the wagon rolled slowly past. By the time they reached the ranch house, they could hear a sharp, piercing whistle.

Billie glanced over at Gabe. "What was that?"

"Just Aaron summoning Kitty from the fields. He used to call all of us that way." Gabe lifted his hat in salute, then urged the horse into a trot until, in a swirl of dust, they stopped outside a small corral, where an old bearded man was forking hay to a herd of mustangs dancing nervously around him.

"Hey, Aaron." Gabe climbed down, then offered a hand to Billie, who stepped down to stand uncertainly beside him.

"Good to see you, Gabriel." The old man finished his chore, then let himself out of the corral, walking slowly with the aid of a walking stick. He shook the sheriff's hand. "I see you brought company."

Billie found herself looking into dark, probing eyes.

"Aaron Smiler, this is Billie Calley."

The old man gallantly tipped his hat. "Miss Calley."

She felt herself blushing at his courtly manners. "You can just call me Billie."

"Only if you call me Aaron."

Her blush deepened, but she managed to nod her head. "All right."

They looked up at the sound of a horse's hooves pounding the hard ground. A voice gave out a wild hoot as a figure in buckskins astride a big spotted mustang came racing toward them at a dead run. At the last moment the horse veered and the figure leaped to the ground with a laugh.

"Where've you been, Gabe?" came the decidedly feminine voice. "You haven't been by in weeks."

"Sorry. I got busy." When she stepped closer Gabe tousled her hair before slapping her arm the way he might greet another man. Then he stepped back a pace. "I brought someone to meet you."

For the space of several seconds the two young women stared at each other as Gabe said, "Kitty, this is Billie Calley. Billie, meet my little sister."

Billie wondered if she looked as surprised as Kitty did. But she'd never before seen a girl in buckskins. Especially one as pretty as Kitty Conover. Despite the fact that her face was as dirty as her clothes, and her hair was tied back with a strip of rawhide, there was no hiding that yellow hair and those big blue eyes. Alongside her, Billie felt as plain as dirt.

She tried a tentative smile. "Hello, Kitty."

The girl nodded. "Billie." Then she returned her attention to her brother. "You staying for supper?"

"If you don't mind the extra work."

"Don't mind a bit." She walked along beside him,

matching her strides to his. "Aaron promised to bake corn bread."

At the old man's cough she turned. "Don't tell me you forgot."

Aaron looked contrite. "Sorry. I meant to, but those mustangs got jittery and I came out to soothe them, and never gave the corn bread another thought."

Kitty put her hands on her hips. "And me with a hunk of ham smoking. It's just begging for some corn bread to go with it."

Billie said softly, "I could make the corn bread. That is, if you don't want to eat that ham right away."

Kitty stopped in her tracks. "You can bake?"

Billie shrugged, feeling her cheeks grow hot when she realized they were all looking at her. "Enough to get by."

Kitty suddenly smiled. "Well, then. What are we waiting for? Come on inside, Billie, and make yourself at home."

As Kitty and Gabe strode ahead, Billie walked more slowly, keeping pace with the old man.

"How'd you hurt your leg?"

He shrugged. "It started years ago. Tossed from a stallion with a mind of his own. Now it's just old age. Seems to get worse every winter. One of these springs I just won't be able to get out of my bed."

Billie glanced at the man and woman up ahead. "Do they like each other?"

"Of course they do." Aaron turned to look at her. "You think, because they don't hug and kiss, they don't care?"

She shrugged in embarrassment.

He smiled. "That's just the Conovers for you. They had to be tough when they were still so young, they're not sure how to act any other way."

"Why did they have to be tough?"

"They lost their ma when they were just pups. Gabriel was the one who held them together and got them across some pretty rough country. It took him years to let go and stop being the boss of the family. But you can see that he's still more comfortable giving orders than taking them."

Billie couldn't help smiling. Apparently she wasn't the only one who noticed that Gabe Conover liked to be in charge. "What about their pa?"

The old man shrugged. "They were searching for him when their mother died along the trail. But from the time they came to live with me, they seemed to have some sort of unspoken code of silence about him."

Before Billie could ask anything more, Aaron held the door. "Like Kitty said, come on inside and make yourself at home."

Chapter Six

Billie glanced around the crude shack. There was a
fire burning in the fireplace. Pulled in front of it were
two rocking chairs. Along one wall by the door was
a long wooden bench. Aaron took a seat there and
began to pry off his boots. Off to one side was a
scarred wooden table and four chairs. Through an
open doorway could be seen a bed made of timbers.
Across the room a wooden ladder led to a loft, pro-
viding a second bedroom. Several fur throws had
been tossed carelessly over the rail to air.

Seeing the direction of her gaze Kitty said,
"That's my place up there. With his bum leg, Aaron
had to give up the loft. Years ago he and my brothers
slept up there and I had the bedroom."

"You don't mind sleeping up there?"

Kitty smiled. "I've really learned to like it. I like
the sound of the wind and rain at night. There's just
something soothing about being all alone, just under
the roof."

Billie nodded, thinking that sounded like heaven.

Kitty pointed to the wooden table. "The corn-meal's in a sack in the corner. You can make the dough in that bowl over there. There're eggs in that basket. I gathered them fresh this morning."

"You have chickens?"

Kitty nodded. "Pesky little critters. Leave their eggs all over the fields, where half of them are eaten by wild animals before I can gather them up. The other day I found a nest of young ones way off in a bramble patch. I figure they'll be food for the coyotes in a couple of days."

Billie's eyes went wide. "You didn't move them out of harm's way?"

"Where to?"

She thought a moment. "Why don't you bring them up to the house?"

"Bring chickens in here?" Kitty looked at her as if she'd lost her mind. "Do you have any idea how dirty they are?"

"But to just leave them out there for the coyotes…"

Kitty laughed. "Don't waste your time worrying about a few critters. There'll be plenty more in the next few weeks. Seems like all the hens are nesting lately." She paused a moment. "You want some baby chicks?"

"Could I?"

Kitty gave her a puzzled look. "Sure. Come on. I'll take you to them." She turned to her brother and Aaron. "Want to come along?"

The old man shook his head. "Too far to walk. You go along, Gabriel. I'll wait here."

Gabe nodded and followed as Kitty led the way across the dusty yard and past a thicket of trees to where a hen clucked contentedly to the little yellow balls of fluff that poked their heads out from under her wings.

"Oh, look at this." Billie was down on her knees in the brambles as the baby chicks began tumbling over one another to climb into her lap. Soon she was laughing and scooping them up, pressing her cheek to the soft down and crooning to them in that breathy voice. "Oh, aren't you just the cutest thing. Don't you worry. I'm not going to let some mean old coyote gobble you up for his supper. How would you like to come home and live with me?"

Gabe stood to one side watching and listening. The transformation in her was amazing to behold. She seemed, for the moment, to have forgotten that he and his sister were there as she played with the chicks like a child with a toy.

Kitty turned to her brother. "Aaron's got an old pen in the shed. If we put the hen inside, the chicks will stay with her."

He walked away and returned a short time later with a pen. Scooping up the hen and her nest, he called to Billie, "I'll leave the chicks to you and Kitty. You can put them in the back of the wagon with their mama."

"How are we supposed to carry all these?" Kitty called to his retreating back.

"That's your problem," he said over his shoulder.

"I have an idea." Billie began filling her skirt with peeping chicks until all of them were clustered together. Then standing, she gathered up her skirts and followed Gabe, unaware that as she did, she displayed a great deal of shapely ankle and leg.

Gabe turned to watch her approach and felt his throat go dry. And though he knew he ought to look away, it was impossible. Though he was always striving to be superhuman, he was forced to admit that he was a mere man. Especially whenever he looked at Billie.

"Here you are," she said in that breathy voice as she lifted each little chick from her skirt and sent it racing toward the clucking hen.

Once in the back of the wagon, the babies gathered around their mother, tucking themselves under her wings until they were fast asleep.

Billie leaned her chin on her hands, watching until even the hen had closed her eyes. "I can't believe you're giving them to me."

"I can't believe you'd want them. They're a lot of work."

"I don't mind. I'm used to hard work."

Kitty touched her arm. "You'd better get inside and start that corn bread, before we all starve."

"All right." Billie turned away, happy for the chore. It had been such a long time since she'd been able to cook in a real home.

Inside she rolled her sleeves and washed in a basin, then began preparing the dough for corn bread.

Soon, while Aaron and Gabe and Kitty talked about ranch chores, the little cabin was filled with the most delicious fragrances. And by the time they sat down to supper, their mouths were watering.

Gabe took one bite of meat and arched a brow at his sister. "Where'd you get the ham?"

"I bartered it from Jeb Simmons. He's got a hog ranch about an hour from here."

"I've heard Jeb demands a high price for his pork. What'd you use for barter?"

She nodded toward the corral. "You saw those mustangs out there. I tracked them down a couple of months ago, and I've been breaking them to saddle ever since. When I heard that Jeb Simmons was in the market for a good saddle horse, I figured we'd do some business."

Gabe looked at her with respect. "You thought of that all by yourself?"

Aaron winked at Billie before saying, "The girl's a natural. She can break horses with the best of them. And she's not afraid to deal with the other ranchers in the area. Since I couldn't talk you and your brother into staying and working the ranch, I figured Kitty was my last hope."

His words grabbed Billie's attention. She looked from Kitty to Gabe. "You have a brother? Does he live in Misery, too?"

"No." Gabe's tone was clipped. "He took off for parts unknown."

Billie could hear the note of anger and was puzzled by it, but she wisely kept any more questions to herself.

Aaron took a second helping of corn bread and chewed slowly, savoring the rare treat. "I haven't tasted anything this fine since my mama was alive, Billie."

Her smile was warm with gratitude. "Thank you."

"Want to come and cook for us?" Kitty asked. "Aaron and I are always fighting over who's going to fix the vittles. I'd rather muck a dozen stalls than fix a single meal. As for Aaron, I think he'd rather walk all the way to Misery on his sore leg than have to cook."

Billie laughed. "The fact is, I like cooking."

"Is that what you do in Misery?"

Billie felt her cheeks grow warm. "Yes. I cook at the Red Dog."

Aaron glanced up sharply. "I thought old Grunt did the cooking there."

"He does. I just help him." Her voice lowered. "And other things."

Kitty seemed intrigued. "Have you seen that new singer Jack Slade hired?"

Gabe's face grew as dark as a thundercloud. "How'd you hear about that?"

"Everybody in Misery is talking about it." Kitty seemed surprised at his outburst. "I wasn't thinking about going in there or anything. I just wondered what this new singer looks like. But then—" her lips turned into a pout "—I suppose working in the kitchen, Billie has about as much chance of seeing her as I have.''

Billie could feel the heat burning her cheeks as she bent to her meal. She could feel Aaron watching her, and it suddenly occurred to her that this old man didn't miss much. But if he were to believe that she did more than just cook at the Red Dog, he might think badly of her.

Now why in the world should that matter to her? Aaron Smiler was neither kin nor friend. He was just someone she would probably never see again. But she liked him. And she liked Kitty. Much more than she'd expected to. And she wished, oh, how she wished, that she did something more respectable than work in a saloon.

''You want more coffee, Gabe?'' Kitty glanced at the blackened pot, boiling over the fire.

''I'll get it.'' Billie wrapped a piece of linen around her hand and lifted the coffeepot, circling the table as she topped off their cups.

''You sure do look comfortable in the kitchen, Billie.'' Aaron leaned back, watching her. ''Looks like you've had lots of practice.''

She flushed. ''I guess I have.'' She glanced at Kitty. ''If you're through, I'll start heating some water for the dishes.''

''There's no need.'' Kitty drank her coffee. ''You're company. And you already did enough, baking the corn bread. From the looks of it, Aaron and I will have enough left over for tomorrow.''

''But the dishes...''

Kitty pushed away from the table. "When we run out of clean ones, Aaron and I will play poker to see who does them. That's how we always settle on the chores neither of us wants to do."

Billie was already shaking her head as she set a kettle of water over the fire and began to gather up the dirty dishes. "You fed me. And it was just about the finest ham I've ever tasted. The least I can do is tidy up around here before I leave."

Kitty paused, then with a sigh, picked up a faded linen towel. "I guess, if you're washing, I can dry."

From his spot at the table Aaron merely smiled. If there was one thing he admired in a person, it was neatness. He'd spent years trying to instill that virtue in Kitty, but she'd fought him every step of the way. Now, maybe she would see that it didn't take all that much effort.

He winked at Gabe across the table. "I hope you brought me one of those cigars I love."

Gabe touched a hand to the inside pocket of his coat and smiled. "I didn't forget. Why don't we sit by the fire?"

The old man shook his head. "Let's leave these two alone in here and sit out on the porch instead."

The two men walked away, leaving Kitty and Billie working side by side in the kitchen.

Billie filled a basin with hot water, then began to wash, while Kitty dried.

"How old were you when you came to live with Aaron?"

Kitty smiled. "Five. He used to say I was five years nasty."

"Were you nasty?"

Kitty shrugged. "Not exactly. But tough, I guess. Surviving on the trail does that."

"Yeah." Billie nodded. "I know a little about that."

"You, too?" Kitty looked at her with new interest. "Where did you come from?"

"All over." Billie set down a chipped cup and plunged her hands into the soapy water. "My pa and I were on ranches from the Wyoming Territory to the Dakota Territory."

"Why?"

Billie paused to study the delicate design on a cracked plate. "After my ma died, my pa and I moved around a lot. He was a cowboy who helped out on ranches during calving season, or on round-ups."

"What did you do?"

Billie smiled. "Worked in the kitchens, mostly. There were always a lot of cowboys to feed, and by the time I was six or seven, my pa figured I ought to earn my keep."

Kitty carefully dried the plate before looking up. "I guess we're alike, you and me. Except I never knew my pa."

"Why not?"

She lifted a shoulder, clearly uncomfortable talking about him. "He left before I was born. Our ma was taking us to find him, but then she died along the trail, and Gabe just kept us together until we found Aaron. And I've been here ever since."

"You're lucky. I mean, to have a home and a kind man who lets you live here and all."

Kitty nodded. "I know. I can't imagine being anywhere else but here."

Billie scrubbed the wooden table until it gleamed, then scrubbed each chair clean. "What about the other brother you spoke of? Is he older or younger than Gabe?"

"Yale?" Kitty sighed. "He's a year younger than Gabe. And I think he's spent every day of his life resenting the fact that he wasn't born first."

Billie looked up. "Why did Gabe get so angry when you mentioned his name?"

Kitty hung the towel over the back of one of the chairs and lowered her voice so that it wouldn't carry through the open doorway. "Yale was always wild. Not at all like Gabe. And the more Gabe tried to rein him in, the more he just had to push away. He started drinking and gambling and running with some bad characters. The last we heard, he was seen with the Fenner gang."

Billie let out a gasp of surprise. Everyone knew of the Fenners. They'd evaded every lawman from Missouri to Wyoming while they robbed trains and stages, stealing horses along the way, and leaving a trail of terrified victims in their wake. It was rumored that they hid out in the Badlands.

"No wonder Gabe is so mad," she whispered. She turned to see him and Aaron on the porch, smoke circling their heads while they talked easily together. "It must be hard to be a lawman, knowing your brother is outside the law."

Kitty nodded. "It'd kill Gabe if he had to go up against Yale in a shoot-out."

"How would Yale feel?" Billie asked softly.

"The same. I don't care how many people have seen him running with the Fenner gang, he's still my brother. And he's still Gabe's brother, too, even if they have butted heads more often than two bulls in a pasture." She turned worried eyes on Billie. "I just hope it never comes to that."

On an impulse Billie caught Kitty's hand and squeezed. "It won't ever come to that, Kitty. You'll see."

Kitty gave her a timid smile. "Thanks, Billie." She hesitated, then said, "I've been meaning to ask. Why are you wearing that dress?"

Billie glanced down at herself and then burst into laughter. "It's really ugly, isn't it?"

"It surely is. Not to mention way too big. Where did you get it?"

"From a kind lady who was like a ma to me. She was the one who took the time to teach me how to cook and bake."

"And you wear it to honor her?"

Billie shook her head. "I wear it because it's all I have."

Kitty's eyes widened. After a moment's hesitation she said, "I still have some of my ma's old dresses. They're so old they're not good for much more than rags now. But I bet they'd look better than what you're wearing.''

Billie glanced at the buckskins on Kitty. ''Why don't you wear your ma's clothes?''

Kitty shrugged. ''Aaron tried to get me to dress like a girl. But the skirts just got in the way. Finally he gave up and stopped complaining about my clothes.'' She caught Billie's hand and started toward the ladder leading to the loft. ''Come on. Let's have a look.''

Giggling like children the two young women climbed the ladder. Billie watched as Kitty rummaged through an old carpet bag, hauling out several tattered dresses and holding them up until she found one that wasn't falling apart at the seams.

''Try this on, Billie.''

Billie tugged the old gown over her head, then slipped into the one Kitty was holding out to her. Though the once bright buttercup fabric was faded to the color of old gold, and the sash was missing, it fit her as though made for her.

''Come on. There's a looking glass downstairs.'' Kitty snatched up the carpet bag and led the way.

After much searching, she found a lemon yellow sash to tie around Billie's waist. At the bottom of the bag she found a silver comb, which she used to secure Billie's hair out of her eyes. Then she held up the looking glass.

''Oh, my.'' That was all Billie could say as she studied her reflection. Then she turned. ''Are you sure you want to give away your ma's dress? Just think, Kitty. If you were to wear this, there wouldn't be a man in all of the Dakotas who wouldn't fall dead at your feet.''

"The last thing I want is some man falling at my feet." Kitty shook her head. "I don't ask much in this life. But I'd rather have some good horseflesh under my saddle and a rifle in my hand any day, than a man in my bed."

"I know what you mean." Billie looked around the tiny shack. "If I could have a place of my own like this, and a stove for cooking, I wouldn't ask for much more. And all the men in the world wouldn't tempt me to leave it."

The two women fell into a fit of giggles. When Gabe and Aaron stepped inside minutes later, that's how they found them. Clinging together and laughing like children.

Gabe was startled by the change in Billie. But when she caught him staring, her face reddened. "I'm sorry. I know this was your ma's and I have no right…"

Puzzled he lifted a hand, abruptly cutting her off. "I don't care whose dress it used to be, it's a whole lot better than what you've been wearing."

Kitty nodded. "That's what I told her."

Aaron, seeing the blush on Billie's cheeks, felt a wave of sympathy. "I think you look just grand, Billie."

She shot him a look of gratitude. "Thank you."

"Well." Gabe cleared his throat before saying, "We'd better get started for town." He tousled

Kitty's hair, then shook hands with Aaron before striding out to the buckboard.

Billie and Kitty walked out on the porch, with Aaron following. Outside Billie offered her hand to the old man, who grasped it in both of his.

"I hope you'll come back again, Billie. Maybe next Sunday, if Gabriel can get away."

"Thank you. I'd like that." She turned to Kitty and surprised them both by hugging her fiercely. "Thank you for this dress. And for the chicks. And for making me feel welcome."

She saw the way Kitty's jaw dropped at her boldness. Without another word she turned away and raced to the buckboard. Gabe helped her up, then settled himself beside her and flicked the reins.

As the horse and wagon started up, Billie turned to wave to the old man and young woman who stood watching. Then she turned to Gabe. "I like your sister."

"She liked you, too. I could tell."

"Really?"

He nodded. "I'm glad the two of you have become friends."

Friends. She hugged the word to her heart, afraid to speak. Afraid if she did, she might find out that this entire day had been a dream.

Friend. She leaned back against the hard seat of the wagon and smiled. There had been so few in her life. But now she had one. Kitty Conover.

She slid a glance toward the man holding the reins.

His hands were so big. So strong. His profile so rugged. His eyes so fierce.

Her gaze moved to his mouth. It had been so surprisingly soft against hers.

She wondered if he would ever kiss her again. But then, a man who couldn't even bring himself to hug his sister was probably extremely frugal with his kisses, as well.

Whatever had happened that night in her room had no doubt been a momentary weakness. A mistake. One he had no intention of ever making again. But she would be satisfied with the fact that he'd taken her on a ride to the country. For a few precious hours she'd been able to completely forget the Red Dog, and the exotic Belle California.

She sighed and lifted her face to the sun. For this brief time she hadn't felt like Billie Calley, either. For a little while she'd felt like an ordinary woman, doing the things other women did on a Sunday afternoon.

Beside her, Gabe tried not to stare at the gown she was wearing. If he closed his eyes, he could see his mother in that dress. Sweeping the porch of his grandfather's farmhouse. Snapping beans from the garden and tossing them into boiling water on the big old stove. In that long-ago time he'd felt safe and warm and loved.

He'd swept all those memories away years ago, and had tucked them in some small corner of his mind. Now they seemed to come rushing back, as though a door had been opened and a strong wind was blowing them like dry leaves.

Billie was like that, he thought. A strong wind blowing around all the carefully ordered things in his life. He resented her presence. Resented all the prickly little feelings that surfaced whenever she got too close. And yet, despite all the disruptions she'd created, he kept coming back for more.

Like a moth to a flame, he thought. Tempting himself with the fire. And more than likely to get himself burned in the process.

He pulled up behind the saloon and stepped out, then helped her to climb down. If his hand lingered overlong at her waist, he told himself it was merely to steady her. And when she looked up at him and smiled, he ignored the little hitch around his heart.

"Come on. I'll help you find a place for these chickens." He hauled the pen out of the back of the wagon and looked around. "Where would you like them?"

Billie ran ahead, and studied the dusty patch of earth behind the Red Dog. To one side was a spindly tree that offered a bit of shade. "I think they'd like it here."

He set down the pen and opened the latch, allowing the hen and her chicks to be free. As they tentatively stepped out, he walked back to the wagon and returned with a sack of grain over his shoulder, which he set down beside the back wall of the saloon.

At Billie's questioning look he shrugged. "I told

Aaron you'd need some food for all these hungry critters.''

She gave a delighted laugh as she reached into the sack and tossed a handful of grain, sending the chickens scattering to snatch it up.

Still smiling she lay a hand on his sleeve. "Oh, Gabe. This has just been the best day. Thank you.''

If she just hadn't touched him, he might have escaped unscathed. But when a sizzle of heat sparked through his veins, he nearly jumped. And when he looked at her, he felt as if some mighty, unseen force had taken over his will. In that instant he was like a man possessed. His eyes were hot and fierce as he dragged her into his arms. The sound that issued from his throat was more animal than human as he pinned her roughly against the wall, his body pressed tightly to hers, his arms nearly crushing the life from her, while he kissed her until they were both gasping for breath.

"Gabe.'' It was all Billie could manage to say before his lips claimed hers again and took her on another head-spinning, heart-stopping ride. She felt as though she'd been caught up in some wild summer storm. All around her thunder was pounding. Or was that her heart? Wasn't that lightning flashing behind her closed eyes? It was all she could do to hold on and ride the tornado that swirled around them.

She wrapped her arms around his waist and clung, drowning in the most amazing sensations. Heat unlike any she'd ever known. A heat that seemed to sear her flesh and melt her bones, even while a trickle of ice along her spine had her trembling.

Gabe knew he was out of control. Knew he was rough and clumsy, and going about this all wrong. A woman ought to be cherished, and treated like a fragile glass doll. But the feelings that were driving him were unlike any he'd ever known. All he could think about was taking her. Here. Now. And it occurred to him that if it weren't broad daylight, he would probably follow his instincts, and to hell with right and wrong.

He could hear the little whimpers coming from her throat as he took the kiss deeper, and knew that he was taking her too high, too fast. But he simply couldn't stop. Not yet. Not when her lips were so sweet. Not when the feel of her against him was sending all those wild sparks through his system, making him half-crazy.

When she sighed and wrapped her arms around his waist, he thought he'd die from the pleasure. But when she went all still and allowed him to run hot, wet kisses down her throat, he knew he'd gone too far.

With a muttered oath he lifted his head and deliberately stepped back, keeping his hands on her shoulders, as much to steady himself as her.

"You'd better…" His tone was so rough, he barely recognized his own voice. It was the growl of something wild. "…get inside now. There'll be work waiting for you."

"Yes. Of…course." She swallowed, wondering

why he looked so angry, when her own heart was soaring to the heavens. Oh, she felt a bit muddled and unsteady, but that was to be expected, she figured, after being kissed like that.

Was it because she wasn't good at kissing? Was that why his face resembled a thundercloud?

She watched in confusion as he spun away and nearly ran to the buckboard. Without glancing at her he climbed to the driver's seat and flicked the reins.

As the wagon rolled toward the jailhouse, Gabe wallowed in misery. What was happening to him? He'd always had to be so strong, so sensible. He'd always left the foolishness to Yale, who'd been so good at playing the fool. But here he was, doing much the same thing.

As he unhitched the horse and went about his chores, his mood grew even darker. Because, if truth be told, with every breath he took, he could still taste her. And with every beat of his heart, he still wanted her more than anything in this world.

And if he could, he'd go back and kiss her again.

Chapter Seven

"Billie." Jack Slade stuck his head in the kitchen and looked around. "Where's Grunt?"

"He...just stepped out back." She'd noticed the old man slip out the back door. He'd done that several times in the past few hours. Whenever she'd gone looking for him she'd found him with his back to the wall, dozing in the sun.

She dried her hands on her apron. "I'll get him." She didn't want Slade to find the old man asleep.

"No." He put a hand on her arm. "It's you I wanted to see."

She froze, wondering what she'd done wrong now.

"I've hired a new girl. She'll be sharing your room."

"My room?" Billie's heart sank. "But there's only one bed."

"You can double up."

"Double..." Her chin came up. That cramped room and tiny bed had become her refuge. And now she would lose the only privacy she had. Her usually breathy voice lowered with anger. "I work until midnight. And I'm up again at dawn. How am I supposed to get any sleep at all if someone's coming into my room in the middle of the night?"

"Maybe, if you're lucky, she'll be in someone else's room more often than yours." He saw the way her features went all stiff and quiet, and turned away before she could give him an argument. "When you're through here you can go up and meet her. Her name's Grace Sawyer."

Billie watched him disappear, then turned toward the sink and took out her temper on the blackened pots and kettles.

When Grunt stepped into the kitchen a short time later he stood in the doorway watching her. "Somethin' eatin' you, girl?"

She dumped water from a kettle and slammed it down. "This place."

He gave her a toothless grin. "Is that all?" He glanced around, admiring the way the dishes were stacked neatly on a table that had been freshly scrubbed. The linen towels were bleached white from the sun, ever since Billie had started hanging them on a line behind the saloon. Even the floor was clean enough to eat on, the wooden boards bleached until they gleamed.

He swayed slightly and paused to steady himself before making his way slowly across the room.

Billie studied his ashen features and the sweat that poured in little rivers down his neck. "Are you all right, Grunt?"

He shook his head. "I think I'm going to have to give up and take to my bed."

"But what about supper?"

He never even paused as he called over his shoulder, "You'll have to take care of things, girl. I need my bed."

Bed, she thought as she carried the basin of water to the back door and emptied it over her garden. She walked to the tiny enclosure she'd made just beyond the garden for the hen and her chicks, and tossed a handful of grain, watching as they scratched and pecked. Grunt had taken to his bed. Even the chickens, she mused, had a bed of their own. She was the only one who had to share. She dried the basin, then hung her freshly washed apron and towel on the line before stepping back into the kitchen.

Squaring her shoulders, she decided to confront Jack Slade. Let somebody else share a room with this newcomer.

She strode down the hall toward the room at the back of the saloon that Jack Slade used as an office. Billie had only been in here once. The day she'd arrived in Misery. Hungry, tired, frightened and desperate, she'd forced herself to walk into this den of iniquity to ask for work, not for wages, but just for food. And despite the fact that Jack Slade more nearly resembled a devil, with that dangerous smile and his swarthy good looks, and his ever present black suit and fancy ruffled shirt, she'd been so relieved to be offered a place to sleep and all the food she wanted, she would have agreed to anything.

She knocked and waited until she heard the deep voice call, "Come in."

She stepped inside and halted when she realized Slade wasn't alone.

"Billie." He looked up from his desk. "I'm glad you're here. This is Grace Sawyer. Grace, you and Billie are going to share a bed and a room."

Billie looked into frightened dark eyes that couldn't quite meet hers. The hands that were clasped together over a pathetically tiny waist were trembling.

Trembling? She'd come here resenting this girl. She'd primed herself for a fight. But she couldn't help but be moved by the desperation she could read in this stranger's face.

"Hello, Grace." Billie tried a smile. "Come on. I'll take you upstairs and show you our room."

Slade nodded. "I'm through with you for now, Grace. You can see Cheri about something to wear tonight when you start work."

The girl turned away and followed Billie without a word.

Upstairs Billie led the way to her room and stepped inside. "This is my...our bed."

Grace kept her hands clasped together, afraid to touch anything. "It looks so clean."

Billie swallowed. "I washed everything myself. The bedding. The curtains. The floor." She nodded toward the gown and plumed hat hanging on pegs beside the door. "There's plenty of room for your things. But see you don't wrinkle those. I…wear them every night.''

Grace hadn't moved. She stood frozen to the spot. In a small voice she said, ''The only things I have are what I'm wearing.''

''Well.'' Billie smiled again. ''What I'm wearing is even better than what I had when I came here.'' She ran a hand down the faded buttercup gown before pulling herself out of her thoughts. ''I've got to get down to the kitchen. I help the cook. Cheri's room is just down the hall. She'll figure out what you should wear tonight.''

As she turned away she saw the way Grace struggled to hold back tears. She touched a tentative hand to the girl's arm. ''What's wrong? Are you in some kind of trouble?''

Grace sniffed and wiped a dirty hand over her eyes. ''My husband—'' her voice wavered ''—was old, but he was good to me. He married me when I was thirteen. He was a friend of my pa's, and when Pa died he married me and took me to his ranch. It wasn't much. Just a little patch of land. And now he's dead. He just laid down next to the fresh earth he'd just plowed and…died. And I was left with no food and no money. I've got two little kids and nothing to eat. So I took them to a neighbor's ranch and came into town to find work.''

Billie sucked in a quick breath. ''You left your children? How old are they?''

''My boy is four. My girl three.''

Billie's heart lurched. "And you left them with neighbors? Are they good people?"

The young woman shrugged. "I don't know them well. Only saw them working their fields now and again. They were miles from our ranch. But I didn't know what else to do after I buried Nathaniel."

Billie took several deep calming breaths, remembering all the strangers who'd drifted in and out of her younger days. Some had been kind. But some… "Your children will be fine, Grace." She knew it was what this young woman needed desperately to hear right now. "Did Slade tell you what you'd have to do here at the Red Dog?"

Grace couldn't meet her eyes. She struggled with a bravado she didn't feel. But she couldn't hide the tremors. "I don't care what I have to do. I'm not going to watch my babies starve."

Billie saw the way the young woman glanced longingly at the bed. "How long has it been since you slept?"

Grace shrugged. "I don't know. Two days, maybe. I've been walking a long time. All the way from Bison Fork."

Billie turned back the covers. "You lie here, Grace. Sleep awhile. And then—" she pressed her down and drew the blanket over her thin shoulders "—you'll have the strength to do whatever you have to."

Billie closed the door softly, hoping to drown out the sound of Grace's weeping. She made her way to the kitchen. While she prepared for the next wave of cowboys coming in for supper, she thought about the young widow upstairs. Hadn't she arrived feeling exactly the way Grace felt? And if fate hadn't stepped in, in the form of Belle California, she'd already be working alongside the other saloon women. Selling her dignity and her soul, just to stay alive.

It wasn't fair, she thought. A man could just walk away from his responsibilities, and hire on as a cowboy or shopkeeper. And before he knew it, he could start over. But what about the ones he left behind? What would happen to Grace Sawyer and her two children?

Just thinking about the plight of those two children brought back a flood of memories. Of sleeping upright in the saddle in front of her father while shivering in the cold or wilting in the heat of the sun. Of working from sunup to sundown for the sake of a meal and a bed.

As she set a pan of biscuits in the oven she found herself thinking about Aaron Smiler who, despite his age and circumstances, had made a home for three frightened orphans. According to Kitty, he'd asked nothing in return. Maybe that's what attracted her to that old man. It was his generous spirit. There weren't many who would open their homes and their hearts to the abandoned and the desperate, without demanding payment of some kind.

Maybe she would take a walk to visit Emma Hardwick, and see if her rescue mission could offer some help to Grace Sawyer.

The thought had her smiling as she bustled about

the kitchen, cutting up chunks of meat for stew and tossing them into a blackened pot. She looked up when Jack Slade walked into the kitchen.

She brushed the hair from her eyes, trying to gauge his mood. "Is something wrong?"

He nodded. "Doc Honeywell is with Grunt. It doesn't look good."

"What do you mean?" The towel slipped from her hands and dropped to her feet. She didn't even notice. "What's wrong with Grunt?"

Slade shrugged. "Doc thinks it might be his appendix."

Billie had no idea what that was, but she'd heard about people dying when the appendix started leaking poisons into the body. "Can't Doc Honeywell fix it?"

Slade shook his head sadly. "Doc says it would mean cutting, and he's not trained for that."

"But he's a doctor, isn't he?"

Slade frowned. "I guess he knows a little about doctoring. But mostly he just knows how to patch up bullet wounds and such."

"Is Grunt going to…" Billie swallowed, unable to speak the word.

"Doc doesn't know. But he says it's a hard way for a man to go." He cleared his throat. "Grunt's asking to see you."

"He is?" Billie was already heading toward the door.

Upstairs she found the old cook lying on a mattress soaked with his own sweat. With that mane of white hair spread around his wet pillow, and his face as pale as marble, he looked more dead than alive.

Billie paused beside the bed and shot a questioning glance at the doctor, who stepped back, allowing her to touch a hand to Grunt's.

He opened his eyes. His breathing was so labored, he could barely speak. "That you, girl?"

"It's me, Grunt."

"I recognized you. As soon as you started working at the Red Dog, I knew you."

"You—" she felt a rush of sheer terror "—recognized me?"

He gave a half smile. "Runnin' from something bad. Like me. We're alike, you and me." He paused to run his tongue over his parched lips. "Nothin' soft about us, is there, girl?"

On a wave of relief she shook her head, fighting not to give in to the whirlwind of emotions that were tugging at her heart. "That's right. We're tough, Grunt."

"And we both like to cook. I never told you, but you're a better cook than I am. I want you to take my place, girl, cooking for those cowboys downstairs."

"Don't talk foolishness, Grunt. You'll be back in the kitchen tomorrow, cooking the way you always have."

He gave a slight squeeze of her hand, all that he could manage in his weakened state. "Don't ever play poker, girl. You'd give away your hand every time."

She sat down on the edge of the mattress and took his hand in both of hers. ''All right, Grunt. I promise. No poker.''

He lay a long time, eyes closed, breathing ragged, while the fever raged through his body.

Doc Honeywell closed up his black bag and walked quietly from the room, having done all he could.

Jack Slade stepped inside long enough to urge Billie to get back to work. But when he saw the look in her eyes, he realized that nothing short of the old man's death would budge her.

Gradually word went around the saloon that Grunt was dying. One by one the cowboys and the gamblers took the news with a simple nod of their head. Most stayed, drinking and eating more out of habit than concern, and waiting for word of the crusty loner who had been in Misery for as long as anybody could remember.

The girls who worked the saloon considered it an inconvenience, since they were forced to ladle the stew that was simmering on the big stove and serve the hungry crowd, while Billie kept her silent vigil beside the bed.

When Gabe heard the news, he walked down the dusty street and stepped inside the Red Dog. He'd been avoiding this place for days, choosing to sleep on one of the bunks in the jail, rather than face Billie after that scene behind the saloon. He'd even deputized young Lars Swensen, putting him in charge of the jail each morning, so he wouldn't have to be there when Billie brought his meals.

Now, as he climbed the stairs, he braced himself for what he knew he would feel when he saw her again. But nothing could prepare him for what he heard as he opened the door.

"Whatever trouble you've been in, it hasn't hardened your heart, girl." Grunt's voice was little more than a whisper, as his breathing became more strained. Each word was a supreme effort now. "You just can't help yourself. Got to take in every stray you meet. But watch yourself, girl. Sometimes strays can bite."

"I'll be careful, Grunt." Billie was kneeling on the hard wooden floor, her hands holding his.

Gabe studied the way the light from the lantern spilled over the slight figure on her knees beside the bed. He'd once thought her slim and frail. But she was proving him wrong once again. Most people would run from the sight of such a painful death. Especially when the one dying wasn't even kin. But here she was, doing what she could to ease an old man through the worst moments of his life.

She tried to urge a sip of water on the old man, but he refused.

"Don't waste time waiting for the preacher. Bury me as soon as I've taken my last breath. And beside my grave, sing one of those pretty songs you sing as Belle California."

She gave a gasp of surprise. "You knew that was me?"

He nodded.

"But you never let on, Grunt."

"Figured it would just shame you." He saw the bright color that came to her cheeks and closed his eyes to spare her. "I never told you, but I like those songs. They remind me of a time when the world was green, and so was I, before I withered and died."

"Don't say that, Grunt."

"I've been dead a long time now. At least my soul's been dead. This land took everythin' from me. My wife. My babies. My ranch. The Badlands'll do that. After a while, I stopped caring. Turned away from people. Hid in that room back there. I've been dead so long, I'm not afraid of it now."

"Stop it, Grunt. You're not dying. You'll be feeling like your old self by tomorrow."

His eyes snapped open. "There's no tomorrow for me. But you've got plenty of 'em. So don't waste 'em. And don't look back on yesterday." He saw the tears she couldn't hide and said sharply, "You hear me, girl?"

Billie choked back the sob that lodged in her throat. "I hear you, Grunt. I won't look back. I'll…make the most of my tomorrows."

He smiled. "That's good, girl. That's real good. 'Cause that's all anybody's really got. A few special tomorrows."

He gave a long, deep sigh. His hand went slack in hers. And though his eyes were still open, they seemed to go flat. The sharp piercing light had gone out of them.

Billie touched a hand to his throat, searching vainly for a pulse. Finding none, she began to weep.

Without a word Gabe strode across the room and hauled her into his arms.

"Oh, Gabe." Seeing him, feeling his strength, she wrapped her arms around his neck and hugged him fiercely. For just a few minutes she would let him be strong for both of them. "He's gone. Grunt's gone."

"I know, Billie. I know." And though he wasn't certain he knew how to be tender, he was determined to try, holding her in his arms while she wept as though her heart was shattered.

And then, when the tears had run their course, he helped her wash the old man's face, and comb back his long white hair, before wrapping him in a clean blanket for burial.

When the word of his death passed through the crowd downstairs, six cowboys carried the blanket-clad body to a wooden box beside a hole freshly dug in the ground just beyond the saloon, on a hillside where the lights of the town could be clearly seen.

Though most of the respectable people of Misery stayed away, a few of them came. Doc Honeywell was there, as well as Sheriff Gabe Conover and young Lars Swensen, his new deputy.

The men removed their hats, and the saloon women bowed their heads. And as they lay Grunt in his grave, and shoveled dirt over the simple wooden box, Billie, dressed in the fancy gown and plumed hat of Belle California, spoke the words from her childhood lullaby.

The words, that had once sounded so simple, now skimmed ever so lightly over their minds, dredging up long-forgotten childhood memories. Every word seemed to take on new meaning. Everyone there felt something whisper over their souls as a breathy voice, trembling with tears, led the old man to his final rest.

Afterward, when everyone had walked back to the saloon, Gabe watched Billie standing alone at the gravesite. He had every intention of leaving until he heard the sound of her weeping.

He walked closer and touched a hand to her arm. She looked up at him, her eyes wet with tears.

It seemed the most natural thing in the world to open his arms and gather her close. And with each sob that shuddered through her slender frame, he found himself wanting to soothe and comfort.

"He would have liked your song, Billie."

"You think so?" Her voice was choked.

"I do. He cared about you, Billie."

She looked up, her lashes glistening with diamond drops. "How do you know that?"

"He let you share his kitchen."

"You mean I'm the first?"

"You're the first one he didn't drive off after a day or two."

"He—" she sniffed "—he tried. At least, looking back, I think that's what he was trying to do. But I wasn't going to let him. And I'd like to think that after a while he didn't mind having me around."

Gabe framed her face with his big hands and

brushed at her tears with his thumbs. In the moonlight she could see something come into his eyes. A look that softened all his features as he studied her with that quiet intensity that always caused a flutter around her heart.

"I'm thinking you'd be easy to have around, Billie."

Before she could make a reply he lowered his head and took her mouth with his. This time his kiss was different from the others. Softer. Gentler. Like the quiet whisper of a butterfly's wings.

His hands, too, were gentle as they slowly slid from her face to her neck and across the slope of her shoulders.

He held her as though she were a fragile doll. Cautious. Careful, lest she break.

He was, she realized, forcing himself to move slowly, without all the flash and fire and passion, in order to soothe. The knowledge that he was doing this for her brought the threat of fresh tears. She swallowed them back as she lifted a palm to his cheek.

"Thank you, Gabe."

He drew back to stare down into her eyes. In his own was a look of stunned surprise, as though he'd just uncovered something so new, so puzzling, he needed to put some distance between them until he'd had time to mull it over.

"I'd better go now, Billie." He took a step back. "You'll be all right?"

She nodded, and even managed a smile. "I'm fine now, thanks to you."

She remained beside the fresh grave and watched as Gabe strode away. When he reached the saloon he turned and looked back, then rounded the building and disappeared into the night.

She found herself alone, thinking back over all that had happened in the space of a single day.

Chapter Eight

Billie paused on her way to jail, balancing the heavy tray as she knocked on the door of the tiny cabin. While she waited, she studied the carefully lettered sign. Rescue Mission.

The door was opened a crack, and the woman's eyes widened before she stepped aside and held the door wide.

"Welcome, lamb." She offered a hand. "My name is Emma Hardwick."

"I'm Billie. Billie Calley." Billie flushed in embarrassment. "I can't shake your hand. Mine are too full."

Emma smiled and pointed to a table. "Would you like to set down your burden?"

Billie placed the tray on the table, then stood twisting her hands around and around, while she noted the tiny room, with a bed, a table and a single chair.

"You've come to seek shelter?"

"Yes. I mean no. Not for myself. There's a woman at the Red Dog. She lost her husband, and she has two little children. I was thinking maybe you could fetch them and put her and the children up here."

Emma indicated the chair. "Why don't you sit down and tell me about your children, Billie?"

Billie perched on the edge of the chair. "They aren't mine. They belong to Grace Sawyer. And she cries every night over them. I thought, since this is a rescue mission—"

Emma held up a hand. "I have no money, except what I earn sewing for the good women of Misery. And as you can see, I have no room to put up a woman and her children. This single room is all I have. But I can pray with her, and encourage her to find employment that isn't demeaning, and—"

Billie sighed. "I don't know those big, fancy words. I just was hoping that you could rescue Grace and her babies." She rubbed her hand on her skirts before offering it to Emma. "But I do thank you for your time."

"I hope you'll come back one day and talk with me," Emma said.

Billie shrugged. "If I can find the time I will."

She walked away, deep in thought. And realized that if she wanted to help Grace, she'd have to see to it herself.

Billie stepped into the jail with her tray and glanced around. Young Lars was in the back, sweeping out an empty cell. Seeing her, he set aside his broom and quickly removed his hat.

"'Morning, Billie."

"Lars. The sheriff isn't here?"

"No, ma'am. But he should be back soon if you'd like to wait for him."

She set the tray on the sheriff's desk. Since the night they'd buried Grunt, Gabe hadn't once been in the jail when she brought his breakfast. It was obvious that he was avoiding her. Though it rankled, she told herself to be patient. Gabe Conover was a man who needed a great deal of space.

Besides, today she'd been counting on his absence. "I don't need to see the sheriff, Lars. It's you I'd like to talk to." She paused beside the desk. "I notice that you still handle the deliveries of supplies to the ranchers for your pa."

"Yes'm. The sheriff doesn't need me most days, except when there's a prisoner."

Billie reached into her pocket and withdrew a precious dollar she'd palmed when a cowboy had tossed it the previous night. She'd consoled herself that it wasn't stealing, since Slade hadn't paid her a thing yet. When he did, if he ever did, she would see that the dollar was returned.

"If you're ever over near Bison Fork, I have a favor to ask."

The young man listened respectfully to her request, then nodded. "Yes'm. I'd be happy to do as you ask." He stared hungrily at the money. "But you don't need to pay me."

Billie pressed the money into his hand. "What

you're doing is important to me, Lars. And I'd feel better if you'd let me pay.''

He watched as she hurried away. Then he scratched his head in dismay. What she'd asked was simple enough. But she'd also asked him not to tell anyone, especially the sheriff. He'd been torn between loyalty to the man who'd hired him, and the chance to earn himself a little extra money. In the end he'd found himself agreeing with Billie that he would be doing nothing wrong. Now he was stuck with their bargain. For, though it bothered him, young Lars Swensen prided himself on keeping his word.

Grace stood outside the room she shared with Billie. She dabbed at her tears and straightened her gown, before combing her fingers through her tangled hair. She was sick and tired of crying herself to sleep each night, but she just couldn't seem to stop. It shamed her to think about what she was doing, just to keep body and soul together. In fact, the cowboys, with their hard hands and eager mouths sickened her. But what hurt even more, right down to her soul, was the thought of little Ned and Nell living with strangers. It was eating at her heart, stealing her spirit. Her will to survive.

She sniffed, wiped at her eyes, and opened the door, ready to face another miserable night trying to hide her tears from Billie. When she stepped inside she felt her jaw drop at the sight of Billie sitting in bed, with Ned on one side of her and Nell on the other. Both children were laughing and clapping as Billie finished a funny story.

For the space of a heartbeat Grace's throat clogged with tears, and though she opened her mouth, no words came out.

"Mama." The little boy and girl leaped up and threw themselves at Grace with a fierceness that had her swaying backward before she regained her footing.

"Ned. Nell. Oh, my babies. My sweet, sweet babies. Let me look at you." With tears streaming down her cheeks she hugged and kissed them both, then wrapped them tightly in her arms as she looked over their heads at Billie. "Why did you...? How did you...?"

"The why's easy. I got tired of hearing you crying yourself to sleep every night. The how took a little planning. I bribed Lars Swensen. He delivers supplies all over the territory, and I figured one of these days he'd pass by the Spooner ranch. Your young ones told me he let them ride up front with him, and when they got tired, he let them lie in the back, on the flour sacks. I gave them supper, then brought them up here when nobody was looking."

"But what'll we do with them all day, Billie?"

The young woman smiled. "I've figured it all out, Grace. During the day, while you're sleeping, they'll stay downstairs with me in the kitchen."

"But Slade..."

Billie touched a finger to her lips. "Hush now. Jack Slade never comes near the kitchen. After he counts the money, he goes off to his room and doesn't come back out until late afternoon. By then you'll be awake, and you can spend some time here in the room with little Ned and Nell. And at night I'll stay up here with them while you work, except while I'm singing. By then they'll surely be asleep.''

"Oh, Billie." Grace sat down on the edge of the bed and clutched her two children to her, unsure whether to laugh or weep. "I don't know if you're right or wrong, but I do know this. I really needed to hold them again."

"And they needed you, Grace. They lost their pa. They need to be with their ma."

Grace became alarmed as another thought struck. "Where are you going to sleep?"

Billie shrugged. "I've slept on the floor plenty of times in my life. I'll just make myself a nice bed over in the corner."

Grace bit her lip. "You're sure about this?"

"As sure as I am about anything. Now kiss them good-night. They've had quite an adventure today. Their little eyes are closing."

Grace tucked the little boy and girl into bed, then knelt on the floor, watching as they drifted into sleep. Then without a word she rounded the bed and hugged Billie, weeping softly into her shoulder. For the first time in weeks, they were tears of joy instead of despair.

Billie wiped damp hair from her eyes as she climbed the stairs to her room. She'd been working nonstop all day, first making breakfast, with the help of little Ned and Nell, who'd rolled the dough for biscuits, and had delighted in tossing grain to the chickens. Then she'd spent some quiet time in her room, telling stories to the children until they fell asleep. Now, after cooking supper and cleaning up the kitchen, she'd given four performances in the saloon as Belle California.

As she stepped into her room Grace looked up from the bed, where she'd been watching her children sleeping.

"Look, Billie." She held up a fistful of dollars. "In no time my babies and I will be in St. Louis with my brother and his wife."

It was all she talked about. She never complained about the work. And never mentioned the husband who had died. After her initial fear of having the children discovered, she had pulled herself together, making plans to start her life over with her brother. To Billie's delight, she seemed to grow stronger each day. All she cared about now was the future.

"That's good, Grace." Billie slumped down on the floor where she kept a pillow and blanket, too tired to even worry about wrinkling her gown.

Grace tucked the money down the front of her dress. "You look tired, Billie."

"Hmm." Mechanically Billie removed her plumed hat and wig, tossing them aside before beginning to unbutton her gown. "I don't think I have the strength to move."

"Here. Let me hang those for you." Grace hung

the hat and wig on a peg, then took the gown that
Billie handed her, running a finger admiringly along
the ruffled skirt. As she turned away she said, "I'm
tired, too. But I know this. For enough money, there
isn't anything I wouldn't do right now. All I care
about is making all the money I can, and getting out
of here forever with my babies."

Billie lay back against the pillow, watching as
Grace moved restlessly around the room. With her
long dark hair and those big sad eyes, she looked
more like Belle California than Billie did, even in
her wig and gown.

The thought had Billie sitting up, her weariness
forgotten. "Would you, Grace?"

The girl turned. "Would I what?"

"Do anything for money?"

Grace shrugged. "Anything within reason. I
wouldn't rob a bank, but I might..." She stepped
closer. "What's wrong? What're you thinking, Billie?"

Billie gave a mysterious smile. "Maybe I just
thought of a way to lighten my burden, and give you
a way to earn money even faster."

Jack Slade drew on his cigar and listened in silence. When Billie was finished he merely dismissed
her request with a wave of his hand.

"Nobody could take the place of Belle California.
You think those cowboys won't know the difference?
You've got something special, Billie. Nobody else
can pretend to be you."

Her mind was racing now. She'd been so certain he would agree to her suggestion. After all, she was cooking all day, singing late into the night, and lately, not able to give her full attention to either. Several times she'd almost fallen asleep at the stove.

"All along you've been telling me that what I do isn't important. You insisted on keeping all the money the cowboys tossed at me, saying I didn't earn it. Now you're saying nobody else can take my place?" She brought her hands to her hips. "Grace can do this, if you'll give her a chance. She's just about my size. And she won't even need to wear that awful wig. All she has to do is learn the words of those songs, and speak them."

Seeing that she had his attention she paced, paused, turned. "Maybe you could announce that Belle California has been having some trouble with her voice. That would explain why she didn't sound like me. And then, in a couple of weeks, nobody will even be able to remember what the old Belle sounded like."

Slade drew on his cigar and studied the smoke that curled toward the ceiling while he considered her suggestion.

"You said yourself that the main thing is to keep the cowboys coming back for more."

He looked over at Billie. He'd known, of course, that she wouldn't be able to keep up this pace much longer. And the truth was, he needed her services in the kitchen more than he needed her at night. There wasn't anyone else willing to do what she did, even for twice the pay. Saloon girls were easy to find. Good cooks were worth their weight in gold. Still, she didn't need to know that. He said angrily, "I'll have to cut your pay."

She shot him a look. "You haven't paid me at all yet."

"I haven't?" He gave that a moment's thought before setting aside his cigar in a crystal ashtray. Lifting a strongbox from a locked drawer, he counted out some money, hoping to placate her. "All right. Here's your pay. But from now on, you'll have to make do on less."

Billie counted out the money, then looked up. "Twenty dollars? For all the work I've done?"

"I had to hold out some for the bed and the gown and the food."

"You already had the dress. I share my bed. And I'm the one who cooks the food. Besides, I know for a fact that those cowboys tossed more than that at me on any single night, and you kept it all." She thought about the dollar she'd palmed, and the guilt she'd suffered for it.

Slade placed the strongbox back in a drawer and locked it before getting to his feet. "You knew the rules when you took the job. As I recall, you didn't care how much you'd make as long as you had a place to sleep and enough food to keep body and soul together."

He saw the blush that stained her cheeks and knew he'd struck a nerve. "Now, if you want Grace to take up the slack at night as Belle California, I'm willing to give her a try.''

Billie considered. ''I won't work for less money.''

His eyes narrowed. ''All right. Twenty dollars a month.''

''And I want a better choice of food.''

''What's that supposed to mean?''

''There's a hog farmer on a ranch north of here. Jeb Simmons. I want a smoked ham now and again. And more chickens. And…''

He held up his hand to silence her. ''One ham. And maybe a few more chickens, if you're willing to see to them. But that's it. And besides your duties in the kitchen, I'll expect you to give Roscoe Timmons a hand serving drinks during the day so he can get some sleep. Like you, he's been working day and night.''

Billie considered the offer, wondering what she would do with the children. But desperate times called for desperate measures. She nodded.

''Good. Now go teach Grace the words she'll need to know as Belle California.''

''On one condition.''

His eyes narrowed as his patience thinned. ''What's that?''

''That Grace gets to keep half of what the cowboys toss at her.''

''You can't be serious.'' For a minute he looked like he might explode. His face reddened and his eyes narrowed to tiny slits. ''You think you can just walk in here and start telling me how to run my business?''

When she didn't offer any defense he studied her in silence before asking, ''What's Grace to you?''

''A friend,'' she said simply.

There was something about the way she said it that had Slade thinking she just might walk out if he balked at her request. Swallowing back his temper he gave a curt nod of his head. ''All right. She keeps half. But if I catch her stealing, I'll have her tossed in jail so fast it'll have her head spinning. You tell her that.''

Elated, Billie raced up the stairs to share her news with Grace. The young woman would be a step closer to taking her children to St. Louis. As for herself, Billie would be able to sleep while the other women worked. And work while they were sleeping. And all the while, doing what she loved.

''Sheriff Conover.'' Cheri paused beside Gabe's table. ''Do you want a drink with your supper?''

He shook his head. ''Just supper, Cheri.''

A short time later she set down a tin plate heaped with thick slices of smoked ham, as well as potatoes mashed with turnips and onions and biscuits drizzled with honey.

For a moment all he could do was stare at the food. Then, picking up a fork, he tasted. Then he savored each successive bite. By the time the plate was empty, he was feeling positively mellow.

Rocking the chair back on its legs he pulled a cigar

from his pocket and held a match to the tip. As smoke curled over his head he closed his eyes, wondering if he'd just died and gone to heaven.

His eyes snapped open when the cowboys around him began stomping their feet and shouting. He watched as Jack Slade kept a protective arm around Belle California, herding her through the crowd, lifting her to the piano. As Slade stepped away, the piano player gave the usual introduction, then paused, waiting for the singer to pick up the note.

As a soft voice began speaking the words, Gabe's eyes narrowed on the woman atop the piano. This wasn't Billie. In fact, she wasn't even a good imitation. For one thing, she was exposing a good deal too much ankle and leg. For another thing, she was looking directly at the cowboys, meeting their eyes, even returning their smiles.

Gabe pushed away from the table and threaded his way through the throng to the door leading to the kitchen.

Inside he saw a lone figure standing at a scarred wooden table, her hands immersed in a basin of soapy water.

"How did you get Slade to agree to this?"

She whirled to see Gabe leaning casually against the closed door. Smoke curled from the cigar in his hand.

"I told him the cowboys wouldn't notice the difference. And it would allow me to spend more time cooking."

"Who's the new Belle?"

"Her name's Grace Sawyer."

"She's not as good as you were."

Billie felt a rush of warmth and blamed it on the heat from the stove. When she could find her voice she managed to say, "Let's just hope those cowboys out there don't agree with you, or I'll be right back where I started."

He took a step closer. "That was a fine meal tonight, Billie. In fact, it was just about the best I've ever tasted."

She felt her face grow hot and knew her cheeks were flaming. "Thank you. That's just about the nicest thing you could say to me."

He stepped even closer, stopping just short of touching her. "I'm sorry I've been keeping my distance since that night we buried Grunt."

"That's all right. I know you're busy and all and I—"

He pressed a finger to her lips to silence her. Even that simple touch had them both taking a step back, as if to escape the heat that engulfed them.

"I was afraid to see you, Billie."

"You? Afraid?" Her eyes widened in surprise. "Why?"

"I found out that I like holding you in my arms. Especially when I take my time and go nice and easy." He heard her little gasp of surprise and rushed ahead, determined to say what was on his mind. "I liked holding you so much, in fact, I was afraid if I came back here I'd have to do it again. And I was afraid if I did that, I might never stop until we…crossed a line. So I've been avoiding you."

He saw the water dripping from her hands and picked up a linen square, handing it to her. As she accepted it, he felt the sudden rush of heat and turned on his heel. "I'll say good-night now, Billie."

"Good…" She watched in dismay as he disappeared even before the word was out of her mouth.

She leaned a hip against the table and dried her hands, wondering what in the world had just happened. Had he been apologizing for wanting to do more than just hold her? Or was he simply annoyed at himself for wanting such things with a woman like her?

She tossed down the towel and tackled the blackened pots with renewed vengeance.

Men, she thought. She just couldn't figure them out.

Upstairs, Gabe prowled his room like a caged panther. It was time to face the fact that he just wasn't good with women. Well, some women didn't seem to mind that he didn't know how to express himself. Like Cheri. But she didn't count. She treated all the men to a smile and a tumble. But Billie was different. She may be working in the Red Dog, but anybody with half a brain could see that she didn't belong here.

Why in hell did she have to come along and complicate his life like this? She was costing him a great deal of sleep. Not to mention a wagonload of common sense.

He'd always prided himself on his discipline. But lately he'd been behaving like some empty-headed ranch hand, letting his paperwork accumulate dust in a drawer, while he spent more and more time in the saloon watching her. Only now she wouldn't be there at night, feeding his fantasies.

He might tell Jack Slade he spent his nights in the saloon just to keep the peace, but he knew in his heart that was a lie. He was there for only one reason. To look out for a female who didn't know how to look out for herself.

It may be true that she'd pulled a pretty slick deal with Slade, getting him to accept someone else to entertain the cowboys so she could spend more time cooking. But she was still working for him in his saloon. On his terms. And Jack Slade was a man who prided himself on being a shrewd businessman. If there was a dollar to be made, no matter what the cost to his girls, Slade would see that it found its way into his pocket.

Gabe stopped his pacing long enough to unfasten his gun belt and slide his pistol under his pillow. With a sigh he kicked off his boots and undressed before blowing out the lantern and lying on the bed. With his hands under his head he closed his eyes and saw Billie's face in his mind.

What was it about that ornery female that touched him so? She wasn't a great beauty. In fact, her skin was so pale it would probably blister in the summer sun. And her eyes were too big for her face. Or maybe it was her face that was too small for her eyes. Such expressive eyes. They mirrored all her feelings. And then there was that pointy little chin that was always stuck out, ready for a fight. And that turned-up little nose with that parade of freckles running across it. And that pouty little mouth.

How he hungered to kiss it. How he yearned to kiss every one of those damnable freckles.

He rolled to his side, punching a fist into his pillow, determined to put Billie Calley out of his mind. At least until tomorrow. When he'd probably act like a damned fool and see her again.

Jack Slade kept an eye on the poker game as he threaded his way between the tables. "You're in the Red Dog pretty early, aren't you, Sheriff?"

Gabe nodded and tried not to stare at Billie behind the bar. "I noticed a couple of unfamiliar horses at the hitching post outside and figured I'd see if you were having any trouble."

"No trouble. Just a couple of gamblers passing through who wanted to try their luck on the locals."

"High stakes?" Gabe glanced over and could see piles of money in the middle of the table.

"High enough that tempers could get hot. Glad to see you'll be keeping an eye out." Slade made his way back to the poker table.

When Gabe paused at the end of the bar, Billie hurried over. "Would you like a drink, Sheriff?"

He shook his head and pinned her with a look. "Slade has you slinging drinks now, Billie?"

She knew, by the rush of heat, that her cheeks were flushed. That only added to her embarrassment. "It's part of our deal. I agreed to let Roscoe get some sleep during the day, when things were slow."

He glanced at the way his mother's faded dress looked on her, freshly washed, the sash tied snugly enough to display her tiny waist and soft curves. "I see you're not wearing one of Slade's saloon dresses."

Her blush deepened. "I guess Mr. Slade doesn't think I'm worth it."

Or maybe, Gabe thought, Slade was smart enough to realize that a revealing gown wasn't nearly as provocative on a woman like Billie as a simple dress that sent a man's mind spinning off in a dozen different directions.

"Whiskey," came a man's voice from the other end of the bar.

Billie hurried over to fill the cowboy's tumbler and spent several minutes answering his questions, all the while aware that Gabe was still watching her.

It gave her a prickly feeling to know that he was there.

"You married?" the cowboy asked.

Billie flushed. "You think I'd be working here if I was?"

"Just thought I'd ask." He glanced at the sheriff, standing tensely at the other end of the bar, watching and listening. "Wouldn't want to have to deal with a jealous husband."

Billie corked the bottle. "If I had one, why would he be jealous?"

"Because of the things I'm thinking about you." The cowboy lifted the tumbler and drained it in one long swallow. Then, seeing the look of surprise on her face, he set down the glass and said with a chuckle, "Go ahead and fill it again. And this time take your time, Red. I like watching the way your hair tumbles in your eyes when you bend forward."

Gabe felt such an unreasonable surge of hatred, it caught him completely by surprise. He found himself wishing this cowboy would do something stupid, like get himself drunk and disorderly, so he could take him out back and beat some sense into him.

The very thought had him fisting a hand at his side.

What was wrong with him? Could he possibly be jealous?

The mere thought had him shaken to the core. Of course it wasn't jealousy. That was an emotion that was completely foreign to him. He'd never been jealous of anyone in his life.

It just went with the job, he told himself. After all these years, he had to be prepared to deal with the worst of humanity.

He was almost disappointed when the cowboy picked up his glass of whiskey and strolled across the room to join in the poker game.

Gabe uncurled his fist and decided to take a walk

around the town. It might not cool his temper, but it would certainly help to clear his mind. Not to mention working out some of the knots he could feel in his shoulders.

Because of Billie, he thought glumly.

What was he going to do about her?

Chapter Nine

"You're not going to believe this." Cheri came rushing into the kitchen of the Red Dog, where Billie efficiently moved from slicing the enormous ham on the table to turning the potatoes browning in a skillet, to checking the steaks sizzling on a grate over the big open fireplace.

Billie looked up. "Believe what?"

"There are so many hungry cowboys out there nursing hangovers, and so many ranchers in town for Sunday services, I had to wake the other girls to give me a hand serving the tables."

Billie's eyes widened. "Really?"

Just then Grace darted inside, her cheeks flushed. "The preacher just had breakfast. Can you imagine a preacher eating in a saloon? He said he came here because he'd heard that the new cook was turning out the finest meals in the Dakota Territory. And after he finished he pronounced it the truth. He said it was the best he's ever tasted."

Billie wiped strings of damp hair from her eyes. "You mean it?"

"I do, honey. He even said he would miss this when he moved on to Bison Fork tomorrow."

Cheri shook her head from side to side. "You're going to make the Red Dog famous."

Billie's smile grew as Grace and Cheri loaded their trays and hurried away. A short time later they returned, looking puzzled.

"What's wrong?" Billie asked.

"It seems the food's so good, the ranchers want some for their wives and children." Grace bit her lip.

Billie shrugged. "Fine. Tell them to bring their families over."

Cheri shook her head. "You don't understand. Those men out there will never allow their wives and children to eat in a saloon."

Though Billie felt a twinge of annoyance, she understood their dilemma.

Grace hiked up the apron she'd tied over her faded dress. "They were wondering if they could take food back to their wagons."

Billie looked around, until her glance fell on a stack of clean tin plates. "All right. Let them carry the food in those. But explain that they'll have to bring the plates back. Otherwise Jack Slade will have my head."

Cheri and Grace raced back and forth from the kitchen, filling plates with food, with a promise from the ranchers that the plates would be returned later.

While she started another batch of biscuits, it occurred to Billie that she was having the time of her life. It was almost like being a little girl again, and cooking for a pack of hungry cowboys just coming in off the range.

How she'd loved that, she mused. Seeing her pa come striding in with the other cowboys, looking flushed and happy from a day of hard work with the herds. Sometimes he'd even stop and pat her on the head before going off to join the other men at the long tables spread out under the trees. It had been a hard life. But as long as her pa was happy, she was happy, too. And besides, she'd always pretended that she was cooking in her own kitchen. It was a dream that had sustained her all these years. And some day, she vowed, it would come true.

As she sliced more ham and set down plates for little Ned and Nell, she decided to put some aside for Kitty and Aaron. Maybe, if Gabe planned to ride out to their ranch this afternoon, she'd send them a little gift, to thank them for their hospitality.

She smiled as the children cleaned their plates. They were so sweet. And so grateful to be here with their mother, that they were willing to do whatever was necessary to keep their presence a secret from Slade. They stayed for hours in the kitchen, helping with the chores. Whenever possible, Billie took them out back in her little garden, knowing Slade never ventured out there. At night, once they were tucked in their bed, they knew they had to be as silent as little mice.

Cheri and the other saloon girls had quickly caught on to Billie's little scheme, and had gone along with it. Now, Billie noticed, whenever their schedules permitted, the women began dropping by the kitchen, something they never used to do. But the presence of little children seemed to have a softening effect on all of them, including the hardened Cheri, who boasted of having never even touched a child until she'd met these two. Now she enjoyed cooing over them, and even combing little Nell's silky hair.

The biggest surprise of all had been Lars. Ever since bringing the children here, he'd been stopping by, bringing them little treats from the dry goods store. A spinning top. A length of rope, so they could jump. And of course, rock candy, which he always seemed to carry in his pocket for them. He was so easy and natural with them. Until their mother would appear. Then his face would grow red and his voice choked, and he would beat a hasty retreat back to the store.

Seeing that the children were finished with their breakfast, Billie cleaned the table before leading them outside where, much to their delight, she allowed them to feed the chickens.

She leaned her hands on the top of the fence, resting her chin there and smiling as Ned and Nell darted here and there, giggling as the chickens followed closely, pecking at their bare feet. It did her heart good to see their little faces wreathed in smiles, and hear the sound of their laughter.

Billie felt a quick tug at her heart. She'd fretted

that a saloon wasn't a proper place to bring two little innocents. But with every passing day she grew more certain that she'd done the right thing, reuniting these children with their mother.

When, minutes later, Lars Swensen arrived with a pocket full of rock candy for the children, they were delighted, dancing around him as he offered them their treat.

He looked up timidly. "Is Grace busy?"

Billie shrugged. "I can go see. Would you like to stay here with the children?"

He nodded.

Minutes later she found Grace cleaning off tables in the saloon.

Billie leaned close to whisper, "Lars is out back with the children. He was asking for you."

Grace's face turned three shades of pink as she touched a hand to her hair before hurrying away. A short time later Billie walked outside to find Grace and Lars standing so close their shoulders were brushing, while the children sat at their feet, their hands and mouths sticky from rock candy.

It occurred to Billie that she'd never seen Grace looking so flushed. Or Lars looking so happy.

Billie stepped into Swensen's Dry Goods and looked around in surprise. Inga and Olaf were no-where to be seen. Usually Inga was behind the long wooden counter, cutting cloth from bolts of fabric, or singing the praises of the latest shipment of Gray's honey or Mrs. Baxter's fruit preserves. Olaf would be hauling sacks of flour and sugar or grain out back to waiting wagons. But today the place appeared to be empty.

When she heard the sound of singing coming from the back room she remembered. It was the one Sunday a month that the town of Misery held special services. Hadn't Cheri told her the visiting preacher had stopped by for a meal? She inched closer and peered through a crack in the wooden door. The people stood in neat rows, sharing books, and singing at the top of their lungs. In the very first row was Emma Hardwick, all neat and buttoned up, her voice lifted in song.

When the song ended, they crowded together on wooden benches, staring expectantly at a black-clad figure in the front of the room. As he began speaking, they listened in rapt attention as his rich voice rolled over them.

Intrigued, Billie pulled up a small wooden stool and pressed her ear to the door. The preacher read fancy words from a book, that didn't seem to make any sense to her. About beating swords into plowshares. But when he spoke about turning lives around, about turning away from violence and embracing goodness, about feeding men instead of killing them, she closed her eyes and smiled. Could there be some hope for her after all? Could it be that she was doing good work, even though she worked in a saloon?

As his voice droned on and on, Billie dozed, missing much of what he was saying. But when she heard a sudden silence, followed by the shuffling of many feet, her head came up sharply, and she leaped up, prepared to race out of the store, before anyone could see her.

When she turned she slammed against a solid wall of chest and looked up to find Gabe staring down at her, his big hands at her shoulders to steady her.

"What got into you?" His voice was gruff.

"I didn't mean to eavesdrop. I just came over to buy some things and I overheard the preacher. And I liked his voice and thought I'd listen for a minute."

"Why didn't you join the others inside?"

She was shaking her head and trying to back away. Except that she couldn't, because he was holding her. "I wouldn't do that. After all, the good people of Misery might be ready to turn away from violence, but I don't think they're ready to have a saloon girl in the midst of their Sunday services."

They could hear the sound of the benches being moved and stacked against the far wall, and the voices of children, relieved to be allowed to run outside and chase each other around the waiting wagons. Soon the store would be filled with men and women hoping to stock up on supplies before beginning the long trek back to their distant ranches.

Billie shot him a pleading look. "Please, Gabe. Let me go. I don't want to be here when the others come in."

"All right." He continued holding her a moment longer. Not, he told himself, because he was enjoying the heat that always accompanied her touch. But simply because she smelled good. Like sugar and flour and some forgotten memory from his past. "On one condition."

She shot him a look. "What is it?"

"I'm riding out to see my sister. I'd like you to come along."

She was already shaking her head as she turned to run. "I don't think I can spare the time. But if you'll stop by the kitchen, I have something for Kitty and Aaron."

And then she was gone, just as Emma led the first wave of people filing into the room. Gabe stood in the doorway and watched as Billie fled across the street and disappeared inside the back door of the Red Dog. He took his time, pausing to chat with the ranchers and their wives, as well as the preacher and Emma, before stepping outside. Minutes later he stopped his horse and wagon outside the back door of the saloon.

Billie hurried to meet him, carrying a linen-covered tray.

He took it from her hands. "What's this?"

"Some food for Kitty and Aaron. Ham and potatoes and such. I wanted to thank them for making me feel so welcome when you took me to visit." She looked down at his mother's faded gown as though it were a treasure. "And for this dress."

He set the tray in the back of the wagon before turning to her. "I guess this means that you've already got supper started?"

She nodded. "That's right. As soon as I was finished with the morning crowd."

"Then come with me. You can spare the time."

She was already shaking her head and backing away. "I only have a few hours free and then I'll have to start serving supper."

"I'll get you back here in plenty of time for that." He caught her hand, drawing her toward the wagon.

She dug in her heels. "Promise? I can't be late."

He actually smiled. "I give you my word, Billie."

She knew the children were with their mother and Lars. He'd taken them along in his wagon while he delivered supplies. Roscoe Timmons was already serving drinks. Her chores were finished for the next several hours. And the truth was, the thought of spending time with Gabe and Kitty and Aaron was just too tempting.

"All right. As long as we're back in time for me to serve supper."

He helped her up to the seat of the wagon, then climbed up beside her and lifted the reins. In no time they had left the dusty town of Misery behind, and were rolling across the hills toward Aaron's ranch.

Along the way Gabe found himself thinking about the surprise he'd felt at finding Billie hiding out in the empty store, listening to the preacher. The fact that she hadn't wanted to show herself to the others touched his heart in an unexpected way. For the longest time, after he'd learned the truth about his father, he'd felt that way. As though maybe he deserved all the pain and heartache that he and his family had been forced to endure. Was it the same for Billie? Did she think she wasn't good enough, because she was forced to work in a saloon?

It pained him to realize he'd been guilty of the same thing. Hadn't he been more than willing to dismiss her as a saloon girl when he'd first met her?

Beside him Billie lifted her face to the sun and breathed in the fresh air. "Oh, it's good to be outside, isn't it?"

He nodded. And realized that, with Billie beside him, the day had just become brighter. The air sweeter. And his mood considerably lighter.

He stretched out his long legs, holding the reins loosely between his knees. "Everyone's talking about the good food at the Red Dog."

She turned with a smile of pleasure. "Are they?"

He nodded. "If you're not careful, you may find yourself too busy to do anything except cook from morning till night."

"I wouldn't mind."

He glanced at her. "You like it that much?"

"I do. It makes me feel—' she searched for the words "—the way the preacher probably feels when he lifts people up with his words." She looked over at him. "Do you like what you do, Gabe?"

He shrugged. "Not always. But I like knowing that what I do is necessary. Without men to keep the peace, the outlaws would soon run all the good people out of the territory."

She lifted a hand to shade the sun from her eyes. "Have you ever arrested an innocent man?"

Gabe nodded. ''Plenty of times. But it's not my job to judge a man's guilt or innocence. If a wanted poster comes in with a man's name on it, I have a duty to arrest him. Then it's up to the judge to decide if he's guilty or innocent.''

She gripped the edge of the seat as they crested a hill, struggling to keep the panic from her voice. ''Do you get those posters from all over? Or just from the Dakotas?''

''In a town as small as Misery, most of the wanted posters are about local crimes. But occasionally I hear from surrounding states, especially if it's a serious offense, like murder.''

She swallowed. ''Have you ever killed a man, Gabe?''

''I have. I'm not proud of that. But I'm not ashamed, either. I knew when I took this job what I'd be expected to do.'' He looked over at her. ''It's a serious thing, to take another man's life. It's not something I'd ever do lightly.''

Billie looked away from those intense, all-knowing eyes and was relieved when the Smiler ranch came into view.

They caught sight of Aaron sitting on the porch, his legs propped up on the railing to ease the pain in them. The minute he saw them he put his fingers to his lips and gave a shrill whistle. By the time they had drawn up alongside the house and were climbing down from the hard wooden seat, Kitty was racing up on horseback, whooping out a welcome.

She leaped from her mustang and paused for

breath alongside Gabe, who tousled her hair before slapping her on the arm. But when she turned to Billie her shyness disappeared. Kitty threw her arms around her and swung her around and around. "You came back. Aaron said you would."

"Well, he knew more than I did." Billie huffed in a breath, more than a little surprised by Kitty's exuberance. "I expected to be in Misery right now, working."

"What changed your mind?"

"Your brother." Billie watched as Gabe lifted the tray from the back of the wagon before walking up onto the porch and shaking hands with old Aaron, who was getting slowly to his feet.

"I'm glad." Kitty turned to Gabe. "What've you got there?"

"Billie brought you a surprise." He tore aside the linen cover to reveal a platter of thick ham slices, fancy potatoes and a basket of biscuits.

"You made us supper?"

At her look of astonishment, mingled with sheer joy, Billie touched a hand to her arm. "What's wrong, Kitty?"

The young woman shook her head, sending honey curls tumbling. When she found her voice she said, "Nobody's ever fixed us supper before."

Now it was Billie's turn to look surprised, before a smile touched her lips. "Then I'm glad I was the first."

Aaron stood on the porch, leaning on his walking stick and looking on with pleasure. "Then, considering the importance of your gift, why don't we step inside out of the hot sun and enjoy this supper before it gets cold?''

In the kitchen Billie placed the food on a warming tray over the fire and chatted happily with Kitty as the two women set the table and filled a basin with fresh water. While they worked Gabe and Aaron settled themselves into rocking chairs and talked over the news of the past week.

When everything was ready the men rolled their sleeves and washed before taking their places at the table.

As he sat down, Aaron glanced at Billie. "Gabriel just told me about Grunt. I'm real sorry, Billie."

She ducked her head. "Sometimes I look over, expecting to see him slicing the meat or stirring the stew. And then I realize he isn't coming back, and I miss him."

The old man pressed a hand over hers. "Of course you do. It takes time to get over grieving."

"I'm not grieving exactly." She blushed. "He didn't like having me in his kitchen at first. But I like to think that before he died, he was getting used to the idea." She passed around the ham and potatoes. "Did you ever lose anyone close, Aaron?"

He nodded and helped himself to a biscuit. "I had a wife and two boys. And my mother, who always made her home with us. Outlived them all. They're buried out beyond the barn. I visit them sometimes, just to talk."

Kitty looked over at him. "You never talk about them."

He gave her a gentle smile. "You never ask."

"You see that, Billie?" Kitty held the platter while Gabe forked a thick slice of ham onto his plate. "I've known Aaron all my life, and we never talk about the things he's told you in less than a hour."

Gabe chuckled. "I guess we'd all better be warned. Before we know it Billie might pry all our secrets out of us."

Kitty shook her head. "Ours, maybe. But not yours, Gabe."

He arched a brow. "Now why do you say that?"

"I just don't figure you'd share your secrets with another living soul."

He bent to his food. "I'd say you got that right." He broke open a hot, steaming biscuit and inhaled the fragrance. "Ummm. That smells really good. What is it?"

Billie laughed. "Cinnamon. Haven't you ever tasted it before?"

He took a taste and closed his eyes a moment as memories washed over him. Memories of his mother baking a cake on Christmas morning that smelled this same sweet way. He could recall the laughter, and the excitement, and the whispered secrets of that day as though they'd just happened yesterday.

He took another bite, then slowly nodded. "I do believe I've tasted this before. Back on my grandfather's farm."

"I don't remember," Kitty said with a pout.

"You were too young. But Yale and I—" he smiled, remembering "—how we could eat our mama's cinnamon cake. Washed down with warm, foamy milk straight from the cow."

Billie was amazed at the transformation in him when he gave one of those rare smiles. Those gray eyes were no longer icy, but crinkled with warmth. And his mouth, which could be so stern and tight, curved in the most delicious way, and deepened the cleft in his chin.

When she realized that Aaron had seen her staring, she covered by saying quickly, "Then I'm glad I decided to sprinkle them with cinnamon. I only did that because I couldn't buy any of Mrs. Baxter's preserves at Swensen's."

"Preserves?" Now she had Kitty's full attention. "What're preserves?"

"You've never tasted them?" Billie shot her a look of surprise. "Next time I visit, I'll have to bring you some. On biscuits, they taste better than—" she thought a minute "—better than rock candy."

Kitty sighed. "I had some of that once. Remember, Aaron? You brought us all some candy. And I liked it so much, I offered to do all the chores for Yale and Gabe if they'd give me theirs."

"Did they agree?" Billie asked.

Kitty nodded. "But later on, when I tried to keep my end of the bargain, they wouldn't let me. I do recall mucking a couple of stalls for Yale, but he and Gabe wouldn't let me help with the plowing." She laughed. "Now I get to do all the chores by myself.

The plowing and planting and harvesting, as well as the mucking.''

Aaron sighed as he finished his meal. ''You don't know how much it pains me not to be able to lend you a hand any more, child.''

Kitty placed a hand over his. ''I wasn't complaining, Aaron. You know I love the work.'' She smiled. ''Well, all except the cooking and washing. If we could just tempt Billie to come live with us, we could eat like this every day.''

They lingered over their meal, talking, laughing, and polishing off the last of the coffee and biscuits. And when they finished, the two men went out on the porch to smoke their precious cigars while the two young women worked together washing, drying and tidying up the table.

''You know, Billie.'' Kitty put away the last chipped plate and hung her towel over the back of a chair before following Billie out onto the porch. ''It's just so much fun when you're here. Why, you even had my brother smiling. And that's something.''

At that Aaron threw back his head and chuckled, while Gabe merely looked uncomfortable.

''Then I'm glad Gabe talked me into coming with him.''

As before Billie offered her hand to Aaron, and was caught off guard when the old man took her hand and drew her close to brush a kiss over her cheek.

''Thank you for a fine supper, Billie.''

"You're welcome, Aaron." She turned to Kitty and the two women embraced.

"Will you come back next Sunday, Billie?"

She gave a shrug of her shoulders. "I guess we'll just have to see what next week brings. But if I can, I'll come back and bring you those preserves."

She allowed Gabe to lift her up to the wagon seat. When he flicked the reins she turned and waved. Then she continued waving until they crested a ridge.

As they rolled across a meadow she glanced at the man beside her. "Kitty's lucky to have someone like Aaron."

Gabe nodded. "We were all lucky to have him. I often wonder what would have happened if we hadn't come across him when we did. We were out of food, out of hope, and nearly out of our minds by the time we stumbled over him."

"But you kept going." She studied the hard, rugged profile.

He turned to meet her eyes. "I had to. Yale and Kitty were depending on me. And I'd given my word to my ma that I'd see to them."

It was, she realized, what defined the man. His word was his bond. It was what she most admired about him. And what she most feared. Gabe Conover, she thought, would never let sentiment get in the way of duty.

When they reached the back door of the Red Dog, Billie started to climb down from the rig. Before she could, Gabe reached up and caught her in his arms.

The moment he touched her, heat flared in his

eyes. He lowered her so slowly, she could feel him in every part of her body. Her breasts tingled at the contact with his chest. She looked into his eyes and could see that he was feeling the same heat, the same shocking need.

As he continued lowering her, she kept her hands lightly at his shoulders, struggling with the desire to wrap her arms around his neck and press her lips to his. She saw the way he studied her mouth, and knew that he was fighting the same battle.

When her feet finally touched the ground, he released her and took a step back. She felt a bitter wave of disappointment.

"I'd…better get back to the jail now. Lars had deliveries to make, and there's no one tending to the town."

She swallowed back her feelings and clasped her hands tightly in front of her. "Thank you for today, Gabe."

"My pleasure." He took another step back, still staring at her in that way that always caused heat to rush to her cheeks.

Suddenly he seemed to think better of it and reached out, hauling her roughly into his arms. His kiss was so unexpected, she had no time to react as he took her on a quick, head-spinning, heart-stopping ride. His hands at her shoulders were almost bruising. The lips moving over hers were far from gentle as he nearly devoured her.

For good measure he pressed her against the rough wall of the saloon, his body plastered so tightly to hers she could feel him imprinting himself on her as he continued kissing her until they were both breathless.

Just as abruptly he released her and stepped back. He could see that she was as startled by this display as he was. But it couldn't be helped. He'd had to kiss those lips, or die of hunger.

His tone was gruff. "Sorry." Then he shook his head. "Hell. What am I saying? I'm not sorry at all."

At his admission she felt herself blushing all the way to her toes. But she managed to say, "Neither am I."

His eyes narrowed. "You talking about the day? Or the kiss?"

She shrugged, and decided she'd be as honest as he. "Both."

Pleased, he spun away and walked to the wagon before pulling himself up to the seat. As he flicked the reins he turned back.

She was still standing where he'd left her. His heart took a hard, heavy dive at the look on her face. If that look was any indication, she was as perplexed by all this as he was. And every bit as shaken.

Chapter Ten

"Good night, Ned. Good night, Nell." Billie tucked the children into bed, then washed out their day clothes and hung them on a little line she'd strung across the room.

Through the open window, a breeze billowed the curtains and carried the sounds of a tinny piano. The muffled laughter and coarse men's voices drifted up from the saloon below.

Assured that the little boy and girl were asleep, Billie walked from the room and made her way downstairs. After washing up the last of the dishes she stepped out the back door and paused to look up at the night sky, awash with stars.

"Quite a sight, isn't it?"

At the sound of that familiar deep voice, Billie spun around, her hand to her throat. "Gabe. You startled me."

"Sorry." He stayed where he was, watching her in that quiet way that was so unsettling.

"I've always loved the night." She looked away

from him and tipped her head to the sky. "Maybe because I always had to work so hard during the day. And at night, when everyone else was asleep, I could just sit and watch the stars, and think."

"What did you think about?" He loved the sound of her voice. Always a little breathy, as though she'd been running hard and fast. It had a way of wrapping itself around his heart and tugging.

She shrugged, and watched the way a cloud scudded across the moon, momentarily obliterating the light. "About all the people who had come and gone through my life. My ma, though I don't recall much about her. My grandma. My pa, who was always on the move. He couldn't seem to settle in one place. Whenever I asked him why, he said it was because nothing seemed like home since my ma died. I guess that's why I tried so hard to please him. I kept thinking if I could just be good enough, and smart enough, and strong enough, I could give him a reason to settle. I'd cook his favorite meal, and he'd pat me on the head and tell me how happy he was with it. And I'd go to sleep thinking maybe this time we'd stay. Then the next day, he'd wake me up to say we were leaving." She sighed. "I guess I've worked on every ranch from here to Wyoming. But I've never really lived on any of them. We were always just passing through."

Just passing through. He'd felt that way once. Until he'd settled here in Misery.

He wondered if Billie knew how sweet she looked,

standing there in the moonlight. A sweetness that caused a pleasant ache in him.

She clutched her hands together at her waist and looked away, aware that she'd revealed far too much about herself. "What are you doing out here, listening to me ramble on, Gabe? Why aren't you inside, enjoying Belle California's songs?"

"Grace will never be Belle California, Billie. At least, not to me."

There was a gruff quality to his tone that had the hair at the back of her neck prickling.

He'd waged a terrible battle with himself after that kiss earlier today. He'd spent the best part of the evening thinking about Billie, and the way she'd felt in his arms. It pained him to admit his weakness. But he hadn't been able to stay away. He needed to see her again. Just see her, he promised himself. And then he'd walk away.

He cleared his throat. "Whenever you sat on that piano and spoke those words, I found I couldn't look away. With your first word you had me."

"But I thought..." She swallowed.

"You thought what?"

She lifted her head. "I thought you hated seeing me in that dress. Whenever I looked at you, you were always frowning. And when the others cheered and shouted, you were always so still and quiet, I just figured you despised me."

"How could you think such a thing, Billie?"

She shrugged. "It was easy. I wasn't proud of what I was doing. I hated myself for it."

"You have nothing to be ashamed of. You needed a job. You took what was offered you. As for me, I wasn't any different from any other man in that room, Billie. With every word you spoke, with every breath you took, I wanted you."

He took a step closer. In the moonlight she could see the glint of something in his eyes. Something so hot, so fierce, it had her pulse leaping.

"It—it was probably the dress. I never wore anything quite that fancy before."

"It wasn't the dress. Grace is in there right now, wearing that dress. I don't feel anything when I look at her."

"The hat, then. Or the wig..." She knew she was babbling. But she had to say something to cover the sound of her thundering heartbeat.

He touched a finger to her mouth. Just a touch, but he felt the heat leap and sizzle as it sang through his veins.

His voice lowered to a whisper. "It's you, Billie. Just you. Every time I look at you, I want you."

She knew her jaw had dropped, but she couldn't seem to control it. Such an admission from this tight-lipped lawman was so out of character, she couldn't think of a thing to say.

"From the time I go to sleep until the time I wake each morning, I want you. Right now, this minute, I want you, Billie. Ever since that kiss, I've thought about a hundred different ways to take you."

He stood, mere inches from her, afraid to move.

Afraid to breathe, for fear of the impending storm building inside him.

"Then why…" She gathered her courage and took a step closer, so that her body brushed his. At once she felt the heat that poured between them, and saw the sheen of sweat on his forehead. "…why don't you do something about it, Gabe?"

He took a step back as though she'd slapped him. But not before his body had already reacted. His throat was dry as dust. His breathing labored. A pulse beat hammered in his temples. And that simple touch had him fully aroused. "I can understand you asking. You're an innocent, Billie. You don't know what you're suggesting. But I know better. I've seen what happens to women in this land, when they foolishly place their trust in a man who betrays them."

Billie gave him a halting smile. "You don't look like a man who would betray a woman, Gabe."

His eyes narrowed with smoldering anger. "I'm a man of the law. I've always held myself to a higher standard. And that's why I'm leaving you now. Before I'm tempted to show you just how weak a man I really am. The fact that I'm here with you now, while I'm in this mood, proves just how weak I am."

He spun away. And though it cost him, he managed to keep from turning back to look at her as he made his way determinedly toward the jail.

Billie pushed her way through the crowded saloon toward the stairway. Nobody took any notice of her as they stared, entranced, at the woman seated on the piano, mouthing the words of a lullaby.

She climbed the stairs to her room and stepped inside, leaning against the closed door as she studied the two sleeping children.

For the longest time she simply stood there, holding back the disappointment that seemed to wash over her in brutal waves. Gabe hated himself for wanting her. And why not? What did she have to offer a man?

She crossed the room and picked up the looking glass, forcing herself to study her reflection with a critical eye. What man would want a woman who looked like this? Stringy red hair. Skin that blistered and burned in the summer sun. A body that more nearly resembled a girl's than a woman's. And those hated freckles, splashed over every inch of her pasty flesh.

She set aside the mirror and crossed to the window, kneeling down so that her chin rested on her hands. She watched Buck Reedy stumble to the hitching post and haul himself astride his horse. His wife and son would pay for the liquor he'd consumed. Had he and his wife been young once, and wildly in love? Or had they merely married so he'd have someone to cook and clean for him, and she'd have someone to provide for her? Did a lover's soft words always fade into cries in the night? Or were there people who managed to keep the flame burning for a lifetime?

She thought about her father. He'd mourned the

loss of his beloved wife until he'd finally joined her in death, after a lifetime of despair. But their love had been real and deep. And seeing it, Billie couldn't help but believe that true love was possible. But how did a body know when the love was real?

Oh, if only her mother had lived. If only she had someone she could ask.

Her thoughts were distracted by two cowboys standing in the middle of the road, fists raised, curses exchanged. Before they could come to blows, Gabe was there, striding from the jailhouse, stepping between them. With a few well-chosen words he had them going their separate ways. One staggered toward a waiting horse and wagon. The other was helped into his saddle and pointed in the direction of home.

When the street was empty, Gabe turned toward the jail once more. Billie watched his progress, drowning in misery. He was the strongest man she'd ever met. Stronger even than her pa. And he stirred such feelings in her. Feelings that had her wanting to throw herself into his arms and beg for his kisses.

Why did he have to be a lawman? And why did he have to matter so to her, when nothing could ever come of it? Hadn't he admitted that he hated himself for wanting her? And why not? Even though she did nothing more than cook in the Red Dog, that made her, in the eyes of everyone in this town, a saloon girl. What respectable man would want to be associated with the likes of her?

She'd seen the repressed anger in his eyes. Had heard it in his voice.

She paused.

Or had it been something other than anger?

At the thought, she went very still, thinking over the words he'd spoken.

It isn't the dress or the hat or the wig. It's you, Billie. Just you. From the moment I fall asleep until I wake, all I want is you.

She clutched her hands together, trying to sort through the feelings churning around inside. So many feelings battering her. Hope. Fear. Confusion. Dread, that what she was thinking could be very, very wrong. But she had to find out. Had to.

At the sound of Grace's footsteps on the stairs she tore out of her room without giving herself time to think.

"Billie?" Grace held up a fistful of dollars. "Look what I earned tonight. Just by being Belle California."

"That's wonderful, Grace. I'm so happy for you." Billie dashed past her and went crashing into Roscoe Timmons, who had just paused at the stair landing.

In his hand was a bottle of whiskey and an empty glass. He thrust it into Billie's hands. "Good. You've just saved me some time. Take this to room three. Russ Hawking." His lips turned into a half smile. "And if you're smart, you'll get in and out fast, 'cause he's liquored up and he'd been boasting all night that the woman hasn't been born who can't be charmed into his bed."

Roscoe turned away and hurried downstairs to tend to the bar.

When he was gone, Billie held out the bottle and glass to her friend. "Would you mind seeing to this, Grace? I have...someplace I have to go."

Grace shrugged as she stuffed the fistful of money down the front of her gown. "I don't mind, Billie. But where are you going at this time of night?"

Billie handed over the whiskey and turned away, as skittish as one of Kitty's mustangs. "To see if I'm right about something, or just a foolish dolt." She gave a nervous laugh. "Wish me luck, Grace."

"All right." The young woman looked puzzled as her friend nearly toppled headlong down the last of the steps. "Good luck, Billie. With whatever it is you're after."

Gabe paced from the door of the jail to the cell, then back again. What had come over him tonight? Confessing all those things to Billie. Like some love-sick fool.

He'd frightened her. He could see the fear in her eyes. And why not? A sweet thing like her. And then he'd toyed with the idea of seducing here there in the moonlight. What was he thinking? A lawman having his way with an innocent in the back of a saloon. Did he really believe this badge and gun gave him the right to just take what he wanted, without regard to the consequences?

He strode to his desk and leaned a hip against the edge, crossing his arms over his chest and kicking the toe of his boot against the floor. Ever since Billie had come to Misery he'd been acting out of character. It just proved how wrong they were for each other. She brought out the worst in him. Made him want things he had no right to. Because of her, his work had suffered. He'd grown lazy and careless. Like those wanted posters piling up in his drawer. And the fact that he ought to be over at the Red Dog right now, seeing to it that some drunken cowboy didn't do damage to the people or the town before leaving.

He couldn't go back there. If he did, there's no telling what he might do. He knew where her room was. And nobody would question the sheriff going up those stairs.

He glanced at the empty cot in the cell. He'd spent many a night sleeping here. One more wouldn't make any difference. But at least Billie would be safe from him for one more night.

At the slight sound in the doorway he spun around, instinctively pulling his pistol from the holster.

"Billie." He froze, wondering if she was really here, or if he'd simply conjured this image to ease his aching heart.

But she was real. Too real, looking like the angel that had been haunting his dreams for so many nights.

Her chest was heaving, as though she'd been running hard and fast. Her hair hung in wild tangles around her shoulders and cheeks. Her eyes looked a little too bright. She held her arms outward, her hands gripping either side of the doorway, as though afraid she might stumble and fall should she let go.

"What are you doing here?" He remained where he was, afraid to move.

"I came to ask you something."

"It couldn't wait until morning?"

She shook her head, sending her hair dancing. "This is too important."

He studied her, puzzled by the warring emotions he could read in her eyes.

"I need to know, Gabe. Do you resent your feelings for me because of who you are? Or is it because of who I am?"

"What kind of nonsense is this?" He struggled to sound indignant, to hide the fear that had suddenly leaped up and begun twisting in his gut.

"You're the most respected man in this town. I know you didn't come by that easily. It would have taken years of hard work, of rock-solid discipline, to gain the trust of so many people. If they were to learn that you were soft on a saloon girl, they might not think so highly of you."

"Is that what you think?" There was such anger in his eyes, Billie took a step back. But it was too late. His hand snaked out, dragging her close.

"Do you really think I would deny my feelings for you, for anyone, for the sake of my reputation?"

"Then it's me." She let out a long, slow sigh and looked away, absorbing a slash of pain to her heart. "I guess I knew all along. A man like you could never feel anything for someone like me."

She started to turn away and was startled when he cupped the back of her head and turned her back, forcing her to look at him.

"It isn't you, Billie. Don't ever think that. You're a fine woman. Too fine for the likes of me." His tone softened, as did his touch. "You think I'm this noble lawman. You think I'm above reproach. And maybe that's what I've tried to be. But I'm just a man, Billie. A flesh-and-blood man. And whenever I see you, my thoughts are coarse and base. I'm no better than the cowboys who frequent the Red Dog. And a woman like you is too good for that."

He brought his hands to her shoulders and held her at arm's length. "Now go to bed, Billie. Before we both do something we'll regret in the morning."

She wasn't listening. All she could hear were the words he'd spoken with such passion.

A woman like you is too good for that.

"You think you'd hurt me, Gabe? Is that what this is about?"

"Of course I would. Anyone with half a brain can see that you're an innocent. And that's the way it should be until you find the man you want to spend the rest of your life with. Now go, Billie. This minute."

He gave her a shove and turned away, feeling the familiar tingling in his fingertips and cursing the fact that even now, in spite of all his noble words, he wanted her. With every fiber of his being.

He felt the tentative touch on his arm and glanced

over his shoulder to see her still standing right behind him.

"What if I've already found him, Gabe?"

"Found who?"

"The man I…want." The fierce look in his eyes had her courage quickly deserting her, but she stood her ground.

He was already shaking his head in denial. "It isn't enough to want someone. There has to be more."

"More?" She looked intrigued. "More of what?"

"More than the wanting. The two have to…care more about the other than they do about themselves."

"The way you care that I'm still an innocent?"

Her simple question had him sucking in a quick breath. "Something like that."

"And the way I bring you a tray in the morning, to see that you get enough to eat?"

She was trying to trap him. He could already see the way that clever mind was working. He crossed his arms over his chest and regarded her with amusement. "As I recall, Grunt used to send me a tray every morning, too."

"But Grunt didn't tuck in extra biscuits, slathered with honey. Or add a few more slices of ham or beef to tide you over until supper."

"That's true." He couldn't keep the smile from his voice. "I'd say that proves that you care more about me than Grunt did."

She laughed, and the sound wrapped itself around

his heart in the most amazing way. ''You see? We care about each other, Gabe. And if you don't mind that I work in a saloon—'' she startled him by running her hands up his arms, across his shoulders, sending the most amazing curl of heat along his spine ''—why don't you kiss me again, the way you kissed me this afternoon, and we'll see what comes of it?''

''You're crazy.'' Even as the words slipped from his lips, he had his hands on her, dragging her closer.

And then his mouth was on hers, moving over her lips with a thoroughness that had them both sighing. His strong, calloused fingers were tangling in her hair, drawing her head back while his mouth continued plundering hers until they were both dazed and breathless.

When she moaned and wrapped her arms around his waist, drawing him even closer, he suddenly lifted his head to stare down into her eyes. ''I don't want you to hate me tomorrow. I couldn't bear it if you did, Billie.''

''I won't hate you, Gabe. I give you my word on it. I want this as much as you.''

He kept his eyes steady on hers as he pressed her back against the hard wall of the jail. Heat was spiraling through him, threatening to erupt into an inferno. He knew that any moment now he would lose his last thread of control.

''I'll hold you to that.''

''As long as you hold me, Gabe.'' She lifted herself on tiptoe and brushed her lips over his.

She heard his quick intake of breath and knew that

he was holding himself together by a thin thread of control.

She brushed her lips over his again and was almost burned by the heat. And though she didn't have the slightest notion what would happen next, she knew that they had crossed a line. There would be no turning back now.

Chapter Eleven

Billie lifted trembling hands to the buttons of her faded gown.

Gabe's eyes narrowed. "What are you doing?"

"I thought…" Those innocent eyes went wide before the color bloomed on her cheeks. "Isn't this what you want?"

"No. Yes. Hell." He fought to keep the anger from his tone, knowing it would only embarrass her more. "I'll get to that eventually, Billie. What I want right now is to just hold you."

"Oh." Her voice was muffled against his chest as he gathered her close and wrapped his big arms around her.

She was trembling. And he knew it wasn't passion, but nerves. Though it would cost him, he vowed to take his time with her. To make this night as perfect as possible. It was, after all, the only thing he had to give her. And soon, if his patience paid off, her only trembling would be from desire. The same shattering desire he'd been feeling for so long now.

"I don't always kiss you the way a woman like you ought to be kissed."

A woman like you. Somehow this time, the phrase didn't hurt. Instead, it sounded like an endearment.

"I don't mind, Gabe."

"But I mind, Billie. You have the most amazing lips. I love kissing them. And now I can take the time to really taste them." He spoke the words against her mouth, moving his lips over hers until they softened, then opened to him.

His tongue met hers and she felt a tingle of surprise, followed by a wave of pleasure. And all the while his big hands moved down her back, soothing, even while they ignited fires along her spine.

He lingered over her lips, drawing out the moment until he could feel her breathing begin to speed up, matching his own. Then he began raining kisses over her eyelids, her cheeks, the corner of her jaw.

When he dipped his tongue into her ear she felt the most amazing tug deep inside. She looked up at him but he merely smiled and returned his mouth to hers. And while the kiss spun on and on, she felt his fingers move to the buttons of her gown. He ran nibbling kisses down her throat, sending icy shivers coursing through her veins.

She was so caught up in the kiss, she barely noticed that he'd parted the front of her dress. But when his mouth dipped lower, she stiffened in his arms and began to back away.

His mouth was back on hers. His voice was soft

as a night breeze as he whispered against her lips, "I want to see you, Billie. All of you."

She didn't flinch as he slid the gown from her shoulders. It dropped to the floor to pool at her feet. Then he untied the ribbons of her chemise and his hands cupped her breasts so gently, as though he'd been given a rare and wonderful treasure.

"I'm scrawny. Always have been," she muttered.

"You're perfect, Billie. The first time I saw you, I knew I was looking at the most beautiful woman in the world."

Beautiful? No one had ever called her that before. She wanted to weep from the sheer pleasure of such words. But he'd lowered his mouth to her breast and the shock that shot through her had all the air leaving her lungs. Deep inside she experienced the most amazing feelings. A tightening, like a fist. And then a flow of liquid fire.

"Gabe." Her arms closed around his waist and she hung on, wondering how much longer her legs would be able to hold her.

He lifted his head. "Do you want me to stop?"

"Stop? No, I…" She dragged in a breath. "No. Please. Don't stop."

She heard the soft rumble of his laughter. "That's good. For a moment there I thought maybe I'd been too rough for you."

She touched a hand to his cheek. Just a hand, but it had his nostrils flaring with need. "You could never be too rough, Gabe. Do you want to take me now?"

He clamped down on the feelings swirling inside, determined not to spoil the moment. "Not yet, Billie. There's so much more I want to show you."

With hands that were none too steady he unbuttoned his shirt and tossed it aside before drawing her close again.

She felt the tingle of his hairy chest against her soft skin. His body was so hard, so muscled. It was almost frightening to be held against someone so strong. Strong enough that if he chose, he could easily snap her bones like twigs. And yet he was so careful with her. So unbelievably tender with her.

He felt her tense and framed her face with his hands, brushing light butterfly kisses across her jaw, then lower, to the soft column of her throat, until she relaxed once more in his arms.

With slow easy movements he slid the open chemise from her shoulders, baring her torso. This time she didn't flinch when he brushed soft kisses between her breasts, before circling each breast with his tongue. But when his mouth closed around one erect nipple, he heard her quick hiss of surprise before she clamped her fingers in his hair and clung. Her breath was coming in quick bursts, and her body gave a sudden, violent tremor.

She wondered how long her legs could continue to support her.

As if reading her mind he scooped her up and cradled her against him as he strode toward the back of the jail and the open cell. He lowered her gently to the cot, then quickly discarded the rest of his clothes before lying beside her.

At once he felt her tension return. To calm her, he drew her close, running his hand lightly along her back. Over the flare of her hip. Along her thigh. And all the while he whispered endearments meant to soothe.

"Do you know how long I've wanted to do this?"

"How long?"

"Since the first time I saw you in the Red Dog, being held in Buck Reedy's arms."

"You looked so fierce."

"I wanted to strangle Buck with my bare hands. And would've, to save you." He pressed a tender kiss to the tip of her nose.

The only light came from the slivers of moonlight filtering through the narrow window of the cell. It gilded her skin and turned the ends of her hair to flame.

Gabe could feel the need building inside, scrambling to be free. A need he'd held at bay for so long now. But though he was desperate to end this terrible hunger, he was even more determined to give Billie what she needed. Any fool could see that she'd been terribly hurt in the past. Now, this minute, what she needed most was tenderness. Patience. And though he'd never before thought of himself as a patient man, he knew he would rather die than spoil this moment for her.

He held her in his arms and kissed her, long and slow and deep, until he could feel her breath begin to speed up, as well as her heartbeat. Then he lowered his mouth to her breast and tasted the sweetness of her skin. Not the cloying perfume of the saloon women, but a fresh soap and water clean that made him think of his childhood home.

Under his patient ministrations he could feel her heart begin to thunder. Her muscles begin to quiver. Still it wasn't enough. He wanted her to experience what he did. The hunger. The desperation. The complete surrender. And the trust.

And so he touched and stroked and suckled, arousing them both until she heard a voice that sounded more animal than human, and realized it was her own.

"Please, Gabe." The sensations swirling inside her were unlike any she'd ever experienced. She moaned and writhed and fisted her hands in the bed linens as he continued driving her to the edge of a high, sheer cliff. She had no idea what lay on the other side. But she knew this much. She couldn't stay here, clinging to the very edge much longer without taking a fall.

"Not yet, Billie." He found her, hot and wet, and took her on a fast, dizzying climb.

She cried out as she felt herself arching up toward a lance of pleasure that seemed to go on and on before bursting free. And then she collapsed against him and heard his voice whispering her name, over and over, like a litany.

He gave her no time to recover as he took her again. This time, as his fingers found her, she didn't fight the feeling, but rather embraced it as twin points of pain and pleasure speared through her until, spent, she lay back, her breathing ragged, her body slick with sheen.

Gabe knew he could wait no longer. His own needs, so long denied, now battered him, desperate to be free. He levered himself above her and entered her as gently as possible.

He saw her eyes snap open, and for the space of a heartbeat saw the flicker of fear. He knew she expected pain and struggled to take her slowly, keeping each thrust a long, easy glide. Suddenly the fear was gone from her eyes as the most incredible pleasure grew and grew until it seemed to take over her will. She wrapped herself around him and began to move with him. He could feel her strength as she gripped his shoulders and began to climb once more. Whatever patience he'd planned was forgotten as she began to shudder and convulse.

He was racing with her now. Soaring. Suddenly they reached the peak and broke free. He whispered her name and closed his hands over hers. Together they flew.

Billie couldn't seem to control the shudders that were still rocking through her body. She felt icy cold and unbearably hot. The body pressing hers to the thin mattress was heavy. His breathing was as ragged as hers.

She'd never felt more wonderful in her life.

For the first time she understood the unspoken pleasure that drove men and women to mate for life.

She would walk through fire, would gladly go through everything she'd already suffered in her young life, just to lie here like this with Gabe.

"You're so quiet." He levered himself on his hands to look down into her eyes. "Did I hurt you?"

"No." She said it quickly, needing to assure him.

"Am I too heavy?"

She shook her head. Smiled. "I like feeling you here."

"You do?" He touched a finger to her mouth. "You're not sorry, Billie?"

"Oh, don't ever think that."

She was almost sorry when he rolled aside. She started to sit up. "Did you want me to go now?"

"Go?" He linked his fingers with hers, loving the feel of her small hand in his. "Why would I want you to leave?"

She looked surprised. "I figured, since you were done with me…"

"Done? Is that what you think?" He lifted her hand to his mouth and brushed a kiss to the palm.

"I don't figure you'd want the folks in town to see me coming out of the jailhouse in the morning."

"Billie." He drew her back down and gathered her into the circle of his arms. "I want you to spend the night here with me."

"You do?"

"There's so much more I want to show you."

"There is?" She couldn't hide her little sigh of

relief as he brushed the damp hair from her face and pressed a soft kiss to the corner of her eye.

"Mm hmm. We haven't even begun to do all the things a man and woman can do together." He lifted her so that she was lying on top of him, her hair swirling around, tickling his cheeks and chest.

"You mean there's more?"

"So much more, Billie." He played with a strand of her hair, twisting it around and around his finger while he studied the gleam in her eyes. "Have I told you how much I like your freckles?"

She blushed. "You're just saying that. No man could like all these ugly blotches on my skin."

"I like them. They fascinate me." He trailed a finger across the slope of her shoulder. "I'd been wondering just how far they paraded. And now I can see for myself. There's a cluster of them here." He pressed a kiss to the spot. "And here." He moved his finger down her throat to circle her breast before pressing his mouth there.

He heard her soft sigh of pleasure and lingered there a minute longer, feeling the passion begin to rise again. He saw the way her eyes darkened and knew that she'd felt it, too.

"Are you going to...?" She started to wriggle off him but he wrapped his arms around her, holding her still. "Gabe, are we going to...again?"

"Would you like to?"

She couldn't help the laughter that bubbled up. "I guess. If you don't mind."

"Mind? Why, Miss Calley, it'd be my pleasure,

ma'am.'' There was a gleam of laughter in his eyes
as he folded his arms under his head and lay back,
allowing her to set the pace. But minutes later he
gripped her hard as she brought them both to a sudden, shattering climax.

Later he lay on his side, holding her against his
chest as gently as a fragile doll, keeping her safe and
warm in his embrace while they both drifted off to
sleep.

The first faint rays of morning light poked through
the bars of the cell. Billie awoke slowly, aware of a
heaviness pressing her to the mattress. She opened
her eyes to find Gabe lying spoonlike against her,
one arm encircling her waist, one leg tossed over
hers.

The thought of what they had shared during the
night had her smiling. Who would have ever believed
that the tough lawman, Gabe Conover, could have
this other side to him? He'd been gentle and rough.
As sweet as a summer morning. As wild as a prairie
storm. There had been such hunger in him. A hunger
she was delighted to feed. He had shown her, in a
hundred different ways, how much he cared.

She eased off the cot, hoping not to disturb him.
At once his eyes opened and his hand snaked out,
snagging her wrist.

''Where are you going?'' His sleep-roughened
voice had her pulse leaping.

''I have to get back to the Red Dog and start
breakfast.''

"Don't leave me." He tugged her down and snuggled her against him. "I want you here."

"And I want to be here." She touched a palm to his scratchy cheek. "If you want, I'll come back when my work's done."

"Yeah. I want." He covered her mouth with his and kissed her until her head was swimming.

When he released her she slid off the bed and hurriedly dressed. She paused beside him and leaned down to brush her lips over his. "I can't wait for tonight."

"Neither can I. If you're not here by the time it's dark, I'll head over to the Red Dog and carry you back."

"Promise?"

"Count on it."

She felt a little thrill as she let herself out of the jail and raced toward the saloon.

Who would have believed scant weeks ago that her odyssey of fear and terror would end so joyously? When it began, her only thought had been survival. Now she was not only looking forward to today, but tomorrow, as well. And all her tomorrows. And all of them spent in the arms of Gabe Conover.

She let herself in the back door of the Red Dog and began mechanically feeding wood to the stove.

She couldn't wait for this day to end, so that she could be with Gabe.

Chapter Twelve

Gabe stood at the little basin in the cell and wiped the last of the soap from his chin before pulling on his shirt. He couldn't remember the last time he'd felt so alive. So eager for the day. He buttoned his shirt and tucked it into his waist, then strapped on his gun belt.

Had the sky always been this blue? He'd never really noticed before. And the air so sweet. Summer, which often became a furnace in the Dakotas, had decided to treat them gently this year.

Or maybe it just seemed that way because of Billie.

Billie.

He paused. Who would have ever believed one woman could make such a difference in his life? But there it was. This morning, after a single night with her, there was this wonderful feeling of expectancy. As though the world had suddenly become a bright, shiny toy. And it was his for the taking.

He was whistling as he walked to his desk. He felt like a kid at Christmas.

He looked up with a smile when Roscoe Timmons burst through the door. "Don't tell me some cowboy's got himself drunk this early in the morning?"

"Not drunk, Sheriff." Roscoe's normally ruddy complexion had turned a shade of pasty white. "Dead."

Gabe gathered up his rifle and started out on a run, with Roscoe struggling to keep up. He pushed through the swinging doors of the saloon. "Who's the cowboy?"

Roscoe drew in a wheezing breath. "Name's Russ Hawking. Room three."

Gabe took the stairs two at a time and saw the door to room three standing open, with Doc Honeywell inside, examining the body. Jack Slade and Cheri, waiting for him in the hallway, looked up expectantly.

Without a word he walked past them and into the room.

Doc Honeywell shot him a glance, then continued his examination of the body.

Gabe stooped down beside him. "What did you find, Doc?"

"Just a single stab wound to the chest. It didn't appear deep enough to cause death; only a great deal of pain, and perhaps weakness. Death may have come later, from a loss of blood."

Gabe studied the dead man on the floor, his body smeared with blood. A bloody knife lay beside his hand. There was more blood in the bed and in a trail across the floor. "You think he dragged himself out of bed after having been stabbed?"

Doc nodded. "I'd say he managed to pull the knife from his chest, which caused the blood to gush even harder. It would seem he made a last, desperate effort to stop his killer. But he probably passed out before making it to the door. Death came later."

"You say the stab wound wasn't very deep. That's puzzling. If someone had wanted this man dead, why didn't the killer stab him again? And again, if that's what it took? It doesn't make any sense to leave a man alive to name his attacker."

The old doctor looked over at him. "Unless the attacker had been driven off by a fear of being found out. Maybe he heard someone coming."

"Could be." Gabe paused. "Did Slade say if this Hawking had been gambling? Maybe somebody downstairs saw him win a big pot and wanted a cut of it."

Doc shrugged. "I didn't ask. But it sounds likely."

Gabe leaned close and checked the cowboy's pockets. He withdrew a handful of money, counting out more than a hundred dollars.

Doc Honeywell arched a bushy brow. "So much for your theory that our cowboy was the victim of a robbery."

Gabe nodded as he carefully folded the money and tucked it into his shirt pocket, to be given to the man's next of kin.

While the doctor lumbered to his feet, Gabe began checking the room. "Look at this. Though it was warm out last night, the window was closed and latched."

The older man followed his line of reasoning. "All right. We know the killer didn't use it for his escape. Though it would have made sense if he'd wanted to sneak away undetected. That only leaves the door. Which means that someone in the Red Dog may have spotted the killer entering or leaving."

Gabe nodded his agreement, then pointed to the full bottle of whiskey and an empty glass atop a scarred nightstand. "Wouldn't that be the first thing a man would reach for after getting himself comfortably into bed?"

Doc's lips twitched. "That, and a warm willing woman."

Gabe checked the drawers below. All were empty. "It appears that Russ Hawking hadn't planned to spend more than a night in town."

"You think somebody followed him here and waited until he'd gone to bed? A grudge, maybe?"

Gabe shrugged. "If so, why not make certain he was dead before running out? Could it be that his attacker just wanted to stop him, not kill him?"

Doc shook his head. "It's a puzzle, Gabe. But I'm sure you'll figure it out."

As he walked away Gabe studied the rest of the room. A faded shirt had been tossed carelessly over the back of a chair. A gun belt hung over the bedpost. One boot lay at the foot of the bed, the other against the wall, where it had probably landed after being kicked off. Everything looked the way it might if a man had come up to his room expecting nothing more than to get himself good and drunk before falling asleep.

With a sigh he turned away, closing the door as he took leave of the room.

Out in the hall, Jack Slade looked more annoyed than alarmed. "How soon can I get that body out of here and the mess cleaned up?"

"Doc's through with his exam of the body. I guess you can have Jesse Cutler come by and see about a burial." The owner of the barbershop ran a side business burying the citizens of Misery in a plot of land just outside of town. For those without families, the territory of the Dakotas paid Jesse a dollar toward funeral costs.

Gabe turned to include Cheri. "I've seen enough to believe the motive wasn't robbery. Anything you can tell me about this cowboy?"

Cheri glanced at Slade before saying softly, "He had a high opinion of himself. But he had a mean mouth. Mean hands, too. Liked to use them on the women."

Gabe turned to Slade. "Did he take one of the women up to his room last night?"

Slade shook his head. "He played poker. Won a hundred and called it a night. Said he was going up to bed alone. I checked my receipts. No woman for room three. The only thing he ordered on his way upstairs was whiskey."

Gabe nodded. "I'll check with Roscoe. See what time he took it up."

Even before he was walking down the stairs, Slade was ordering the body of Russ Hawking to be removed and the room cleaned, so that the Red Dog could return to business as usual.

Gabe paused at the bar, where Roscoe was wiping a tumbler with a dirty towel. "I understand the dead man ordered up a bottle of whiskey. What time was that?"

Roscoe thought a minute. "Midnight, maybe. Right after Belle California sang her last song."

"You took it up yourself?"

Roscoe nodded. Then he paused. "Well, I started to. But then I gave it to Billie and told her to take it instead."

"Billie?" Gabe froze. His hand fisted on the bar. Then, because it was too impossible to accept, he began shaking his head. "Think about this, Roscoe. Are you absolutely sure it was Billie?"

The bartender thought a minute, then frowned. "Yeah. I'm sure. I remember warning her that he was drunk, and had been boasting to anyone who would listen to him that there wasn't a female alive who could resist his charms." The bartender's frown turned into a look of amazement as the truth dawned. "Hell. Little Billie. Who'd have thought she could…?"

Gabe was already storming across the room, heading toward the kitchen.

* * *

Billie was in her glory. She'd sliced thick hunks of steak and had them grilling over the open fire. Potatoes and onions sizzled in a blackened skillet. Biscuits, perfectly browned, rested on a platter.

She felt light as air this morning, dancing through her chores with a smile of pure delight on her face.

And all because of Gabe. She couldn't wait for this day to be over, so she could lie with him again and learn all the ways to love him.

Love him.

The thought was so stunning, she had to stop and press a hand to her heart. Oh, it was so delicious. She did love him. Truly loved him. And from all the sweet things he'd whispered to her last night, she thought there was a very good chance that he loved her, too.

He loved her.

Oh, that was even better. The thought wrapped itself around her heart, sending her into peals of laughter.

Gabe Conover loved her. And she loved him. Who would have thought such a thing could happen?

She couldn't wait to tell Kitty. How amazing to think that, until she'd come here, she'd never had anyone she could call friend. And now she had not one, but two, counting Grace.

She felt a quick wave of sadness at the thought of her friend. She'd dashed up to her room at dawn to share her news with Grace, only to find that she and the children were gone. There had been a note on the bed telling her that they were leaving for her brother's in St. Louis.

She was happy for them, of course. It had been Grace's dream to leave this place and make a new life. And now, thanks to the money she'd earned as Belle California, she was free to start over. Billie wouldn't allow herself to wallow in self-pity at their abrupt departure. It would have been nice to be able to say some proper goodbyes, especially to those two sweet children. But they were about to live their dream.

And so was she.

She twirled around the room, turning the potatoes, lifting out the steaks that were already cooked and placing them on a tray. If she could carry a tune, she thought with a little laugh, she'd be singing.

When the door to the kitchen opened she speared another steak and called, "How many hungry cowboys do we have this morning, Cheri?"

"I don't know about hungry ones. But we have one dead."

At the sound of Gabe's voice she turned. Seeing the look of fury on his face she nearly dropped the heavy platter. At the last minute she was able to balance it, losing only one steak to the floor before setting it on the table.

She lifted a hand to the damp hair at her forehead, then wiped her sweating hands down her skirt. "What's wrong, Gabe? I thought you'd be happy to see me."

"I bet you did." He remained in the doorway,

unwilling to step closer. "I was just upstairs. In room three."

"What for?"

His tone hardened. "I think you know, Billie."

At the anger in his voice she flinched. "What's wrong with you, Gabe? Why do you look like that?"

"Murder doesn't sit well with me, Billie. I'm a lawman, remember?" He clenched his jaw as a sudden thought struck. "But of course, you'd remember. Is that why you dashed over to the jail last night to offer yourself to me? Did you think I'd be so blinded by what you offered, I'd even put aside my duties for more of the same?"

Since he wouldn't make a move toward her, she stepped closer to him, her eyes mirroring the shock that was racing through her system. "You're not making any sense, Gabe. What is it you think I've done?"

He kept his hands fisted at his sides, afraid to touch her. Afraid that if he did, he'd let his fury get in the way of his common sense. "Roscoe tells me that he handed you a bottle of whiskey last night and asked you to take it up to Russ Hawking in room three."

She blinked, trying to recall. Had it really been last night? It seemed ages ago. Her mind had been so filled with confusion about Gabe. She'd just made up her mind to risk everything and go to him. To tell him how she felt and offer her love to him. And she'd been terrified that he might reject her offer.

"Yes. I guess that's so."

"He claims that he warned you about Hawking, saying he was drunk and boasting that there wasn't a female alive he couldn't get into his bed."

She shrugged. "I suppose he did. But it didn't matter because—" She paused. She'd almost told him about giving the bottle to Grace.

Grace. All the color drained from her face as the truth dawned. She'd asked Grace to do her job for her, because she'd selfishly wanted to hurry over to the jail. Because of her, Grace had been put in harm's way. And had...killed a man.

"Because why, Billie? What were you going to say?"

She couldn't tell him the truth. Grace was her friend. And friends were too precious to ever be betrayed. Besides, little Ned and Nell had already lost a father. They couldn't lose their mother, too.

The room took one quick spin, and she found herself sinking to her knees. When she looked up, Gabe was standing over her, with a look in his eyes that tore at her heart.

"Tell me, Billie." His voice was gruff with a passion that went so deep, he didn't even realize he was begging. "Give me a reason, any reason, not to arrest you for the murder of Russ Hawking."

She sat back on her heels, waiting for the light-headed feeling to pass. Ever-so-slowly she got to her feet and took a step back, lifting her chin in the way he'd come to recognize.

"I can't do that."

His eyes narrowed on her. "Do you really believe

that what we shared last night will persuade me to look the other way?''

She shook her head. ''If there's one thing I've learned about you, Gabe, it's that you would never let your personal feelings get in the way of doing your job.''

''Then why?'' His voice was a hiss of frustration. ''Why won't you give me at least some reason why you stabbed that cowboy?''

She gave a long, deep sigh and looked away from those accusing eyes. ''I suppose one reason is as good as another.''

They both looked up as Jack Slade stepped into the kitchen. He looked from Gabe to Billie. ''Roscoe says you were the last person to see Hawking alive. Is that so?''

She swallowed, and held her silence.

He looked at Gabe. ''You going to arrest her, Sheriff?''

Gabe's tone was flat. ''That's my job.''

Slade turned to Billie. ''Look, kid. Judge Hathaway rides through here every couple of months. He's expected back any day now. He's tough, but he's fair. If you can think of anything that might persuade him that you had no choice, he might go easy on you.'' He shot her a challenging look. ''You understand what I'm saying?''

Through a haze of pain she nodded.

''Good.'' He turned away, his mind already on the business of getting things back to normal.

Gabe touched a hand to her arm. She was cold as ice. "Let's go, Billie."

"Go?" She seemed completely bewildered.

"To jail. You're under arrest for the murder of Russ Hawking."

She walked numbly from the kitchen and out into the dusty street of Misery. Past Swensen's Dry Goods and Eli Moffat's Stables, past Doc Honeywell's Surgical Clinic and Emma Hardwick's rescue mission. Past Jesse Cutler's Barbershop and Bath, where the blanket-clad body of the dead man was just being loaded into the back of a wagon for burial.

Billie lowered her gaze, refusing to look at the scene.

When she stepped into the jail, Gabe held the door of the cell and waited until she was inside before turning the key.

He watched the way she stood, still as a statue, staring at the cot with a look of such misery, it nearly broke his heart.

He cleared his throat. "Slade was right. If you can think of anything at all that might persuade the judge that you had no choice, it'll go easier on you, Billie."

"Thank you."

Her words, so stiff and formal, sent an arrow clear through his heart.

Before he could say more Emma Hardwick came running in, coming to a skidding halt when she saw Billie in the cell.

"So. It's true." Her hat was slightly askew, the

only sign that she'd been caught unawares. She turned to Gabe. "May I speak with the prisoner?"

Tight-lipped, he nodded.

Emma walked to the bars. "Would you like to pray with me, Billie?"

Billie shrugged. "I don't know much about that. Don't figure my Maker would want to hear from me."

"He claims to love sinners, Billie. And if we confess our sins, they'll be forgiven. Would you like to confess yours?"

Billie considered. "I guess maybe I'd like you to go first, Emma, if you don't mind."

Gabe turned away to hide his smile.

Emma frowned. "I'm not the sinner here, Billie. You are."

Again that little shrug of her thin shoulders as Billie said, "Seems like the preacher said we're all sinners. And since I'm going to have to confess my crimes in front of a judge, I figure the Almighty will hear along with most of the town. But I do thank you for your concern, Emma. You're a good woman."

Emma backed away, aware that she'd just been gently rebuked. "If you need to talk to me, Billie, you let the sheriff know."

"I surely will, Emma."

When the young woman was gone Gabe crossed the room and sat down at his desk, determined to get some work done. But it was impossible to concentrate on anything. All he could see was Billie, as she'd looked last night in his arms. In his bed. And how she looked now, with the weight of the world on her shoulders.

As much as he tried to convince himself that she'd actually planned that little seduction last night to cover her crime, he wasn't having much luck.

There might be some women who could be cold and calculating. But not Billie. The sweetness, the goodness in her, couldn't be faked. Especially by someone as open, as guileless as she was.

But, if she hadn't offered herself to him to cover her crime, what other explanation was there?

He mulled it over in his mind.

Knowing Billie, it wasn't possible for her to kill a man and then calmly seduce another. What they'd shared last night had been too deep, too special, to be anything less than love.

Love.

For long minutes he stared into space, feeling again the deep and abiding peace he'd experienced in Billie's arms. There'd been so little love in his life. He'd often wondered if it was something he'd ever find.

He huffed out a breath. Maybe that was the trouble. How would he know the difference between real love and something contrived by a clever female?

He knew only one thing. He had a job to do and he did it. The same way he'd always done it. Now it would be up to a judge to determine Billie's guilt or innocence.

Love or no, her fate was out of his hands.

At least that's what he tried to tell himself as he buried himself in his work.

Chapter Thirteen

Gabe seemed relieved when Lars arrived at the jail late in the afternoon.

"Sorry I'm late, Sheriff. I had…business to see to." The young man caught sight of Billie in the cell and whipped his hat from his head. "Billie."

"Lars." She had been standing for what seemed hours, staring at the thin rays of sunlight coming through the bars of the window.

"I…heard the news, Sheriff." Lars stood twirling his hat around and around in his hands, looking as miserable as Gabe felt. "The whole town is talking about…" He cleared his throat. "Is there anything you'd like me to do?"

"Yes." Gabe got to his feet, relieved to be able to escape. "I have some things to do. You can stay with…the prisoner."

"Yes, sir."

Lars watched Gabe pick up his hat before walking out the door. Alone with Billie, the young man took up a broom and began to sweep. Halfway across the floor he paused and glanced at Billie.

"I had to take some supplies to Bison Fork for my pa." He watched as Billie sank down on the edge of the cot and stared at the floor. "I had company on my ride."

Billie folded her hands, one inside the other, holding herself together by sheer will. Though she wasn't paying any attention to the words, she was glad for the sound of Lars Swensen's voice. It was better than the awkward silence that had been her constant companion all morning. Though she and Gabe had been just a few feet apart, there was a wall between them. A wall so high, so thick, nothing could penetrate it.

"Grace and the children said to be sure and tell you how much they appreciate all you did for them, Billie."

For a moment Billie didn't seem to understand. Then her head came up sharply. "You drove Grace and the children to Bison Fork?"

He nodded. "Out to the Spooner ranch. She said Mr. and Mrs. Spooner would give her a ride to a nearby town where she and the children can catch a stage to St. Louis."

"And a new life."

"Yes'm." He walked closer and lowered his voice. "I know Grace has been saving her money so she can join her brother in St. Louis. And I know I have no right to stand in her way but—" he stared long and hard at the broom in his hand before glancing over at Billie "—I don't have a big fancy job. I just help the sheriff out here, and deliver supplies for my folks. But I…'' His Adam's apple bounced once, twice, before he managed to say, ''I have feelings for Grace and the children. And I'm wondering if I should have told her before I left her at the Spooner ranch.''

Billie made a choked sound that might have been a laugh or a sob. ''Oh, Lars. I'm the last one to give advice. I've made such a mess of my life.''

''I just thought—'' he clutched the bars of the cell so tightly his knuckles were white ''—since you and Grace are friends and all…'' He flushed, looking so uncomfortable she took pity on him.

She stood and walked across the cell to close a hand over his. ''I think, if you have feelings for Grace and the children, you ought to tell her.''

''I don't want to stand in the way of her life in St. Louis.''

Billie saw the fear and doubt in his eyes. ''I understand, Lars. But wouldn't it be awful if she went to St. Louis, believing it was her only choice?''

He sounded doubtful. ''I suppose.''

''When does she leave?''

He shrugged. ''Tomorrow.''

Billie felt herself close to tears. ''A wise old man once told me that all we have are a few tomorrows. Maybe this one will be special for you and Grace.''

She saw the thoughtful look that came over him as he resumed his sweeping.

Feeling a wave of such abject misery, she turned away and sank down on the cot, wondering how she would possibly get through the ordeal to come. She didn't know what would be worse. The trial, or seeing the way Gabe looked at her.

Gabe had fire in his eyes as he stormed around town, itching for a fight. He actually hoped Buck Reedy would come into town and get himself good and drunk so he'd have an excuse to use his fists on someone.

He'd stayed away from the jail most of the day, looking for ways to avoid having to see Billie in that cell. Every time he saw her there, so still and hurt, he wanted to tear down those bars with his bare hands.

He'd actually been mulling the idea of turning her loose after everyone was asleep tonight and carrying her off somewhere. They could lose themselves up in the Badlands, and live like outlaws. It wasn't much of a life. But it would be better than what he'd have if the judge sentenced her to die for her crime.

The thought caused such a pain to his heart he had to stop and take in a long, deep breath.

When he did, Cheri fell into step beside him, carrying a covered tray.

"You look as bad as Slade, Sheriff."

"What's eating him?"

"Oh, just another day at the Red Dog. He probably won't be able to use room three for a week, until he can get rid of the blood and the stench. The best cook he's ever had is in jail for murder. And now he's just learned that his evening's entertainment, the lovely Belle California, took off in the night for parts unknown.''

Gabe's head came up sharply. "Grace left? Why?''

"Everybody knew she didn't want to stay any longer than she had to. She told all of us that she'd leave as soon as she had enough money to get her and her kids to St. Louis.''

"Kids?'' Gabe looked startled. "How many?''

"Two. A boy and girl. Cute little things. They were staying at a neighbor's ranch until Billie had them brought here. We were all crazy about them. But Billie most of all. Took care of them like they were her own.''

He mulled over this latest piece of news. It occurred to Gabe that there were a whole lot of things he didn't know about Billie.

When they reached the jail he held the door while Cheri carried the tray inside and set it on the desk. Crossing to the cell she called, "Hey, Billie. How are you doing, honey?''

Billie got stiffly to her feet and stood at the bars. "I'm fine, Cheri.''

"Everybody at the Red Dog is missing you, honey. Slade has Roscoe cooking.'' She made a face and nodded toward the tray. "You might want to skip the stew and just fill up on those rocks he calls biscuits.'' She reached through the bars and patted Billie's hand. "Judge Hathaway's rig just pulled into town. So I guess he'll be holding court tomorrow.''

She could see the way Billie was struggling to

hold herself together. Hoping to comfort her she said, "Everybody who works at the Red Dog will be there for you, honey."

She turned away calling, "I'd appreciate it if one of you men would bring the tray back later, seeing as how we're up to our elbows in work right now."

Lars uncovered the tray and studied the congealed globs before saying, "If you don't need me, Sheriff, I'd better get back. My ma will have supper ready."

"You go ahead, Lars. I'll be spending the night here instead of at the Red Dog."

Lars glanced around. "Where'll you sleep?"

"I'll toss a bedroll on the floor."

Gabe waited until the young man was gone before removing a tin plate and carrying it to the cell.

He unlocked the door and strode inside, setting the plate on the cot. As he moved past Billie he brushed her arm and his body reacted instantly. Without even thinking he turned, touching a hand to her shoulder, and felt her flinch.

"You have to help me, Billie."

She looked up in surprise. "Help you? With what?"

"With your defense. Why don't you sit here?" He led her toward the cot and moved the tin plate aside so she could sit. Then he knelt in front of her, so that his gaze was level with hers, and took her hands in his. They were so cold, he found himself rubbing them between his in a gentle, soothing motion. "Tell me everything. What you said. What you did. And what Russ Hawking said and did."

She shook her head. "I can't, Gabe."

"You'll have to tell the judge tomorrow. With the whole town watching and listening." Beneath his fingertips he could feel the tremors that rocked her, and he wanted desperately to comfort her.

She looked into his eyes. "Do you have to be there?"

He nodded.

"Couldn't you let Lars bring me?"

"That would be cowardly."

"And you'd never take the coward's route, would you, Gabe?"

He heaved a sigh. "I'm not trying to be a hero, Billie. I'm just doing my job. Besides, if you're going to face the judge, I'm going to be there with you."

"Why?"

It was such a simple question. And so complex.

"Because I feel responsible."

She leaped to her feet and turned away from him, annoyed that it hadn't been the answer she'd been hoping for. "You're not responsible for me, Gabe. I'm old enough to make my own choices. And old enough to pay the price for my mistakes."

"That isn't what I meant." He walked up behind her and stood there, fighting a terrible battle within himself. What he wanted, more than anything, was to hold her. Just hold her. But he could never forget that he was a man of the law. And for now she was no longer the woman he loved. She was his prisoner.

"I wish…" He touched a hand to her hair, then thought better of it and lowered his hand to his side.

She felt the curl of heat along her spine and glanced over her shoulder. "What do you wish, Gabe?"

His voice was low with anger. "I wish right now I could be my brother Yale. He wouldn't agonize over what was right and what was wrong. He'd just do what he wanted, and to hell with the rest."

She turned, her face in shadow, her voice little more than a whisper. "If you were Yale, what would you do right now?"

"This." He dragged her roughly into his arms and covered her mouth with his, kissing her in a way he'd never kissed her before. With a depth and a hunger and a fierce longing that had them both trembling.

Forgetting himself, he pressed her against the bars and ravished her with kisses. When at last he left her mouth, it was only to trail hot wet kisses down her throat, then lower, to her breast.

His need for her was so overwhelming it staggered him. What he wanted, right this minute, was to take her. To fill himself with her, the touch of her, the taste of her, the smell of her, so that he could store her up in all the empty places inside himself. And then, in years to come, he would still have her here with him when the loneliness became too much.

With his body pressed to hers, and the need vibrating through him, he gripped the bars behind her and went very still.

Billie closed her eyes. She could feel his hard body

imprinting itself on hers. She strained toward him, wanting, needing to feel him inside her. Her blood was so hot it threatened to burn her flesh and melt her bones. Her breath was coming in short gasps, hurting her lungs.

When she opened her eyes she could see him watching her. Those icy silver eyes staring into her heart, her soul.

"Tell me you didn't kill him, Billie."

When she started to close her eyes he caught her chin. His voice was as cruel as the cutting edge of a razor. "Look at me."

She did as he said.

"Now tell me."

She kept her eyes steady on his. "I can't tell you that."

He let out a long, deep sigh and rested his forehead against hers. Then, slowly, as if in a dream, he peeled himself away and took a step back, and then another, until he'd reached the door of the cell. Stepping out, he turned the key in the lock and crossed to his desk.

Billie stood for long minutes watching him. Then she placed the tin plate on the floor and curled up on the bunk, her face to the wall. The better to hide the hot tears that welled up and spilled over in silent anguish.

Around midnight Gabe made a tour of the town, walking slowly along the dusty street. At the hitching post outside the Red Dog he studied the horses, noting which ones belonged to nearby ranchers, and which ones signaled the presence of strangers. Then he stepped inside and took a long, slow look at the crowd.

Without the lure of entertainment, the crowd was unusually thin. Half a dozen cowboys sat at a poker table where Jack Slade was dealing. Judging by the meager chips on the table, the real players had already cashed in. A few ranchers and cowboys sat at tables scattered around the room. The girls, on their feet since breakfast, were happy to join them for a watered-down drink so they could sit and rest. The few who stood near the bar were stifling yawns.

Roscoe looked up, then seeing it was the sheriff, returned his attention to the tumbler he was washing.

"No trouble tonight, Roscoe?"

The bartender frowned. "I figure we've already had our share." He set down the glass. "How's Billie?"

"She knows what's coming. It's going to be a hard night for her."

Roscoe nodded. "Tell her…" He shrugged. Thought better of it and said, "Just tell her we're all thinking of her."

"Yeah." Gabe walked back into the night and made his way to the jail. Up in the sky the big golden moon and the sprinkling of stars seemed to mock him. It didn't seem possible that in the space of a single day, his emotions had taken such a battering. He'd gone from the happiest man in the universe to the most miserable. If the angel of death came to claim him right now, he'd accept his fate without question. Anything would be better than what he would have to face in the morning.

He stepped into the jail and tossed his keys on the desk. By the flickering light of a lantern he could see Billie lying on the cot exactly as she'd been hours before. He hoped she was sleeping. She needed her strength for what was ahead.

He spread out his bedroll in a corner of the room, then kicked off his boots before blowing out the lantern. He had every intention of slipping between the covers. But the sound from the cell had him looking over. Had she merely sighed in her sleep? Or was she weeping?

Because he couldn't bear the thought that she might be crying, he picked up the keys and unlocked the cell, then walked inside and knelt down beside the figure on the cot.

"Billie?" His voice was hushed. "You all right?"

"Yes."

He could hear the tears in her voice. The sound of it had his heart splintering into millions of pieces. "I'm not."

She stirred, then rolled to face him. "You're not?"

He shook his head. "I don't think I can make it, Billie."

"Oh, Gabe." She reached for him, and he fell into her arms like a broken man.

"I thought I could be strong for you, Billie. I thought I could get through this. But I can't. I can't."

She gathered him against her, rocking him as she'd rocked little Ned and Nell whenever they were frightened in the night. She pressed her mouth to his cheek, murmuring words meant to soothe.

"You'll be fine, Gabe. We'll both be fine. You'll see."

"I can't let you do this, Billie. I can't."

"Shh."

It seemed the most natural thing in the world to kiss him. And for him to kiss her back. And then, as they held each other, the kisses deepened, and the sighs grew.

Softly, gently, carefully, they came together, each offering the other comfort in the only way they knew. And as the hours passed all to quickly, they held each other, ignoring the heaviness in their chests at the knowledge that in just a few hours their fates would be sealed for all time.

Chapter Fourteen

Judge Dexter Hathaway figured he'd seen everything in his fifty-two years. After traveling all over
this untamed land, he could understand why some
men chose to break the law. A hungry man was
sometimes forced to steal in order to eat. For this,
Dexter Hathaway was willing to let the offender off
easy. Though he was fair, he was a strict believer in
the law. There were certain moral laws that should
not, must not, be broken.

The greatest of these was the sacredness of life.
Judge Dexter Hathaway considered the taking of a
man's life a grave crime indeed. That was why, after
reading the sheriff's report, he consented to holding
court in the center of town, under a blazing sun. It
was important for every citizen of this little town to
understand the importance of the crime he was about
to judge.

The ranchers and cowboys arrived early, each vy-
ing for the best view of the judge's table. The townspeople were aware that the presence of so many vis-

itors would mean coin in their pocket. And so the Swensen family moved the pretty bolts of fabric and fancy jars of preserves to the front of their store, where they looked most inviting. Eli Moffat's stables did a brisk business, as did Jesse Cutler's barbershop. The girls at the Red Dog wriggled between tables crowded with thirsty customers who were storing up on their whiskey, since the judge had decreed that once the trial started, there would be no liquor served until the verdict had been announced.

At precisely noon the customers at the saloon were herded outside along with the employees, and the doors closed. Minutes later Sheriff Gabe Conover could be seen walking slowly along the street with his prisoner beside him. Much to Gabe's discomfort, the judge had ordered the prisoner shackled. The chains around Billie's wrists and ankles weighed almost as much as she did, and clanged and rattled with each step she took.

By mutual consent, the sheriff and his prisoner exchanged no words. But the looks that passed between them spoke volumes.

Gabe's heart lay like a rock in his chest. And though he could hear the murmur of the crowd, and the occasional snicker, he looked neither right nor left as he took the longest walk of his life.

If Judge Hathaway was surprised by the tender age of the accused, he carefully covered it by pointing to a chair placed to the left of his table.

"The accused will sit there."

Gabe waited until Billie managed to settle herself

amid the jangling chains. Then he took up a position just behind her, standing ramrod straight, his eyes staring straight ahead, blindly seeing nothing.

The judge read the charges, then asked Billie if she understood them.

"Yes, sir."

"How do you plead?"

She wondered how she would possibly speak the word. But finally, after swallowing twice, she managed to say, "Guilty."

That had the people who had gathered around calling out loudly to one another until the judge rapped his gavel on the table. "If any of you should get out of hand, the sheriff is ordered to haul you off to jail until this trial is over. Is that understood?"

The crowd fell silent.

"Now I'd like to hear from the doctor who examined the body."

Doc Honeywell described the single knife wound, and the loss of blood, and the location of the body. Through it all, Billie listened intently. When he was finished, the judge asked Gabe to testify to what he'd seen. With a written report in front of him, the judge asked half a dozen pointed questions, all of which Gabe answered with as few words as possible. The last thing he wanted was to make this any more dramatic than it already was.

Finally the judge turned to Billie. "Miss Calley. I'd like you to stand up and tell this court what happened in Russ Hawking's room."

Billie looked startled by the command. At a nudge

from Gabe she got unsteadily to her feet and faced the stern man who would decide her fate. She struggled to remember all the details Gabe and the doctor had revealed.

"I'd like you to begin at the beginning, Miss Calley. You entered room three."

"Yes, sir."

"What were you carrying?"

At least she knew this much. "A bottle of whiskey and a tumbler."

"Where did you put it?"

"On..." She tried to picture the rooms at the Red Dog. But the only one she was familiar with was her own. She'd never been in any of the others. "...on the night table."

"Where was the deceased?"

"The who?"

There was a smattering of laughter at her innocent question.

"Russ Hawking," the judge said, glancing around sternly. "Where was he?"

She thought a moment. "At the door, I guess."

"So he opened the door and you walked into the room and set the whiskey on the night table. Then what did Russ do?"

"He..." She tried to picture it in her mind. "He leaned against the closed door and said he'd like me to stay. I told him no and tried to get around him to open the door. We fought. I grabbed his knife...."

"Where was his knife, Miss Calley?"

"Where?" She nearly groaned. "In his hand."

"You mean he was holding it when you walked in?"

"Yes, sir."

"Was he holding it up, in a menacing way?"

"Ye-yes."

"But, even though he was menacing you with a knife, you came into the room anyway?"

"I...had a job to do. Deliver the whiskey. So I did it. And then at the door we fought and I grabbed his knife and stuck him."

"Where did you stick him?"

What had doc said? In her panic she struggled to recall. "In the chest."

"You remember this clearly, do you?"

She nodded.

"And was that the only place? Or were there other wounds?"

Had doc mentioned more than one? She didn't think so. "No, sir. Just that one time." She was watching the judge's eyes, trying to see if she was saying the right things. But he was giving nothing away, and she was feeling terribly lost. "Then I ran out and left him to die."

"So you expected him to die, Miss Calley?"

Was he trying to trap her? "Yes, sir."

"Because he wanted you to stay and you didn't want to. Is that right?"

"Yes, sir."

"But isn't that your job at the Red Dog? To stay with the customers if they ask?"

"No, sir, I'm just the—" She bit her lip. This was

no time to worry about her reputation. It was already destroyed. Now it was simply lie upon lie. "Yes, sir. That was my job."

The crowd laughed and pointed, while the saloon women, standing off to one side, linked hands and stared at Billie as if to lend their support.

"So you were just tired and didn't feel like staying. And that's why you stabbed Russ Hawking?"

"Yes, sir."

"But you didn't tell anyone?"

She shook her head. "I was too ashamed."

"What did you do then, Miss Calley? Did you go and hide out in your room?"

"Yes." She could almost feel Gabe's eyes burning into her back. But one lie was as good as another, and she didn't see any reason to bring him into this and destroy his reputation along with her own. "And I stayed in my room until the morning, when I went downstairs to start breakfast."

"What did you do about the blood, Miss Calley?"

"The blood?"

"On your hands and clothes."

"I washed myself in a basin, and then my clothes, and hung them to dry in my room. They were dry by morning."

"Ah, yes. Morning. When you calmly went down to start breakfast."

"Yes, sir."

"Do you like to cook?"

For the first time she almost smiled. "Yes, sir."

"So, you cook on top of your…other duties at the Red Dog."

"Those are my duties, sir."

"Your only duties?"

She looked away. "Right now. Unless Jack Slade says otherwise."

"And if Mr. Slade asked you to do something more, you would?"

She shrugged. "He gave me a job, and a place to sleep, and enough to eat. I owe him."

Judge Hathaway set down the sheriff's report and stared at her for long, silent minutes. Then he said, "Very well, Miss Calley. You may take a seat."

When Billie was seated he glanced around at the townspeople who were lining the street. "Last night Jack Slade was kind enough to give me a list of several of your finest, most upright citizens, who might be willing to testify to the character of the accused."

He glanced around. "Who is Olaf Swensen?"

At forty-five, the handsome, blond-haired giant felt that he was in the prime of his life. He had been married for twenty-five years to his beautiful Inga, and their only child, Lars, a younger mirror image of his giant father, was the light of his life. Olaf Swensen stepped forward, proud to have been singled out.

"I am Olaf Swensen. My wife Inga and I own that store." He pointed to the hand-painted sign, and the fine display of goods that could be seen through the open door.

"I surmise by your speech that you come from Sweden, Mr. Swensen?"

"Yah." He nodded vigorously.

"When you and your wife first came here, were you accepted by the good people of Misery?"

The question caught Olaf by surprise. "Yah." He flushed. "Maybe not right away. Some made fun of the way we talked and dressed. But we overcame that with hard work. And now we are regarded as fine, upright citizens of this town."

"Most commendable, Mr. Swensen. It's the reason why so many of your countrymen, and men from other countries, come to our shores. With enough work, anyone can make a good life for himself here. Isn't that so?"

When Olaf nodded the judge smiled. "Did you ever meet the defendant before she started work at the Red Dog, Mr. Swensen?"

Another surprise. Olaf glanced at his wife, then at the judge. "Yah. She came into our store and asked if we had any work."

If Gabe was surprised by this admission, he kept it from showing. Except for a slight narrowing of his eyes. But in the blazing sun, nobody noticed.

"Did you have any work?"

Olaf shrugged. "Maybe. But this girl...she looked..."

"How did she look?" the judge asked.

Olaf stared at the ground. "She was dirty. And her dress was little more than a rag."

"Was she asking for too much money?" the judge asked.

Olaf's voice lowered. He kicked at a pebble on the ground. "She said she would work for food and a place to sleep."

"But you had no work for her?"

"No, sir."

The judge folded his hands. "Thank you, Mr. Swensen." He looked around. "Is Jesse Cutler here?"

The barber, rail-thin, with a hawkish, angular face and a monk's cap of dark hair stepped forward, pleased that he was also considered a leading citizen of the town. It would be good for his wife and four children to see him held in such high esteem.

"You own the barbershop and bath?"

"Yes, sir. And I perform burials for those who can't see to their own."

"I suppose all that work would require a great deal of help."

Jesse smiled. "I've hired a good number of young people in Misery."

"Did the accused come to you for work?"

Jesse's smile faded. "Yes, but…I didn't have any need of her."

"Nothing at all?" Judge Hathaway leaned forward. "Not even hauling water from the well for the baths?"

Jesse Cutler shrugged, embarrassed to be caught in the same situation as Olaf Swensen. "Look at her. You think she could haul heavy buckets of water?"

"Did you give her the chance to try?"

Jesse frowned. "You don't know how bad she looked, your honor. Like she'd been sleeping in a manure pile. Dirty. Her clothes were rags. Her hair matted and dirty."

"But all she wanted was a chance to work, isn't that so, Mr. Cutler?"

"Yes, sir. But I didn't have any work for her."

The judge nodded and waved a hand. "Thank you, Mr. Cutler." He glanced around at the crowd. "Is Eli Moffat here?"

The stable owner stepped forward. A big man who had long ago gone to fat, his hands were workworn, his boots caked with mud and manure.

The judge studied him for a minute before saying, "Did Miss Calley come to you for a job, Mr. Moffat?"

The big man nodded.

"Did you have any work for her?"

Eli Moffat glanced at Billie. "What I do requires muscle. You think she can muck stalls and carry feed and water for a dozen or more horses?"

"Did you ask her if she could, Mr. Moffat?"

Eli looked away. "No, sir."

"Did she ask for wages, or just for food and lodging?"

"Just food. She said she'd sleep in one of the stalls."

"And still you told her no."

"I didn't need her kind working in my stable."

"What is her kind, Mr. Moffat?"

"She works in a saloon, doesn't she? And besides, she's a killer. She said so herself."

At a murmur from the crowd Judge Hathaway called for silence before asking Emma Hardwick to step forward.

Next to Billie, Emma was an amazing contrast. Her prim dark skirt just brushed the tips of perfectly polished boots. Her crisp white shirtwaist showed not a speck of dust. Every hair had been slicked back into a perfect knot, and topped by a neat little hat.

"You run a rescue mission, Miss Hardwick?"

"I do."

"Who is it you hope to rescue?"

"Women like this, who turn to work in a saloon because they believe they are unsuited for anything else."

The judge frowned. "From what I've heard here today, this young woman didn't consider herself unsuited for other work. It was the people of Misery who considered her unsuitable."

Emma kept her composure. "I care not the reason why a woman chooses such work. My only hope is to persuade them to leave that life behind and choose something more worthy."

"And what do you offer them in place of such work, Miss Hardwick?"

"My strength of will. My words of encouragement. And the knowledge that they are turning away from evil and returning to a righteous path."

"Do you also offer them a place to sleep, and enough to eat?"

She shook her head. "Alas, I have nothing of that nature to share with them."

"I see." His tone gentled. "Noble intentions, Miss Hardwick, are to be admired. But without matching deeds, they won't feed the hungry or comfort the homeless."

Judge Hathaway sat back, glancing around at the crowd that had fallen eerily silent. Many, who had been staring at Billie, now looked away.

The judge turned to Billie. "Do you have anything to say in your own defense, Miss Calley?" His tone seemed almost pleading. "Anything at all?"

She shook her head. "No, sir." She stared at the ground.

"Very well. The defendant will rise and remain standing while I weigh the evidence and return my verdict."

Billie wondered if her trembling legs would hold her. Especially since each of the chains felt as though it weighed more than a boulder.

Out of the corner of her eye she saw Gabe staring at her with that strange, intense look that always made her spine prickly. With every word from the town's leading citizens, his look had grown increasingly angrier.

For long silent moments the judge folded his hands, almost as though in prayer, and closed his eyes, as he mentally went over all that had been said. Then he opened his eyes and fixed them on Billie.

"I'm truly sorry that life has dealt you such a losing hand, Miss Calley. But that cannot excuse the

fact that you made your own choice on the night of
the murder. If you had given me one good reason
why you felt the need to take Russ Hawking's life,
I may have been persuaded to spare yours. But you
seem almost determined to shoulder the blame and
suffer the consequences. Therefore it is the judgment
of this court that…''

He looked up at a commotion, as a wagon rolled
right into the center of town, raising a curtain of dust.
When it came to a halt Lars Swensen stepped down
and lifted a young woman to the ground, and then
two little children, who came racing across the distance that separated them until they clung to Billie's
skirts.

Judge Hathaway looked thoroughly annoyed at the
interruption. ''You will step back and remain silent,
or I'll have the sheriff haul the lot of you off to jail.''

Grace Sawyer, wearing a clean modest dress,
stepped up to the judge's table to say, ''I came as
soon as I heard that Billie had confessed to killing
Russ Hawking. She isn't guilty, your honor.''

''And how would you know that, young lady?''

She glanced at Billie, then back at the judge. ''Because I killed him.''

It took half an hour to restore order to the electrified crowd. They had come expecting a little excitement. But this strange twist in events would give
them something to talk about for many years to
come.

At last, with the banging of the judge's gavel, and

a threat to jail anyone who disturbed the peace, the crowd settled down to hear Grace's story. With her children standing on either side of Lars Swensen, she stood humbly before the judge.

"I was just going to my room, after singing my last song."

"You were a singer at the Red Dog?"

"Yes, sir. I entertained as Belle California. And before me, Billie was Belle."

Even while the townspeople gasped and craned for a better look, Jack Slade groaned as the secret was revealed. It was, he knew, the end of the mystery that had caused the success of the exotic Belle.

"It had been one of our best crowds, and I had a fistful of money." Grace smiled, remembering. "I showed it to Billie, who was just about to race off somewhere. Just then Roscoe Timmons, our bartender, came up to Billie and asked her to take a bottle of whiskey to room three. But she never got there."

"How do you know that?"

Grace swallowed. "Because I took it for her. I thought I'd only be a minute, and then I would go to my room and count my money. But when I got in the room, Russ was lying on his bed. As I set down the bottle of whiskey, he saw the money I'd tucked into the front of my gown. He grabbed a handful, and when I tried to take it back he started laughing and said I could have it back after I'd pleasured him."

"Then what did you do, Miss Sawyer?"

"I started crying. I told him I'd worked so hard for that money. It meant everything in the world to me. My freedom. A better life for my children. I started pummeling him with my fists, and all he did was laugh harder. Then suddenly he turned vicious and put a knife to my throat. He said he was going to slit it wide open and watch me bleed. And when I was dead he was going to do the same thing to my babies."

Despite the shackles, Billie stepped close to Grace and took hold of her hand, squeezing hard. Grace glanced at her, then back at the judge.

"I don't know how I got the knife away from Russ. I think it was the thought of him hurting my babies that gave me the strength. But I just wanted to stop him. So I stuck him, and then I ran to the door. I saw him coming after me and slammed the door. I figured he'd run down and report me to Jack Slade, so I packed up my children, left a note for Billie, and ran through the darkness to find Lars Swensen to take us to Bison Fork."

"Why did you go to Lars Swensen? Weren't you afraid this young man might tell other people about your deed?"

She shook her head and glanced at the shy young giant who stood to one side, watching her. "I needed someone who could get me out of town at once. It was Lars who, at Billie's request, brought my children to me. He knew where the Spooner ranch was. And I thought…since he'd been so kind to me on other occasions, that he would help me. But he didn't know about Russ. I just told him I wanted to go home."

Olaf and Inga were already stepping closer to their son, their eyes full of questions.

The judge rapped for silence. "Why did you come back to Misery, Miss Sawyer?"

Big tears streamed down Grace's face, as she said, "I never dreamed Russ would die and Billie would be blamed for his death. Billie is the finest woman I've ever known. She told me that the little bedroom in the Red Dog was the first one she'd ever had. Yet when I came along she was willing to share it with me. And when she heard me crying in the night over my babies, she paid Lars to fetch them so I wouldn't miss them anymore. Billie slept on the floor so my children could have a bed."

The crowd, already silent, now went pale and still at her words.

"Billie is my friend. My very best friend. It was Billie who rescued me from despair. And when Lars told me what had happened, I knew I had to come back here and make things right, no matter what happened to me."

Judge Hathaway looked at the two young women who stood clasping each other's hands, then rapped for attention.

When he spoke, every person in the crowd listened respectfully.

"The taking of a life is a serious thing. This court will not deal with it lightly. But every one of us has the right to do whatever necessary to preserve our own lives. By your account, you were fighting for your life, Miss Sawyer. But even more important here, Russ Hawking had threatened the lives of your innocent children. I believe there isn't a mother here who wouldn't have done what you did. For that reason, this court will not try you for murder.''

He turned to Billie. ''This court does not take lightly a lie made under oath. For that alone, you could be sent to prison, Miss Calley. But the court understands why you did this. According to Miss Sawyer, you are the kind of friend who would give up, not only her comfort, but also her life, in order to give this woman and her children the opportunity to pursue their dream. I consider this a true rescue mission. Greater love than this I cannot imagine. Because of your generous spirit, Miss Calley, this court finds you innocent of all charges.''

He turned to Gabe. ''You will unshackle the prisoner, Sheriff Conover. She is free to go.''

Gabe knew the entire town was watching. But the need to touch her, to hold her, was so great, he could hardly restrain himself.

As he removed the chains from around her wrists he leaned close enough to whisper, ''Will you forgive me for what I believed?''

She swallowed hard before nodding.

His voice was choked with remorse. ''Will you come to me at the jail tonight?''

Billie felt the weight of the chains removed as he knelt and unlocked the shackles from her ankles. At the same time she felt all the weight that had been around her heart slip away as well. "If you want me."

His eyes were so hot, so fierce, they seemed to burn with the heat of the sun. "I do. I want you, Billie. Only you."

Those were, Billie realized, when all was said and done, the only words that mattered to her this day. They meant even more than the words the judge had just spoken.

The judge had given her back her freedom. Gabe's words had just given her back her hope.

Chapter Fifteen

When Billie was free of her shackles, the judge studied the two young women who were now locked in a tearful embrace. He pounded his gavel and intoned, "This court is adjourned."

Jack Slade offered a round of drinks on the house. At once the crowd thinned considerably, the ranchers and cowboys hurrying inside the Red Dog, the housewives heading back to their homes, heads bent as they chewed over what had taken place. Emma Hardwick, silent and shaken, returned to her tidy cabin, mulling the judge's words.

Billie knelt to hug Ned and Nell, who came hurtling into her arms, while Lars came to stand quietly beside Grace.

"Where will you go now, Grace?" Billie got to her feet, with the children clinging to both her hands.

"Lars has asked me to stay in Misery. He wants to speak to his parents about staying with them until he can build us a place of our own."

"Is that what you want?"

Grace smiled shyly at the handsome young man beside her, then nodded. "My marriage to Nathaniel was..." She paused, not wanting to say anything against the father of her children. "He took care of me out of a sense of duty to my pa. But what I feel for Lars is unlike anything I've ever felt before. This is my dream. To have someone love me and my children, and want to be with us forever."

The smile on Lars's face rivaled the sun. "And it's all because of you, Billie. You're the one who told me to take a chance."

She shook her head. "I didn't do anything, Lars. You're the one who had to choose. But I'm so happy you chose Grace. I'm happy for both of you."

The young man picked up little Nell and caught Ned's hand. "Come on, Grace. It's time we spoke to my parents."

"They may not be happy about this," she said softly.

He merely shook his head. "I know it's sudden. And they've had no time to prepare. They always wanted me to carry on a long courtship, so that they would get to know the girl's family. But once they meet you, Grace, they're going to love you as I do."

As they walked away, Billie had to swallow back fresh tears.

Just then Jack Slade stepped through the swinging doors of the Red Dog and hollered, "Billie. You coming back to work? Or are all these folks supposed to starve in here?"

Her eyes grew as big as saucers. "You mean you still want me to work for you? I thought—"

"That's the trouble with you, girl. You do too much thinking. Time to get back to work. A deal's a deal."

She gave a laugh. "I'll be right there. Just give me a minute."

"A minute's all I can spare."

When the doors closed behind him she turned to see Gabe and the judge just disappearing inside the jail. At the door he turned and for the space of a heartbeat their gazes met. She shivered. Despite the distance, she could feel his touch as surely as though he had reached out a hand to her.

With a shaky little laugh she pulled herself together and hurried to the back door of the saloon.

When she stepped into the kitchen she looked around. Roscoe had left it as filthy as when old Grunt had been here. The floor was littered with debris. Blackened pots half-filled with congealed food and dirty dishes covered every inch of the table and work space. Meat scraps lay rotting in the heat of the day.

With a sigh of sheer happiness she fed wood to the stove and began heating pots of water. As she cleaned and scrubbed and started her first batch of biscuit dough, Billie felt a wave of pure happiness.

She'd been given a reprieve. For at least another day, she could go about doing what she most loved. And tonight, when the town slept, she would go to Gabe.

But despite her relief, there was still a dark cloud

hovering. She brushed it aside. She refused to allow even a moment's unhappiness to mar this day. She'd be a fool to waste time thinking about what might be. For now, for these few hours or days, she'd been given a gift. She intended to savor every precious moment of it.

"I think that's the last of them." With a flourish Judge Dexter Hathaway signed yet another document, and waited for Gabe to add his name as a witness. Then he straightened and offered his hand. "As always, this has been an interesting day, Sheriff."

"Yes, sir."

"I don't believe I will soon forget the town of Misery, or Miss Calley." He lowered his voice. "I'm not a man who believes in divine intervention. But if I were such a man, I'd believe I witnessed it this day. How else to explain her friend arriving just in time to spare her a death sentence?"

He saw the way Gabe blanched and put a hand on his shoulder. "Too much sun, sheriff?"

"I guess so." He paused. "Would you really have sentenced her to death?"

"She left me no choice when she offered no defense. You and I both know that Lady Justice is blind. As a judge I'm permitted some leniency. But I must always take into account the facts of a case."

He turned away. "I'm heading over to the Red Dog for a quick meal before leaving town. Jack Slade assured me that the pig slop I tasted last night is not their usual fare. Would you care to join me?"

Gabe shook his head. "Sorry. I've fallen behind in my paperwork." He grimaced. "Not my favorite part of the job."

"I know what you mean. Sometimes I fear I'll be buried under all the legal documents I'm forced to read on my way from one town to the next." The judge turned toward the door. "I'll see you next month, Sheriff."

When he was alone Gabe sank down into his chair, grateful for the chance to clear his mind. He'd known, in that one terrible moment before Grace arrived, that Billie's sentence would be harsh. He'd felt that he was quietly going mad. That he would be forced to stand by and watch helplessly as she was taken from him forever.

What would his life be like if he lost her, after having just discovered her love?

Billie had changed everything. One night with her and he knew that she was what he wanted, needed, in his life. She filled him up. Soothed him. Made his heartbeat quicken, his pulse leap.

Now her ordeal was over. And he was going to see that she remained safely by his side, no matter what.

He pulled open the bulging drawer and spread a pile of wanted-posters over every inch of his desktop. He was determined to work his way through the mountain of tedious paperwork that was the bane of his existence.

Billie worked her way through the afternoon and evening, happily cooking and cleaning until the kitchen was spotless, and the customers of the Red Dog were satisfied.

Just as dusk fell she looked up to see Grace and Lars standing in the doorway, holding hands, wearing matching smiles of pure delight.

"We're going to be married, Billie." Grace dashed across the room and threw her arms around her friend. "As soon as the preacher returns to Misery."

"Oh, Grace." Billie gave a delighted laugh. "How are Olaf and Inga taking the news?"

"They were surprised, of course. And I'm not sure they liked the idea of Lars having an instant family. But Ned and Nell are with them now, weaving their magic."

Billie turned to Lars. "How can your parents help but lose their hearts to those two little charmers?"

He nodded. "Mama already asked them to call her Nana. That's what I always called my grandmother. It might take my papa a bit longer. But there's something different about him tonight. I don't know what it is, but he seemed changed. He gave none of the old arguments about marrying our own kind. And he promised to help me build a house on the edge of town."

"Oh, Lars. I'm so happy for you." She hugged the young giant, then turned to hug her friend. "I'm happy for both of you."

Grace returned the hug, then stepped back and squared her shoulders. "Now Lars and I have to face

Jack Slade with the news that I'm never coming back to work for him.''

Billie watched the happy couple walk away, and felt such a warm glow in her heart for them. It took a special kind of man to love a woman who had once worked in a saloon. It would seem that Grace had found a man worthy of her love.

She sighed and found herself wishing Gabe would pay her a visit. She had hours yet to go before the day's work would be done. But just seeing him, touching him, would go a long way toward easing her weariness.

She turned away, chiding herself for her impatience. And soon lost herself in her work.

Billie couldn't wait any longer. She had cleaned, scrubbed, polished. She'd put a hambone in the big old blackened kettle and left it to simmer over the fire all night. She'd even peeled a peck of potatoes and left them in a bucket of salted water so they'd be ready to fry in the morning.

She raced up to her bedroom where she took the time to wash herself and run her fingers through the tangles of her hair. Then, with a last glance at her reflection in the chipped looking glass, she hurried down the stairs and out the back door of the saloon.

She gave a delighted laugh as she glanced heavenward. Even the weather, it seemed, was determined to be perfect tonight. The fierce heat had fled, leaving the air cooled by a fresh breeze. The moon was a big golden ball of light. And the stars flickered and blazed in the night sky, looking like sprinkles of diamonds.

Her heart was so light she lifted her skirts and started to run. By the time she reached the jail she was breathless and giggling.

She burst through the door and looked around in surprise. Gabe wasn't there. Lars was standing beside the desk

"Lars." She took a moment to catch her breath. "I thought you'd be home with Grace and the children."

"I was. Until Gabe came to fetch me."

She looked around. "Where is he?"

The young man shrugged, obviously as puzzled as she. "He told me he had to leave town right away. Important business. And that I'd be in charge until he returned."

"Where was he going?"

"He didn't say."

"How long will he be gone?"

Lars shrugged. "I don't know."

"Did he—" she ran a tongue over her lips "—did he leave a message for me, Lars?"

The young man nodded. "He did. In fact, I was just going to lock up here and stop by the Red Dog to give it to you."

She was nearly twitching with impatience. "What was his message?"

Lars considered, then said, "I hope I get this right. He made me repeat it so I wouldn't make any mistakes. Sheriff Conover said to tell you that he was going to make certain that lightning didn't strike twice."

Puzzled, Billie watched while Lars set a lantern on the desk, then turned away to tuck the pile of wanted posters into an already cluttered drawer. As he did, one of them fell to the floor. Billie bent to retrieve it, then seeing it, quickly folded it and tucked it into her pocket.

"I guess that's it, then." Lars lifted the lantern and led the way to the door. He locked it before dropping the key into his pocket.

"You want to walk along with me as far as the Red Dog, Billie?"

"No. That's all right, Lars. I'll...just take my time."

She waited until he'd gone ahead, then she moved numbly along the familiar street, feeling the familiar flutter of fear in the pit of her stomach.

She was relieved when she reached the saloon and could slip inside. But instead of pausing in the kitchen she raced up the stairs to her room and closed the door. With trembling fingers she held a match to the wick of a lantern and hastily withdrew the wanted poster from her pocket. Smoothing out the folds she studied the poorly sketched likeness of her, with the words, "Wanted, for the murder of Linus Ebberling, a rancher and lawman in the Wyoming Territory. This female is considered armed and dangerous."

Billie knelt by the window, staring into the darkness. She'd learned to love this town and the people in it. She'd actually made friends. Grace and Lars. Kitty and Aaron Smiler. Even Cheri and Jack Slade had become her friends. And there was Gabe, of course. But he couldn't afford to be her friend. Every time he extended the hand of friendship, all he got for the effort was another shock. Like the one he'd had to endure tonight when he found that wanted poster.

Hadn't she known that sooner or later her past would catch up with her? The judge had actually praised her for offering to give up her life in exchange for Grace's. What he hadn't known that she was already living on borrowed time. Dying for one crime was as good as dying for another.

But she hadn't wanted Gabe to find out. She couldn't bear the thought that he would now hate her. What's more, he would use the power of his badge to see that she paid for her crime.

Wasn't that what he'd been telling her with that message? He was going to see that lightning didn't strike twice. She'd been given leniency by one judge. Gabe would see that it didn't happen again.

She tried to mentally calculate how long it would take Gabe to get to Wyoming Territory. Several days if he went by horseback. Less if he caught a train just over the border of the Dakota Territories.

That gave her time to take stock of what she had and what she would need to make good her escape before he returned.

Chapter Sixteen

"Mr. Moffat." Billie stepped through the doorway of the stables and waited for her eyes to adjust to the dim light.

Eli Moffat looked up from the stall he was mucking, then glanced down, avoiding her eyes. He'd been suffering pangs of remorse ever since the truth had been revealed at her trial. Not the truth of her innocence, but the truth of his refusal to hire her because of the way she'd looked. The knowledge that he'd been so narrow-minded would stay with him for a lifetime.

"Sorry." He forced himself to look at her. "Was there something you wanted?"

"I was wondering if you had any horses for sale."

"You interested in buying?"

"I might be."

"Well, now." He set aside the pitchfork and led the way past several stalls until he came to one at the end of the stable. "This here's Russ Hawking's horse." When he realized the irony of the situation, he turned away and patted the nose of an old roan gelding. "Not much to speak of. Probably put to the plow for a few years before being turned to saddle. But he's still got some life left in him. Where're you thinking of taking him?"

"I just—" she'd prepared herself for the question "—want something to ride out to the Smiler ranch now and then."

"Oh. Aaron's place, huh?" He nodded. "This old horse would be fine for that. And for getting you around to neighboring ranches. He wouldn't be much good for distance, but as I said, there's still some life in him." And it would feel like some sort of perfect justice to see that she got Hawking's horse, after all the grief his death had caused her. "I can sell him for ten dollars."

She looked crestfallen. "That's more than I thought. And I still need a saddle."

Eli Moffat wasn't known as a generous man, so his offer surprised even himself. "I'll throw one in. And I'll even throw in food and water whenever you need to board him here."

"That's…more than fair, Eli." She dug into her pocket and counted out the money.

He wiped a hand on his filthy britches before accepting it from her and stuffing it into his pocket. Then he offered his handshake. "You made yourself a fine deal, Billie."

She dimpled and accepted his hand. "Thank you."

As he followed her past the row of stalls he cleared

his throat. "I'm sorry about not giving you that job when you first came to town."

"That's all right. I understand."

"Thank you. That's...real nice of you, Billie." He paused before adding, "It looks like you made the right choice, cooking at the Red Dog. Everybody in town is talking about your fine cooking, even if it is in a saloon."

She tried not to let the pain of his remark show. "Thanks, Eli. It's something I've loved doing."

She stopped, realizing how final that sounded. She cursed her choice of words. But when she glanced at him, she thought he'd missed her meaning entirely.

When she'd concluded her business with Eli Moffat she started toward Swensen's Dry Goods. It would mean facing more townspeople, but it couldn't be helped.

Even before she walked in, Olaf Swensen stepped out. He stood blocking her way, those light-blue eyes fixed on her with such intensity, all she could do was stare.

"I want you to know how sorry I am, Billie. And how ashamed."

"Mr. Swensen, there's no need—"

"Yah, there is." His accent deepened. "When I came to this land I was made to feel foolish for the way I talked. That should have taught me something, but I guess I forgot. Now I'll remember for as long as I live. I won't be so quick to judge a stranger by the way he looks or talks. And if he needs a hand up, I'll offer mine.'' He stuck out his hand and Billie accepted it.

"Thank you, Mr. Swensen." She took a deep breath. "I'll be needing a sack of flour and sugar for the Red Dog."

"I'll take it over myself." He paused. "Do you need anything else?"

She nodded. "I'll want to look around first."

"You do that, Billie." Before walking away he gave her a tentative smile, which she returned.

Inside she stared straight ahead as several women nudged each other and looked her way. As she started up an aisle she could hear the whispers.

"That's her."

"Looks pretty enough, I'd say. And clean."

"For a saloon girl."

Instead of the usual laughter following such comments, Emma Hardwick's voice could be heard saying, "You were at the trial, Martha Sweeney. This town left her no choice but to work at the Red Dog."

Inga Swensen's voice chimed in. "That's right. At least, while the rest of us looked away, Jack Slade kept her from starving."

Billie could have hugged both women. Instead she walked along the aisles, looking over the assortment of canned goods, her mind on the days looming ahead of her.

She would need to travel light, and might have to do without a cooking fire. That would mean enough food to sustain her strength, in the fastest manner possible.

She was standing by a display of dried meats, wondering if they would taste as bad as they looked, when Inga Swensen walked up.

"Billie. Olaf carried that sack of flour and sugar to the Red Dog's kitchen."

"Thank you. And be sure to thank Olaf."

The woman paused beside her. "Did you come for those preserves?"

"Oh, yes. I'm glad you reminded me." They would make a grand goodbye gift for Kitty.

"I'll have them ready for you on the counter. How many would you like?"

"Two will be enough."

Billie continued along another aisle until she stopped and pointed. "And a couple of those cigars."

The pretty blond woman looked at her closely. "You thinking of taking up smoking, Billie?"

She gave Inga a quick smile. "They're for a friend."

"The only one I've ever seen buy that brand is Sheriff Conover." The older woman studied Billie more closely. "Are you buying them for the sheriff?"

Billie shook her head, wishing she could do just that. "They're for Aaron Smiler."

"What else does Jack Slade need, Billie?" Inga asked.

Billie looked up. "This is my order, Inga. I'll be paying for it. The flour and sugar can go on the Red Dog's account."

The woman's brow shot up. There weren't many in this town who would be so scrupulously honest with another man's money. "All right. Will there by anything else?"

Billie looked around, wishing she could take a sack of flour and one of sugar for herself, so that she could make fresh biscuits. But that was a foolish dream. Instead she pointed toward the dried meats. "I'll take some of those."

Minutes later she hurried back to the saloon with her supplies. Up in her room she took stock of what she had, and what she still needed. The blanket off her bed would provide warmth when the sun went down, and cover at night. She would leave a dollar on the night table to cover the cost.

She left her supplies in her room and headed down to the kitchen to prepare the evening meal for the saloon. If all went well, she would leave by morning.

The thought brought a heaviness to her heart. She never would have believed that she'd be reluctant to leave such an inhospitable place as Misery behind. But somehow, over the past weeks, it had become her haven.

It wasn't just the town she'd miss. She knew that the hardest part about leaving Misery was leaving Gabe, without a word.

She sighed. She was no better than her pa. Just when a place and its people started to feel easy, it was time to pick up and leave.

"Billie." Grace opened the door to the Swensen living quarters above the dry goods store.

"I thought I'd see how you were getting along." Billie stepped in when Grace stood aside.

"Things are even better than I'd hoped." Grace closed the door and led the way to a small sitting area that overlooked the main street of Misery. Across the way Billie could see the horses hitched in front of the Red Dog. Her own was tied out back, the saddle bags loaded, the blanket roll tied behind the saddle.

"Inga and Olaf have really opened their hearts to us. In fact—" she touched a finger to her lips and led the way to a closed door "—look at this." She opened the door and whispered, "Inga wanted the children to have the bed that Lars used when he was a boy."

Billie paused beside the bed to watch the two children in sleep. They looked like angels. She had to swallow hard to hold back the tears as she brushed a lock of golden hair from little Nell's cheek.

After a few minutes she stepped back into the sitting area and reached into her pocket. "I brought you this."

"What is it?" Grace stared at the small lace square.

"It was my ma's and her ma's before her. Just a bit of a lace handkerchief, but I'd like you to have it."

"Why, Billie?" Grace looked thunderstruck.

"Because you're getting married soon. And I want you to carry it for luck."

"But why don't you wait until my wedding day?

That way I can carry it, and afterward I'll give it back to you.''

Billie was already shaking her head. ''I want you to have it, Grace. To remember me by.''

Grace's eyes darkened with concern. ''You make it sound like you're going away.''

Billie almost broke down and admitted the truth. But then she thought about Gabe, and how persuasive he could be. The first one he'd come to would be Grace. There was no way she would burden a friend with what she was about to do.

She turned away, avoiding Grace's eyes, and headed toward the door. ''I've got to get back to work now. I'll see you tomorrow.''

''All right.'' At the door Grace stared into her eyes. ''You all right, Billie?''

''I'm fine.'' But she couldn't help wrapping her arms around her friend and hugging her fiercely. ''One more thing. Be sure and bring the children around often to play with the chickens, or they'll get lonesome.''

She took a step back and hurried out the door, before she embarrassed herself by weeping.

''Well, look who's here.'' Aaron lifted himself slowly out of the chair on the porch and leaned heavily on his cane as he made his way down the steps, just as Billie slipped from the saddle.

''Aaron.'' She hurried forward and gave him a quick hug.

He looked around. ''Where's Gabe?''

"He's off doing sheriff work." She avoided his eyes. "Is Kitty here?"

"She's down at the corral, breaking a mustang to saddle." He lifted his finger to his lips and gave a shrill whistle. A short time later they saw Kitty striding toward the house.

When she spotted Billie she made a mad dash into her arms. "What're you doing here in the middle of the week? And where's my brother?"

"I just thought I'd take a little time off work to visit. As I told Aaron, Gabe's off doing some lawman's work."

"Well, isn't this a grand surprise?" Kitty eyed Billie's bulging pockets. "What've you got in there?"

"A gift for each of you." She reached in and removed two jars of strawberry preserves, handing them to Kitty. Then she pulled two cigars from her other pocket and handed them to Aaron.

"Well, now." Pleased, Aaron held them in his hand as though they were gold.

"Come on up on the porch," Kitty said, taking her arm. "Sit awhile."

"Only for a few minutes. That's all the time I can spare."

Kitty shot her a glance. "You usually have more time than this. Is Jack Slade working you that hard?"

She flushed. "We've been having good crowds at the Red Dog."

"We heard." With Kitty's help Aaron settled himself in his chair while Kitty and Billie sat on the step at his feet. "Lars Swensen was by with some supplies." Aaron took his time biting the end of the cigar and holding a flame to the tip, puffing until a wreath of smoke circled his head and the rich smell of tobacco filled the air. "He told us about the trial, Billie."

Kitty caught her hand. "Lars said you were a real hero for offering to take the blame for your friend."

Billie flushed clear to her toes. "I'm no hero. Don't ever think that."

"You see, Aaron?" Kitty turned to the old man. "I told you Billie would say that."

Billie's embarrassment deepened. She hated that people thought she was doing something noble, when all along she was merely exchanging the guilt of one crime for another. It shamed her to know that they thought so highly of her, when in truth, she didn't deserve it. "It wasn't like that, Kitty."

The young woman patted Billie's hand. "Whatever you say." She struggled with the lid of the preserves, twisting until it finally gave way. Dipping her finger inside, she tasted, then gave a look of pleasure. "Oh, Billie. This tastes like...pure heaven."

Billie laughed. "I just knew you'd like it. The first time I made them, I couldn't believe how good they tasted either. I had to have them on biscuits, on bread, and sometimes just on a spoon."

"You know how to make preserves?"

Billie nodded. "A sweet lady who was like my own ma taught me. She taught me so much about cooking and such."

"Will you make them for us sometime?"

"You know I will." Billie felt the twinge around her heart at yet another lie. There were so many things she could have done for her friends. But now, she would never have the chance to do anything for them. And there was no way she could explain.

She glanced up at the sun, moving quickly over the towering trees. With a sigh of reluctance she got to her feet. "I'm sorry I have to leave now."

"That's all right. When Gabe gets back, I'll see that he brings you out for supper real soon."

Without a word Billie offered her hand to Aaron, then suddenly bent and kissed his cheek before turning to grab Kitty in a hard bear hug.

"I've loved knowing both of you. You've been…friends to me."

Aaron and Kitty merely stared at her as she ran off the porch and pulled herself into the saddle. Without a word she nudged her horse into a trot.

At the top of the rise she pulled her mount up short for a moment, to pause and look down at the crude ranch and the two people on the porch. She waved, and they returned the wave.

Then, swallowing back a tear, she turned her mount in the opposite direction.

There had been so few people who had ever cared about her. And now, within the space of days, she'd turned away from all of them.

Not all. There was one other, she thought miserably. But he had been more than a friend. So much more.

She wouldn't let herself think about Gabe now. That would only get in the way of what she had to do.

She'd managed to keep her promise to herself to hold her tongue and tell no one about her plans. She knew Gabe well enough now to realize that he'd follow any lead, no matter how slim, to see that justice was done. So she had to outsmart him. And that meant heading, not toward civilization, but as far away from it as possible.

Into the Badlands.

Chapter Seventeen

As the town of Misery came into view Gabe's horse, sensing the end of the trail, broke into a run. Gabe gave him his head, feeling the same sense of elation and relief.

He'd left Misery feeling like a beaten man. He was returning like one reborn. Now, at last, all the stumbling blocks that had stood in the way of his happiness with Billie had been removed.

Finding that wanted poster in his drawer had been every bit as bad as being told that Billie had killed Russ Hawking. But Linus Ebberling's family in the little town of Millersville, in the Wyoming territory, had assured him that their father was alive. Not that any of them seemed to care. From what little Gabe had been able to glean from the tight-lipped bunch, they considered Billie Calley the closest thing to a saint for having nursed their mother through a long and painful illness, and their father a brute and a bully, for having driven Billie away.

But when Gabe had insisted on seeing for himself

that Linus was indeed alive, they took him upstairs to an embittered old man who spent all his time locked away in his room. He came downstairs for an occasional meal, though more often they simply carried a tray to his room. He slipped away from time to time, but always he returned, days or weeks later, looking dazed and confused.

The man Gabe had seen was dirty, unshaven and completely mad. When Gabe had mentioned Billie's name, he'd seen the flare of recognition in the old man's eyes, before they'd become once more veiled in madness.

Maybe that was what living all alone did to a man, Gabe thought. Which was why, as soon as he had time to shave and bathe, he intended to ask Billie to share his life.

It was that sweet thought that had kept him going for nearly three days and nights without sleep. He'd have the rest of his life to sleep in the arms of the woman he loved.

The woman he loved.

Despite his weariness, he smiled. Maybe he wouldn't take the time to shave or bathe. Maybe he would just burst in on her in the kitchen of the Red Dog and declare his intentions.

He looked down at his clothes, coated with the dust of the trail. The least he could do was make himself presentable. It wouldn't be time wasted. Not if it brought a smile to Billie's lips.

He hoped she'd understood his message. But he hadn't wanted to take Lars into his confidence. And so he'd hinted that she would never have to go through another painful trail like the one they'd just survived.

He'd had every intention of telling the former sheriff in Millersville that the woman mentioned on that wanted poster no longer existed. Which wouldn't have been a lie, since Billie really was a different person from the one he'd first met that fateful day. Besides, he intended to ask her to change her name to his. The sooner the better.

He rode up to the jail and was relieved to see Lars inside. Sliding from the saddle he retrieved his rifle and bedroll and stepped through the doorway.

"Afternoon, Lars."

"Sheriff."

"Would you mind taking my horse to the stables?"

"Sure thing, but—"

"On the way would you stop at Jesse Cutler's and ask him to get a bath ready? And I'll need a shave. I'll just hunt up a change of clothes, and I'll be along in a few minutes."

"Yes, sir, but first—"

Gabe was already shaking his head. "If there's any business to see to, Lars, you do it. After a bath and a shave I'm heading to the Red Dog for dinner. And when I'm done I figure I'll try to get maybe twenty or so hours of sleep and then I'll feel human."

"Sheriff..." The young giant stood in the doorway, looking like he couldn't decide whether to come in or go out. "There's something you've just got to know."

"What is it?" Gabe asked tiredly.

"Billie's gone."

Gabe's eyes narrowed. "Gone where?"

"Nobody knows. When the customers at the Red Dog couldn't get their supper, Jack Slade went looking for her, and found her things gone from her room."

"She didn't tell anyone about this?"

Lars avoided his eyes. "Grace said Billie stopped by there earlier today. Grace thought she was acting funny, but when she asked, Billie just said she had to get back to the saloon."

"Nobody saw her leave?"

"Yes, sir." He swallowed. "She told Eli Moffat, when she bought the horse—"

Gabe lifted a hand to interrupt him. "Billie bought a horse?"

"Yes, sir. Russ Hawking's old nag. She told Eli she wanted it to ride out to visit your sister at the Smiler place."

Gabe was already rushing out the door, rifle in hand. As he pulled himself into the saddle he called, "I'm heading out to Aaron's place. I don't know how long I'll be, but until I get back, you're in charge."

There was no telling how far he'd have to go to catch Billie. There was a terrible fear in his gut. A fear that this time, his luck just might have run out.

"I just knew something was wrong." Despite the pain in his leg Aaron got up and began pacing in front of the fire. "When Billie left I told Kitty that there was something troubling our young friend."

Gabe turned to his sister. "Did she give any hint of where she was headed?"

Kitty shook her head. "We thought she was heading back to town."

Aaron paused. "Why is she running now, when the trial is over?"

"Because of a wanted poster from Wyoming territory, showing Billie's picture, and claiming she killed a man. But the claim was a lie, made by a crazy old man whose own family can't abide him."

"If it's a lie, why didn't she stay?"

Gabe sighed. "She shot him and ran, thinking she'd killed him."

Aaron sank down on his chair. "She was already acquitted of one crime, and now she's running from a crime that didn't even happen." He pinned Gabe with a look. "How are you going to find her, Gabriel?"

Gabe glanced at his sister, who was busy filling his saddlebags with whatever supplies she had. Food. A spare pouch of bullets. A knife which she always carried in her boot. "I'm going to try to think the way Billie does."

The old man managed a smile. "That's not so easy, is it?"

Gabe shook his head. "Not easy at all. But I have to find her, Aaron. I have to."

Hearing the vehemence in Gabe's tone, Aaron walked over to close a hand on his shoulder. "You're the best tracker in these parts. If anyone can find her, it's you."

"I hope to heaven you're right."

Gabe stepped outside. When he did, he was surprised to see that Kitty had unsaddled his tired mount and turned it into a corral. In its place was a freshly saddled mustang.

At his arched brow she smiled. "When it comes to horseflesh, I'm an expert. Until a few weeks ago, when I broke him to saddle, this stallion was running free up in those hills. He's strong enough take you wherever you need to go, and bring you safely back home."

Instead of slapping her arm, Gabe surprised them both by dragging her close and pressing his lips to her temple. "Thanks, Kitty. You're the best."

He pulled himself into the saddle and started off at a brisk pace.

Kitty climbed the steps and stood beside Aaron to watch until horse and rider were out of sight.

When the old man started to turn away he spotted a tear in her eye. He leaned close to whisper, "He'll find her. Don't you worry."

She brushed aside the tear with an angry fist, embarrassed by this unexpected rush of emotion. "'Course he will. He's a Conover, isn't he?"

"That's my girl." Aaron smiled. "With Gabriel on her trail, Billie doesn't stand a chance."

Gabe reined in his mount and stared around, unable to shake the feeling that he was being followed. Except for the wind ruffling the leaves of a tree, there seemed to be nothing moving. He glanced at a pile of tumbled boulders, wondering if a horseman could be hiding behind them. Then he chided himself for his foolishness and turned to stare at the trail that led to the Missouri River, and from there to civilization.

In the other direction, far off in the distance, were the Black Hills, looking dark and forbidding.

He had told Aaron that he intended to think like Billie. The only trouble with that was, she wouldn't be using her mind to plot strategy. She would be going on pure emotion.

His heart, so in tune with hers, kept calling him to the wilderness. A long shot, he knew. But there it was.

As best he could tell, he was only hours behind her. If he made a wrong choice now, he would lose her. That thought was too terrible to contemplate.

Closing his eyes a moment, he fought a terrible war within himself. Then he turned his mount southwest, away from the trail leading to civilization and toward the barren land known to all as the Badlands.

Billie eased her horse across the eerie lifeless ridge of rock and across a dry mesa, while the sun slowly sank behind a tall spire of red boulders. Her journey so far had been slower than she'd anticipated, but without incident. Unless she counted the flask of water that she'd dropped, spilling its precious contents. Still, she had another jug of water, and she intended to ration it until she found a pool or stream.

She found herself wishing she could enjoy the strange beauty of this place. It was unlike anything she'd ever seen before. Wide, deep gorges of pink earth. High rocky ridges, giant pyramids of rock that seemed to change color and form with each movement of the sun. And now, with daylight fading and the sky growing dark, the landscape seemed more forbidding, the rocky outcroppings looming like ghostly specters.

In the distance she could see the dark, somber outline of the Black Hills. She shivered and realized that the air had grown considerably cooler. She decided to stop and make camp for the night.

Up ahead she caught sight of a stand of tall junipers. When she reached the spot she reined in her horse and slid wearily from the saddle.

She tethered her horse, then ate a little of the dried meat from her saddlebag. Afterward she wrapped the blanket around herself and curled up on the ground beneath the tallest of the trees. The low-spreading branches offered shelter should it rain, and shielded her from the chill breeze that swept down from the hills.

After the emotions of the past days, and the exhausting hours spent in the saddle, she was asleep almost instantly.

Gabe felt his heartbeat quicken as he bent to the darkened stain across the rocky trail. Though it was nearly dry, it was unmistakably water, where no rain had fallen. And nearby, almost obscured, hoofprints.

A horse and rider had passed this way within the past hour. He was betting it had been Billie.

As he was pulling himself into the saddle he felt again, as he had so often lately, the prickly sense that someone was watching. He turned to peer over his shoulder. Except for the bleak landscape, there seemed to be no sign of life.

If he had more time, he would conceal himself and watch and wait. He was a man who had always trusted his instincts. But there was no time to waste. He only concern now was finding Billie. And to hell with any drifter who might be following him, hoping for a scrap of food.

He urged his horse into a slow walk, keeping his gaze fixed on the ground. Up ahead he found dull gray threads clinging to the sharp edge of a towering stone. His heart stirred with excitement. From their location these could very well have come from a blanket tied behind a saddle, much like his.

He was getting close, he thought. He glanced at the darkening sky with a sense of resignation. Darkness came early in the hills. Another hour or two of light by which to see the trail and he would have caught up with her. But the ground was already cloaked in darkness.

He could feel his energy flagging. He'd been too long without sleep. Still, the thought that Billie might be close by was so enticing, he climbed to the very top of a mound of rocks and stared around, hoping to spot a fire. Seeing none, he decided to give in to his weariness. He would stop and make camp for the night. With any luck, he would catch up to Billie by morning.

Gabe heard the sound. No more than a whisper in the night. But he'd spent years on the trail of outlaws, and had trained himself to recognize a hundred different signs of danger.

Someone was nearby, working very hard at being as quiet as possible. It could be a wanderer hoping to steal his horse.

He cursed the fact that extreme weariness had

made him careless. Had he been more rested, he would have heard the intruder minutes ago.

In the darkness he reached for the gun in the bedroll beside him. But just as his fingers curled around the barrel, he felt the press of something cold to his temple, and the familiar, blood-chilling sound of a pistol being cocked.

"They all think I'm crazy." There was the cackle of wild laughter. "Crazy am I? I figured that wanted poster would bring some fool lawman around who could lead me right to her. I thank you for that, Sheriff. And now I'll show my appreciation."

Gabe struggled to roll aside, but the explosion of gunfire sent his head backward with such force he felt pain crashing through him. Wave after wave of pain, until he felt his head exploding. Felt the warmth of blood surrounding him. Felt all the life draining from him. And then there was nothing. No pain. No sound. Only darkness. A long, long tunnel of darkness.

The land was shrouded in a thick blanket of night. In her sleep Billie heard thunder and sighed, drawing the covering more tightly around her. Nearby her horse blew and snorted and sidestepped, causing her to roll to her other side.

It was the storm, she thought dazedly. Her horse was troubled by the approaching storm. She briefly considered getting up to check the tether. The last thing she needed was to have her horse frightened off by thunder.

She started to toss aside the blanket. As she did, she felt a hand suddenly close over her mouth. She tried to scream but the sound died in her throat as the grasp tightened.

Her eyes flew open. It was too dark to see more than the shadow of a man, but it was enough to have her clawing furiously at the hand while she struggled to scramble to a sitting position.

A voice from her past whispered, "You didn't really think I'd just let you go, did you, sweet Billie?"

"You can't be... You're dead. I killed you."

She reacted like a wild creature, kicking, biting, scratching. But her strength was no match for his. Especially when he swung the handle of his pistol in a wide arc and connected with her temple. For a moment she saw stars and moaned. Before she could recover he hit her again. This time she saw a brilliant white light before it faded into flickering lights. And then she felt herself sliding down a long, dark mountain trail into total blackness.

Chapter Eighteen

When Billie regained consciousness, she couldn't be certain if minutes had passed or hours. Dawn light streaked the sky. Enough to reveal that she was lying on her blanket, her wrists and ankles tightly bound.

Her captor, Linus Ebberling, was seated a short distance away, the contents of her sleeping bag spread out around him. He had helped himself to dried meat and stale biscuits, and was now washing it down with whiskey.

When he realized that she was awake, he walked over to kneel in front of her. Leaning close, he nuzzled his face to her hair. The stench of his sour breath had her shivering uncontrollably.

"Well, now. Isn't this something. Here I am, back from the dead, and ready to finish what we started, pretty little Billie."

"How did you...?" She shook her head to clear it.

"Survive? That was easy enough. You were a lousy shot, sweet thing."

"But the blood…"

"You hit my shoulder. The shock of it knocked me out cold. Hurt like hell when I woke up. Enough to make me real mad, Billie. So while I got back my strength, I started plotting my revenge." He grinned, revealing yellow teeth. "They all think I'm crazy. My kids. My neighbors. Even that sheriff who came out to check up on me." He tipped back his head and took another swallow of whiskey. "Thinks he's such a shrewd lawman. I guess I showed him. He's the one who led me here."

"Gabe is here?" Billie couldn't hide the little thrill of excitement that raced along her spine at his words.

Her captor grinned. "Gabe Conover. The toughest sheriff in the Dakotas, according to all the legends. Hell, he wasn't so tough. One bullet's all it took."

"You—" she felt her heart come to a sudden, screeching halt "—you shot him?"

His smile grew. "Didn't you hear it? I figured the sound of gunfire would spook you and start you running again. But there you were, still sleeping like a baby."

She shuddered as the realization dawned. "The thunder I heard. It was really…"

"Thunder, was it?" He threw back his head and cackled, sending chills along Billie's spine.

She couldn't hide the tears that sprang to her eyes. Seeing them, he caught her chin and leaned close.

"Tears? Don't tell me that lawman meant something to you?"

She tried to pull back, but he held her fast.

"Answer me." His tone hardened. "Were you sweet on him?"

"What if I was? What does it matter now?"

His eyes narrowed. "Did you go to his bed? Did you give yourself to him?"

Billie felt such a deep welling of pain at the thought of Gabe dying because of her. Suddenly, nothing mattered anymore. Not her life. Not the freedom she'd been hoping to find. Not even the things she was certain this man intended to do to her before he killed her.

"Gabe Conover was the finest man I've ever known. I loved him. And yes. I gave myself to him. Despite what you tried to do to me, he was the first. And the only one who'll ever own my heart."

"And you thought you were too good for the likes of me." He slapped her hard enough to snap her head to one side. Then, as he watched her, he suddenly laughed again. "Oh, this just gets better'n better. You tried to kill me because I wanted you. Now I've killed the man you wanted. And my revenge is going to be all the sweeter, knowing I'm the only one left who'll ever have you. When I'm through with you, you'll beg me to kill you. And I'll be happy to oblige. Then I'll go back to my ranch. And nobody will be the wiser. They'll just let the crazy old coot live alone, just the way they always have. But at least I'll have my memories of sweet little Billie Calley."

He took another pull of whiskey, watching her

face as he did. "I used to watch you, feeding Sarah, bathing her, treating her like some kind of fine lady."

"Your wife was the finest woman I've ever known. She taught me everything. How to cook. How to bake. She was so patient with me. So kind. I loved her like my own mother." Tears filled Billie's eyes again. "I didn't mind the work. Not for Sarah. I thought it was a privilege to care for her during her illness. All I could think was that she didn't deserve such a slow, painful death."

"Yeah. Too slow. She should have died sooner. It was making me crazy, watching you, wanting you, and knowing I couldn't make my move until she was gone."

At her little gasp he leaned close and grabbed a handful of her hair. "Don't act so surprised. You had to know what I was thinking."

Billie shook her head. "I didn't. I never dreamed—"

"You're a fool then. You could have had everything. My ranch. All Sarah's things. I'd have given you anything if you'd have just agreed to stay on as my woman."

"Don't you understand? I didn't want Sarah's things. Or you. But you just wouldn't accept that, Linus."

"Oh, I understood well enough. But now it's you who doesn't understand, pretty Billie. I am going to have you." He laughed again, a high, shrill sound of madness that sent chills trickling like ice along her spine as he pulled a pistol from the waistband of his pants.

Billie recognized it as Gabe's.

Seeing her look of recognition, he caressed her cheek with the barrel of the pistol and cackled as she flinched. "I didn't figure a dead lawman had any need of these. So I helped myself to them. His pistol. His rifle. And believe me, I'm a lot better shot than you are. Isn't it sweet irony that I intend to use your lover's guns to force you to pleasure me?"

He tipped up the whiskey and took a long drink, then sat down beside her and started unlacing his boots.

"I'm in a powerful hurry to get started, seeing as how I've been waiting for this for such a long time now."

Beside him, Billie fought the terror that was building inside her, turning her blood to ice.

Gabe moaned and lay very still, wondering why someone had set him on fire. It had to be fire causing this unbearable heat crashing through his body in waves. His ears were still ringing from the gunshot that had exploded so near. Had it shattered his head? Tentatively he lifted a hand and was relieved to find that his skull seemed intact, except for the sticky warmth of blood.

At first he thought he'd gone blind. Everything was shrouded in darkness. But when he looked up at the sky, he could make out the moon and the stars and realized that little time had elapsed since the attack.

What had the attacker wanted? He struggled to make his befuddled mind work.

Billie. He sat bolt upright and let out a string of curses at the pain that shot through him like fiery arrows straight to his brain.

Struggling to ignore the pain he pulled himself to his feet and stood swaying as wave after wave of nausea swept over him.

He fumbled at his waist for his pistol. Not finding it, he dropped to his knees, though it cost him dearly. After scrambling around the dirt searching for his pistol and rifle, he realized both were gone.

His attacker had been thorough, he thought with disgust, as he reached into his boot for the knife Kitty had given him. It wasn't much against a madman with firepower. But it would have to be enough.

Once again he pulled himself to his feet and stumbled toward his horse. Every step was sheer torture. But the knowledge that Linus Ebberling had come all this way to vent his rage on Billie had Gabe moving doggedly forward.

He could have already killed her.

That thought had Gabe pulling himself into the saddle and urging his mount forward, even though he felt his head exploding with each movement.

Billie. He had to reach her in time. If he proved to be too late, this pain would be nothing compared with the pain he would be forced to suffer for the rest of his life.

* * *

As Linus worked off his boots, and then his clothes, Billie swallowed back her terror and steeled herself for what was to come. Whatever he planned to do to her was nothing compared with what he'd already done.

The thought of Gabe lying dead back there on the trail had a sob backing up in her throat. But the more she thought about it, the more she decided to turn her grief into something far more useful. She would not lie back and allow this monster to indulge his fantasies. Instead, she would feed this deep, abiding rage until it gave her the strength she needed to fight him. Linus Ebberling had just taken the life of the finest man she'd ever known. Added to that was the fact that he'd despoiled his beautiful wife's memory. He didn't deserve to walk away from such despicable deeds without paying a price for them.

He kicked off his boots and tossed aside his shirt, then knelt over her. "Now you and I are going to have us a time, pretty Billie."

She indicated the rope at her ankles. "I've learned this much about pleasing a man. It can't be done as long as I'm tied like this."

He grinned. "Maybe I ought to thank that lawman, after all. Looking forward to it, are you?" He reached into his pocket and withdrew a knife, slicing neatly through the ropes that bound her ankles.

She held up her hands. "What about these?"

His eyes narrowed. "I told you. I'm not crazy. And I'm not stupid."

Billie shrugged. "Suit yourself. I just thought it might be nice to put my arms around you."

"I don't need them around me. In fact, if you don't cooperate, I'll just tie them over your head." He gave a chilling laugh and pressed the blade of the knife to her throat as he caught her bound hands and drew them up.

He watched her eyes. Saw them darken with fear. In one swift move he slit open her gown from neck to waist. Finding the chemise beneath it, he cut that away as well.

His gaze was suddenly riveted on that pale flesh. He tossed aside the knife and lowered his face to her breast.

Billie steeled herself not to flinch as her fingers fumbled in the dirt until they encountered a heavy stone.

Her captor's words were muffled against her skin. "Now this was worth waiting—"

She used that moment of distraction to bring the stone against his head with all the force she could muster.

He let out a screech of pain and got to his knees just as Billie scrambled to her feet and started running.

"Oh, no you don't," he shouted as he came after her.

Billie was jerked backward when he caught a handful of her hair, yanking it hard enough to bring tears to her eyes. She turned to him biting and scratching, and brought her knee to his groin. Though the shock momentarily had him doubling over, he reached out before she could flee and spun her around, slapping her so hard she stumbled and fell.

He was on top of her at once, his arm around her throat, cutting off her breath until she could feel herself beginning to fade.

"Now you're going to pay, sweet Billie." With his hands around her throat he lowered his face to hers.

He stiffened when he felt the sharp pain of a knife blade at his back, and a voice thick with rage mutter, "Let the woman go, and get up real slow. Or I'll forget I'm a man of the law and kill you where you stand."

Billie was filled with elation as she felt the weight of Linus lifted off her. But when she caught sight of Gabe she let out a cry of despair.

"Oh, Gabe. Oh, what has he done to you?"

Blood streamed from his head, staining his shirt and pants. His face and hands were smeared with it. His eyes nearly blind from it. So much blood he appeared to be drenched in it.

"Get on your horse, Billie. And start back the way you came. I'll catch up when I'm through here." Gabe swayed, and Billie knew he was barely able to stand. Still, he held the knife steady as he faced her attacker.

"You're under arrest, Linus."

"Am I?" The old man sneered. "You're already out on your feet. All I need to do is..." He lashed out with a foot, sending Gabe sprawling. And was on him in a flash, one hand at Gabe's throat while with his other hand he struggled to get hold of the knife.

"You heard me, Billie. Get out of here," Gabe shouted.

There was no time to see if she heeded his command as he concentrated all his energy on fighting off the man who attacked him like a mad dog, with brutal blows to his already bleeding head.

The knife slipped from his fingers as he felt a fist smash into his face. When Ebberling scrambled around in the dirt, trying to retrieve the knife, Gabe managed to get to his knees and shake his head, hoping to clear it.

He managed to dodge a wild kick, and leaped to his feet just as Linus brought a doubled fist to his midsection. For a moment all the wind was knocked out of him, and he struggled to breathe. Linus took that moment to retrieve the knife, and moved in for the kill.

"This time I'll finish the job," he cried as he swung his arm in an arc toward Gabe's heart.

Suddenly there was a terrible explosion, which echoed across the hills. Linus Ebberling stiffened, then gave a look of amazement as he sank to his knees.

He glanced over his shoulder. "You, Billie?"

Billie stood behind him, holding Gabe's rifle in her hands. She could hardly see for the tears that were streaming from her eyes. Her hands were trembling so violently she couldn't fire off a second shot.

With a gurgle of pain Linus fell forward in the dirt, while his blood spilled out around him forming a muddy pool.

Billie saw the way Gabe was swaying. Tossing aside the rifle she raced to his side and caught him before he could fall.

"Oh, Gabe. Please don't die."

He clung to her, barely able to feel his legs. "...not going to die. Got too much to live for now."

As he slid to the ground, he gave her a lopsided smile. "That was some shooting. Looks like your aim just got better." His brain had gone all fuzzy, and he knew that at any moment he was going to pass out cold. "Will...marry me, Billie?"

"Gabe. Oh Gabe, did you just say what I think you said?" She cradled him in her arms, her tears mingling with the blood that ran in rivers down his face.

But he was beyond repeating anything. The pain, and the relief that they had come through this together, took him under.

Safe in her arms, he collapsed.

Knowing Gabe was too weak to sit a horse, Billie dragged him to the shelter of a rock cave. Then she buried Linus beneath a mound of stones. Afterward she held his bottle of whiskey to Gabe's lips to ease his pain. Finally, exhausted beyond belief, she slipped into the bedroll beside Gabe and held him while he slept.

Days later, as his strength slowly returned, Gabe and Billie passed the hours together, talking quietly, or sleeping in the comfort of each other's arms.

Billie told him about Sarah.

"Sarah Ebberling was the mother I never had. I first met her when I was about six or seven. Pa worked for Linus as a wrangler, and I helped out in the kitchen. Sarah treated me the same as her own children. I can still remember the first time she put her arms around me and hugged me. I thought I'd died and gone to heaven. After that, I couldn't do enough for her." Billie closed her eyes remembering. "Every couple of years we'd drift back to Wyoming Territory, and the Ebberling ranch, and I'd be so happy. I truly loved Sarah. And when my pa died, and Sarah asked me to come and care for her, I felt as if I'd come home. I bathed her, fed her, dressed her, and cooked all the meals for the family and the cowboys."

Gabe, who had remained silent, took her hand in his. "So much work for one little female."

She shook her head. "I would have done anything for Sarah. But I could see her growing weaker, and knew it was only a matter of time. The day she died I was so filled with grief, I could barely stand beside her grave. I remember falling to my knees and sobbing. Later that day Linus came to me and tried to—"

"You don't have to speak of it, Billie." Gabe drew her close. "I know."

"But I need to say it out loud." She took a deep breath. This time, she would face her demons. "I was so shocked, at first all I could do was stand there and cry. I felt that he was doing dishonor to his wife. But then, when he went crazy and tore away my clothes, I panicked. His rifle was on a chest by the bed, and I picked it up and fired. He fell backward and lay there so still, so silent, his blood pouring like a river. I was certain I'd killed him. And I was so afraid, I could hardly stand. But I grabbed one of Sarah's dresses and put it on, then ran out of the house. On the porch was a pair of someone's muddy boots, and I stepped into them and kept on running. And I never looked back until I'd run all the way from Wyoming Territory to Misery."

"How did you survive?"

She shrugged. "There are fish in the rivers. Chickens and eggs and milk on farms. I stole. Begged. Worked some. But mostly stole, because folks thought I looked like some kind of wild woman. I didn't like the fact that I stole, but I knew I had to get far away from the Ebberling ranch."

"Not far enough, it seems." He kissed her. Then kissed her again and murmured against her lips, "I hate the fact that I was the one who brought Linus here."

"Hush, now." She kissed him back. "It wasn't you. It was just…" She struggled for the word. "It's the way life was supposed to work out.

"You mean fate?"

She nodded. "I believe we were meant to meet."

He wrapped his arms around her and noticed that his head didn't hurt nearly so much when she was touching him. "I believe that, too. It was fate that brought my sister and brother and me to Aaron Smiler."

To Billie's amazement, Gabe began to talk about his childhood, and the pain of learning that his father hadn't been a hero, but an outlaw, hiding in the Badlands.

"Is that why you became a lawman?"

He nodded. "I believe that was part of it." He shrugged. "Who knows? Maybe it was that fate you talked about. And maybe it was fate that kept me in Misery all these years. I never expected to love anybody the way I love you, Billie. You make me feel good about myself. Like I can do anything, as long as you believe in me."

She pressed her lips to his throat and whispered, "It's the same for me. You make me feel clean and shiny-new. Reborn, my pa would call it."

He gathered her close. "That's it exactly. With you, Billie, I've been reborn."

And then, because they'd waited so long, and had endured so much, they came together with a reverence that eased their pain and began the healing of two shattered hearts.

Chapter Nineteen

Aaron Smiler sat behind the sheriff's desk in the jail, watching as Gabe stood in the tiny cell, sliding his arms into the sleeves of his Sunday best jacket.

When he stepped out the old man nodded his approval. "Well now, Gabriel. Don't you look like the picture of a nervous groom."

"I'm not nervous."

"That so?" Aaron got slowly to his feet and crossed the room to straighten Gabe's tie. "Is that why you got your boots on the wrong feet?"

Gabe looked down, then grinned. "I thought something didn't feel right." He kicked off his boots and started over. Then he straightened. "Okay. So I'm a little unnerved by all this fuss. It just doesn't seem natural. Why did Billie have to invite the whole town of Misery?"

"Because everybody loves a wedding. You've been sheriff here so long, they all think of you as family. As for Billie, look how the town has taken her to their hearts."

Gabe smiled. "She's pretty amazing, isn't she?"

"That she is." Aaron pointed to the two fancy cigars in Gabe's pocket. "You saving them for something special?"

"I'd say today is special enough." Gabe grinned and reached into his pocket, handing one to Aaron, and biting the end of the other before striking a match. He held it first to Aaron's cigar, then his own. The two men stood together, quietly smoking until Lars burst through the doorway.

"Jack Slade said to tell you that he has free whiskey for the two of you over at the Red Dog."

Gabe looked up in surprise. "Free whiskey? I wonder what's got into Slade?"

Aaron just grinned. "Maybe he's found himself a new cook. At any rate, I wouldn't question it if I were you, son. Let's just go and enjoy ourselves."

The two men followed Lars up the street and through the swinging doors of the saloon. Inside they walked to the bar, where Jack Slade was waiting.

Cowboys and ranchers from miles around were seated at tables, eager for the festivities to begin.

Roscoe Timmons began filling glasses with whiskey and handing them around until everyone was holding one aloft.

"Here's to the best danged sheriff in the Dakota Territory," Slade said.

Amid murmurs of agreement, the others lifted their glasses and drank.

"Who happens to be marrying the best danged cook in the Dakota Territory," Slade added.

There were nods and more words of agreement as everyone drank again.

Several of the men pushed Olaf Swensen forward, since he had become the unofficial leader of the town. He looked slightly embarrassed as he said, "Sheriff, the people of this town feel that, since you're taking a wife, you need something better than a room in the Red Dog." He glanced at Slade's scowling face and hastily added, "Not that there's anything wrong with living here, of course. But with a wife and all—" he turned to the others for encouragement, before adding "—we all agree that it's time the town of Misery built you a real house. We were thinking of a piece of land down the street from the jail, if you and your bride agree."

Gabe couldn't hide his look of surprise. "That's awfully generous of you folks."

Jesse Cutler shook his head. "Not at all. It's just good business, Gabe. We want to make certain you and the missus stay in Misery."

The others laughed and nodded.

Jack Slade cleared his throat before interrupting. "I was hoping, Sheriff…" He paused a beat, wondering if this was the right time. Then, determined to plow ahead, he said, "Seeing as how Billie loves to cook, and seeing as how the townspeople and drifters need someone to feed them, I was wondering if you'd consider letting Billie come back to the Red Dog. Just as a cook, you understand. She'd have no other duties here."

Gabe looked down into his drink, before meeting

Slade's eyes. "You know Billie well enough to know that she doesn't need my approval to do what she wants. So I guess you'll just have to ask her yourself."

"All right. I will. Right after you and she exchange those vows."

Gabe looked around. "What's happened to all your women?"

"Upstairs." He made a sound of disgust. "Fussing over the bride with your sister and Grace."

Gabe handed his whiskey to Roscoe, and turned to Aaron. "I have a powerful need to see Billie. Are you coming with me?"

Olaf Swensen put a hand on his arm. "They're busy with female foolishness, Gabe. The last thing they want is a man around. You can't go up there."

Gabe's eyes narrowed slightly. "You don't want to try and stop me, Olaf."

The others merely smiled as Olaf took a quick step back, an instant before Gabe strode past him and up the stairs, with Aaron Smiler following.

The cowboys involved in their poker game paused to make bets on whether or not the sheriff would successfully run the gauntlet of women.

"A ten-dollar gold piece says the ladies bar his way."

Jack Slade slapped a coin of his own on the table. "I'm betting on the sheriff." He grinned. "I've had a lot of chances to see him in action. After all these years, I recognize that look in those eyes. A man like

Gabe Conover won't be put off, once he's made up his mind, boys."

"Oh, Billie. You look so beautiful." Kitty stood back to admire her mother's faded lace gown, which she'd fished out of the old carpetbag. Then she draped the length of matching lace over Billie's cloud of hair, giving her the look of an angel. "And to think I almost made curtains out of this."

"You wouldn't." Grace, standing beside her, dabbed at her eyes with a handkerchief, until she realized it was the one Billie had given her for her wedding. Quickly smoothing out the wrinkles, she pressed it into her friend's hand.

Billie glanced down. "What's this?"

"The handkerchief that belonged to your mother and grandmother."

"But I gave it to you."

Grace was shaking her head. "You loaned it to me. It's yours. Save it for your own daughter one day."

"A daughter." The word had Billie sighing. "Oh, do you think we might have one someday?"

Kitty, dressed in her usual buckskins, was shaking her head. "I still can't believe you'd want to give up your freedom to marry my brother."

Billie gave her a gentle look. "I may have felt that same way once, Kitty. But not anymore. I'm not giving up anything. I'm getting everything I've ever wanted. Gabe doesn't want to own me. He just wants to love me. And I feel the same way about him."

"I'm just glad it's you and not me standing in front of that preacher today. If I ever start acting silly over a man, just shoot me."

Cheri and the other women merely smiled, knowing that if a man like Gabe Conover ever offered to take them away from this place, wild horses couldn't stop them from going.

Grace closed a hand over Kitty's. "I guess I felt that way after my first husband died, Kitty. I'd been married so young, I never even had a childhood. The last thing I wanted was to tie myself to a man. Any man. And yet, here I am, happily wed to Lars for almost a month now. And I've never been happier."

"A month's not the same as a lifetime," Kitty said doubtfully. "I'll ask you again a few years from now, and see if you feel the same way."

The women were still laughing when they heard a knock on the door moments before it was yanked open. Gabe stood in the doorway, wearing a look of grim determination.

"Well. Here's the happy bridegroom now." Kitty's words had the others grinning. "What's the matter, big brother? Having second thoughts?"

"I came to see Billie. And I've brought Aaron with me."

"For support?" His sister asked with a laugh.

"I think your brother will manage just fine on his own." Aaron moved around Gabe and caught sight of Billie. His eyes went misty. "Oh, my dear." He stepped forward and caught her hands. "You look like a picture."

"You don't think it's—" she looked down at herself and blushed "—too fancy for me?"

"It's perfect, Billie." He stepped close to brush a kiss over her cheek. "And that's as it should be, since you're perfect for Gabriel."

She leaned close to whisper, "Why do you always call him Gabriel?"

Aaron smiled. "When I first met him, I saw an angel. An avenging angel, who would do whatever it took to keep a promise to his dead mother. And who, through all these years, wanted to look out for his brother and sister." He closed a hand over Billie's. "And now he'll have you to look out for, just as you'll look after him. You'll make him so happy, Billie. You're exactly what he's needed in his life."

She looked into those wise old eyes and felt her heart settle. "Thank you, Aaron. That means a lot to me." Then she looked beyond him, to where Gabe stood glowering at the others.

"Out." Gabe motioned to his sister, then to Grace and the other women. "I need to be alone with Billie."

At his look Grace backed up a step, prepared to defend her friend. "It isn't right to be alone with the bride before you two say your vows."

Billie touched a hand to her arm. "It's all right, Grace. I need to see him, too."

Grace paused long enough to say sternly, "Just so you know. The preacher said the service would begin at high noon. Don't you go making us wait."

As soon as Aaron managed to herd the women

over the threshold, Gabe shut the door and leaned against it, staring at Billie with that strange, intense look she'd come to know so well.

Then he shifted away from the door and took a step closer, all the while studying the way she looked in his mother's white lace dress and veil.

"Billie, you look so beautiful."

His words touched her as nothing else could. "And you look so handsome in your suit." She lifted a hand to his face, remembering for an instant how he'd looked in the Badlands. She'd been so afraid that he would die without knowing just how desperately she loved him. And now, here they were, just weeks later, about to bind themselves together for a lifetime.

"Was Kitty right? Are you having second thoughts about what we're doing?"

"Never." He closed a hand over hers, then brought it to his lips. "I just needed to see you. To touch you." He caught her other hand, holding her a little away. His voice was low with feeling. "I love you so much, Billie, it scares me."

"I love you, too, Gabe. But it doesn't scare me. It just fills my heart to overflowing."

"Oh, Billie." He drew her close and pressed his face to her hair. "I never thought I could feel this way. Don't ever stop loving me. Even when I get all gruff and blustery."

"I promise." She laughed, and the sound trickled over his senses and wrapped itself around his heart.

There was a quick knock on the door, and Kitty's

muffled voice called, "The preacher's waiting. So is the whole town. Come on, you two. Time to get hitched. Unless you've changed your mind."

With a sigh of frustration, Gabe brushed his mouth over Billie's and felt the familiar rush of heat. Would it always be this way? he wondered. Would the mere touch of her always have the ability to touch his very soul like this?

He drew back and took Billie's hand, linking his fingers with hers. As they stepped out of the room and started down the stairs, they could hear the crowd out in the street. Because of the size of the crowd, even the back room of Swensen's Dry Goods couldn't accommodate them. So the preacher had agreed to hold the service in the middle of the dusty main street.

Not a breath of air stirred as the handsome sheriff led his beaming bride out into the heat of the afternoon. They nodded to friends and neighbors as they made their way toward the preacher.

As they began to speak the words that would tie them together forever, Billie glanced around at the tiny town of Misery, and at the Black Hills in the distance and thought again about the strange twists and turns her life had taken. She'd come here an outcast, fleeing for her life. Alone, afraid, without a friend in the world. But here she was, surrounded by people who not only accepted her, but treated her with friendship and respect. All those burdens she'd once carried had now slipped away, leaving her with such an amazing sense of freedom.

Best of all, she was about to begin a whole new life with the man she loved.

The man she loved.

This was, she realized, the sweetest gift of all. She had found, in Gabe's loving arms, the home of her heart. And it was, she now knew, sweeter than any childhood dream.

* * * * *

Meet Yale Conover,
Gabe's rakish younger brother, in

BADLANDS LEGEND,

available in October 2002
from Harlequin Historicals.

Chapter One

Yale Conover picked up his money and smiled at the gamblers who sat around the poker table, glowering at him. He'd been on a winning streak that appeared to have no end in sight. Some might call him lucky. But those who'd stayed around for the entire forty-eight-hour poker marathon knew it took more than luck to earn his reputation as one of the shrewdest gamblers in the Dakotas.

He looked the part of a charming rogue. Expensive black suit, soft white shirt, wide-brimmed black hat and boots polished to a high shine. While his opponents cast furtive glances at one another each time the cards were dealt, he merely smiled and drew on his cigar, looking as relaxed as a man after a good meal. And though he always ordered a glass of whiskey, he never drank it. It was just one of his props. Now he indulged himself, draining it in one long swallow.

"Thank you, gentlemen. It's been an…interesting and profitable experience."

He shoved away from the poker table and moved with catlike grace across the room. When he stepped through the swinging doors of the saloon into blinding morning sunlight, he scrubbed a hand over the rough stubble of beard and blinked. For a moment he was tossed back into another time. Another place.

* * * * *

RUTH LANGAN

traces her ancestry to Scotland and Ireland. It is no surprise, then, that she feels a kinship with the characters in her historical novels.

Married to her childhood sweetheart, she has raised five children and lives in Michigan, the state where she was born and raised.

Escape to a land long ago and
far away when you read these thrilling
love stories from Harlequin Historicals

On Sale September 2002

A WARRIOR'S LADY
by Margaret Moore
(England, 1200s)
*A forced marriage between a brave knight and
beautiful heiress blossoms into true love!*

A ROGUE'S HEART
by Debra Lee Brown
(Scotland, 1213)
*Will a carefree rogue sweep a headstrong young lady
off her feet with his tempting business offer?*

On Sale October 2002

MY LADY'S HONOR
by Julia Justiss
(Regency England)
*In the game of disguise a resourceful young
woman falls in love with a dashing aristocrat!*

THE BLANCHLAND SECRET
by Nicola Cornick
(England, 1800s)
*Will a lady's companion risk her reputation by
accepting the help of a well-known rake?*

 Harlequin Historicals®
Historical Romantic Adventure!

 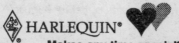